Other Avon Books by
Joanne Greenberg

HIGH CRIMES AND MISDEMEANORS

JOANNE GREENBERG

 A BARD BOOK/PUBLISHED BY AVON BOOKS

"Things in Their Season" and "De Rerum Natura" both appeared originally in *The Denver Quarterly*.

AVON BOOKS
A division of
The Hearst Corporation
959 Eighth Avenue
New York, New York 10019

The Holt, Rinehart and Winston edition contains the following Library of Congress Cataloging in Publication Data:

Greenberg, Joanne.
High crimes and misdemeanors.
I. Title.
PZ4.G7985Hi [PS3557.R378]   813'.5'4

First Bard Printing, July, 1981

To the Tante

"And in that still voice
Onward came the Lord"

CONTENTS

HIGH CRIMES
AND
MISDEMEANORS

CERTAIN DISTANT SUNS

The planning of the Passover Seder was a tradition in our family. My mother and three aunts, dressed in their best, would go downtown. They would conduct their deliberations at a fancy restaurant over drinks, and this included a complete springtime going-over of every other member of the family. Mother usually returned from these sessions snapping with vigor and virtue, but on March 12, 1970, she came home later than usual, slammed the door, slammed into the kitchen, and began to fix supper with a lethal whacking of pots. "Bessie has refused!" she cried to us over a half-cooked, half-burnt meal. "There are four sisters. Each one gives the Seder every fourth year. This is Bessie's year, and she has refused."

"Is something the matter with Abe?" my father asked.

"No! She has the house, the health, the time, and the money. Those are requirements. The rest is her own headache, not a family matter. Not, when it comes down to it, a religious matter; not a requirement!"

In the end we found out that Aunt Bessie, in the fifty-sixth year of her life and three weeks before the Seder, had stopped believing in God.

Had we been Hasidim, Bessie's loss of faith might have been the prelude to one of their thrilling lawsuits against the Almighty. Had we

1

been Orthodox, her denial would have been the occasion for breast-beating and bowed heads, but we were then as we are now: modern American Jews, tangled in compromise, passing the past and the heritage hand to hand like a hot potato and wincing with pain between the toss and the catch. Our belief or nonbelief was different from Bessie's only in degree. She hadn't weakened us spiritually; she had only annoyed us, and she had broken the solidarity of the family. Minnie gave the Seder. Eyebrows were raised but no voices. Bessie stayed away; her husband and children came and sat stiff and uncomfortable at the table. She was a stronger presence there than Elijah. My mother sighed and shook her head. I was nineteen; I thought it was wonderful.

As time passed, we learned to live around Bessie's peculiarity. To all secular family events she came as generously and happily as before. Presents on birthdays, soup in sickness. She would ring the bell with a kind of snap—"Bessie's ring"—and would hurry in as though propelled from behind, her wiry hair unkempt and flying, her plucked eyebrows drawn on again in black pencil with a perpetually upshot line, her voice rich as a singer's (although she couldn't carry a tune—too impatient, I think). When the High Holy Days were glimpsed over the heat-watering horizon of summer and plans were made for the sharing of dinners and the attendance at services, Bessie dwindled to the point of disappearance. As the Lord rose in the web of the year, Aunt Bessie diminished only to reappear when the holy days were past.

The name of God disappeared from her lips. I was the first to notice this—such secular usages that we don't even remember Whose Name it is: Good-bye, Goddammit, for God's sake, Lord knows. No hint of Him. Not any of His Names. She did not tell us what had led to this loss of belief or the more bizarre divorcing of herself from the most common associations with the Name. To my knowledge, no one asked her. Which is, for us, unusual. Ours is a family that allows few secrets and no evasions. We are skilled and merciless trackers. We corner the secret-keepers at funerals and feasts and drive the diffident to the wall. We will not wait for the truth to out; we hector it forth with whatever force is necessary. Except, because we are Jews, for that most subtle of links, broken and rewoven a hundred times a day: belief. We did not examine the broken link.

And Bessie was getting along splendidly without the Lord. She traveled lighter, unburdened of the baggage of belief. We milled away at our compromises, grinding them now coarser, now finer; we were caught surprised as holidays loomed up suddenly from ambush to overwhelm us. We blurred the Sabbath and felt guilty; we violated the laws of kashrut and felt defensive. Bessie sailed past it all and never looked better. Her house was as spotless as ever. The houseplants thrived under her hands; her soufflés fell not, neither did her custards fail. The rezoning of Martin Park stopped four blocks from her house, raising its value by a third.

Occasionally, my mother would mention some religious matter in Bessie's presence and would give one of her significant looks in Bessie's direction. Since belief was not truly an issue—Bessie was incontrovertibly and immutably a Jew by Jewish Law—all that remained for discussion was her uncooperativeness. Unfortunately, Bessie, in secular matters, was remarkably cooperative and the soul of considerate sisterliness. When anyone needed help Bessie was there, and when she heard that my parents were going to the banquet for the national-headquarters people in my father's firm, she came running over with Great Grandma's garnets.

I turned the mammoth ring over in my hand. "Try on the earrings, darling," Bessie said to me. "They're just right with your coloring."

"No thanks," I said quickly and handed the things back. "The ring alone would slow anybody down."

"I'll wear them for the evening," my mother said to Bessie, "and I'll return them this weekend."

"Keep them as long as you like," Bessie said. "Since I gave up the safety-deposit box they're only in my way."

"You're not changing banks again, are you?" (Bessie was a sucker for the free premiums.)

"Which bank is it this time, Aunt Bessie, the one on Tyler Avenue?"

"No," Bessie said cheerfully. "I've decided that I really don't believe in all that anymore, the savings and the safety and the capital and the principal and the interest and the stocks and the bonds and the balances. I've closed my account in the banks and turned in my charge cards. Money is real. Money in the hand is real—coins and bills. The rest I don't believe in, and I don't think I ever did, really. What's a check, after all, but a promise—mine, the bank's. Me, I know, but the bank? You know how quick those tellers change down there; you don't even get to know their names before they leave. Them I should trust?"

"But if you can't think of the convenience," my mother cried, "think of the danger. Money in the house, money in your purse. Think of fire and theft. What if—"

"What if," Bessie said and waved her hand, dismissing it all, "what if no one could be sure of anything!"

Had we been Hasidim we would have waited the lightning stroke or a case of boils. Had we been Orthodox, we would have searched for the first faint whiff of corruption in her, some hint of moral or ethical disintegration, perhaps for symptoms, physical or psychiatric, that would show us that she was despairing or alienated—not that she had ceased believing in banks, but that she seemed actively to be calling down destruction upon herself, a condition from which Jews have always turned in abhorrence. We make poor martyrs and worse ascetics. As it was, we could only wait and watch without knowing what we should wait and watch for.

The months passed. Bessie's housekeeping money went in a coffee can. The stock dividends from the family business were cashed and put in other coffee cans. The IRS got a mailing envelope crammed with bills representing their dividend of her dividends. Bills were paid in person. Neither did fire strike, nor criminals spring from the shadows upon her as my father predicted. In my thoughts, Bessie began to fill a larger space than the other aunts. I saw her as younger, happier, freer than they. The petty details that were weighing my mother down year after year—rules and laws, record keeping, busywork—did not touch Bessie. She had fought free of them, and her courage was keeping her young and heroic and outlined against the family background in sharper relief. When the consciousness-raising seminars came to our school and I sat and heard my "sisters" talk about the heroic women of the past, none of those women were Jews. Sojourner Truth and Harriet Tubman and the Quaker ladies of concern and the early defenders of women's rights held sway, but I was sure that had the underground railway gone through our time and place, Bessie would have been one of the conductors.

Spring came and the women of our family became narrow-eyed and diligent. Roach paste was painted around the bathroom pipes and in the corners. Stiff-jointed ladies bent themselves double to clean the sinister places behind the sinks and toilets and plotted elaborate stratagems against beetles, ants, and silverfish. Bessie knelt at no open cabinets, genuflected beneath no plumbing. As the ground warmed and the hundred million flies of the new generation remembered us, screens went up in all the windows of the neighborhood. Except one. Fly killer in sprays, bricks, strips, candles, flares, and lightbulbs appeared in every shopping cart and was stocked in the newly cleaned cabinets of every dwelling. Except one. Fear of disease, plague, filth, and corruption (ritual and actual) haunted the half sleep of every householder. Except one. Bessie had given up germs.

"My God!, Bessie," my mother cried, "you won't last the summer! Flies in the food—every disease known to man!"

"Germs is a theory," Bessie answered with her usual vigor. "It says so in the books—the germ theory. I stopped believing in the theory, and I won't let it bother me anymore. Think about the people in the olden days. Did they use fly spray? Did they worry about pollution and disease all the time? No. They lived until they were ninety-five, some of them, in the middle of cities that teemed with rats and flies. Show me a rat as big as I am and I'll be afraid of it. Show me a germ and I'll believe in it all."

"In a microscope—"

"I'll live in a microscope and I'll believe in the germs there."

"My aunt is at one, in harmony, with the natural order," I said to my sisters at a meeting. "My sister is crazy," my mother said. "What bad things have happened to me?" Bessie asked. "Am I sick? Have plagues fallen on me? You see that I am fine.—better than ever. I sleep better and eat better because I don't have to worry about supernatural punishments or money or sickness."

And it was true. The cataclysms predicted by my parents were not forthcoming. The flies in Bessie's house came in no greater numbers than those in ours in spite of all our care and her uncaring. I know, because after making a bet with my father, I counted them for him and all the family prophets of disaster who seemed obscurely disappointed that Bessie and Abe lived on unafflicted. In early August Bessie put up six quarts of pickles without steam scouring the crocks or boiling the jars. Mold formed and floated serenely on the tops of the crocks, but when Bessie skimmed it away, I found the pickles delicious and unspoiled. And Bessie wasn't sick. No colds or flu or aching joints or fevers or chills or swollen ears or congestions, inflammations, or eruptions. She was healthier than she had ever been, her skin clearer, her face less lined. She seemed lighter, too, freer, head up in the street even in bad weather while most of the other women in the neighborhood passed by, eyes down, bodies hunched against the rain, frightened by the cough of the passenger next to them on the bus, the dirty nails of the shopkeeper, the sneeze of the postman. Bessie's fearlessness was wonderful to me, and it showed even brighter against the nervousness and hypochondria of the rest of the family. After seeing Bessie, how much poorer and sicker the rest of them looked to me! Aunt Dorothy was afraid of being mugged in the street, Aunt Minnie of what she called "getting a condition" in fear of which she marshaled a pharmacopeia sufficient to supply a city. My mother was terrified of being caught somewhere without any money and died night after night in a hundred old-age homes without the dime for a phone call out. I seldom argued Bessie's case to the family—it only made my father laugh at her more and my mother shake her head. I showed my loyalty by visiting her often and my courage by staying for supper. In my parents' house dark and evil forces went to work on any food left out of a refrigerator for thirty seconds. Bessie's casual attitude was exciting to me. Would there be souring? Sickness? Plague? In a life insufficiently precarious, I felt I was a hostage to comfort. Bessie's danger was a tonic to my soul.

We had one brief cooling, a hiatus in our relationship. It happened when Ray and I, bowing to pressure from both our families, consented to stop living together and get married. Once the decision was made we found ourselves happy with it, eager for the status we had always ridiculed, the granting of full man-and-womanhood to us by our families. We even enjoyed helping to plan the wedding. When I told Bessie, she beamed and invited us over for a meal. Bessie's husband Abe worked long hours at his store. We seldom saw him, but Bessie promised he would be there for the dinner and for my wedding. "Surely you'll be there too . . ."

But the wedding was to be a Jewish wedding—a religious ceremony—and Bessie must have known it. I was the foolish one. I had supposed that because it was to be *my* wedding, because I was her favorite niece, she would come. I had always admired her stand, her refusal to compromise with what she had no belief in, yet when it came to me, I wanted her love to suspend her disbelief. She stayed away. Abe came. He had an easygoing attitude toward Bessie, which was lucky under the circumstances. But I was hurt and Bessie knew it. She had sent us a huge chafing dish. It was the gift I had known it would be—exuberant, impractical, no compromise. I set it up on top of the kitchen cabinet in our small apartment against the day when we would entertain on such a scale. When I next saw her she was so free of guilt or explanation or reproach that I couldn't really stay angry—

my anger seemed unreal. Her absence at my wedding seemed unreal. I soon stopped believing in it.

I did not see my relatives for a while. I assumed that they were standing in the positions in which I had left them, unchanging. It is enough of a shock that the people we see daily change before our eyes; it is unthinkable that the rest of reality is so far beyond our control. One day in April my mother brought over my old summer clothes and some of her own to alter on my machine. We work well together on projects like that, chatting companionably over our decisions, planning the alterations for the things we keep, fitting and refitting. Our tastes are similar, and we laugh and remember the days and events at which we wore this outfit or that. I had been looking forward to a peaceful afternoon. I had taken off from work for it. There was a nice lunch made.

But when I saw her at the door the pleasure went out of the day. She looked worried and frightened. I helped her unload the boxes she had brought from the car. "What's the matter?"

"Later, later," she said.

When we were upstairs, I asked again.

"It's Bessie. It's gone too far this time—Bessie has given up electricity."

I think I laughed. "No one 'gives up' electricity. A person who 'gives up' electricity has no neural function. That person is dead."

"Stop being childish," my mother said angrily. "Bessie is alive enough, but she has stopped believing in electricity, and strange things are happening in that house!"

"What strange things? What does Uncle Abe say?" She was too upset to tell me any more. I could see that she was frightened and a little angry and also that she was angry at me. I had encouraged Bessie with my admiration, goaded her on from one selfishness to another with my shining-eyed approval. She had played to my youth and eagerness; perhaps it is easy for a middle-aged woman to fall into such a trap, to forget that she is middle-aged, too old for nonsense, for beliefs or disbeliefs that put a strain on the family. "Should I go and see her?" I asked before my mother left.

"You might as well," my mother said, as though she meant, "See what you have started."

But I hadn't started it and I wasn't to blame. Could I help it if I admired idealism, honesty, and independence? Could I help it if these were Bessie's virtues and if they are also virtues of the young? I admired her still, I would help and encourage her if I could. The next day I called in sick and went over to Bessie's house.

Bessie's street was a quietly decaying side street of two-family houses with small back gardens and great old trees. Going up the slightly tilted steps I thought I heard the TV with its warm, male drone. Most of the sets in this neighborhood were on during the day. The neighborhood was old, the street full of widows who filled their houses with the sounds of genial, sympathetic men—the suffering doctors of soap operas and the spruce hosts of game shows. If Bessie wasn't using electricity anymore, perhaps the sound was coming from the Galindas in the other half of the house. I rang Bessie's harsh, old-fashioned bell. There was no sound. Oh, yes, electricity. I knocked. After a minute or so I heard Bessie's footsteps going from the worn rug to the foyer floor. Then the door opened.

I studied her for changes. There was something, although I couldn't put my finger on it, and I cursed the curiosity that made me want to peer in through her defenses. Her hair was standing up around her head as usual, her movements were brisk, and she greeted me in that rich, loud voice of hers. "Come on in; you look wonderful! I've been fixing up Danny's old bedroom and I could use a break."

"I thought I heard voices in here when I was at the door," I said. There was silence now. Bessie's face clouded. "I like a little company when I work, that's all. Your mother has been blabbing about it all over town, and my big-mouth sister Minnie, too." She had hurried into the kitchen and was filling a kettle at the sink. I saw her hand tremble a little. It could have been anger at my mother and Aunt

Minnie, but there was something else on her face, an expression I couldn't read. "What if a person wants to hear some programs—have some company while she works! What's so wrong about that?" She was really upset now and almost in tears—not tears of sorrow but of anger and frustration.

"Aunt Bessie, what's the matter?" I cried.

"Well, if you really want to know, I'll show you, but please don't make more of it than there really is!" She took me into the living room.

It was a modest room; Uncle Abe worked hard but he was not very successful. The furniture came mostly from my grandparents' house. Serviceable, Bessie called it. In the corner was an old TV, black-and-white. As I looked at it, I remembered the furor that Bessie had made when my parents had finally gone to color. Uncle Abe liked this set, which he had gotten with the twenty-one-inch screen when the rest of us still had nineteen-inch. Now Bessie sometimes called herself "the only sister without color." I noticed that the set was unplugged. Bessie turned the knob. "What do you want to see?" she asked.

"What's on?" I smiled, thinking that she was perhaps going to tell a joke.

"What do you want to see?" she asked impatiently. "Pick something you want to see."

"I don't know—you pick something."

Medical shows. Doctors. In color—brilliant, clear color. Transfixed, I saw "Medic," "Ben Casey," "Dr. Kildare," "The Nurses." I saw brain operations, heart seizures, epidural hematomas. The crises poured out upon us without snow, flopover, or distortion. All the doctors spoke in Yiddish. All the nurses looked familiar; I realized that they all resembled our family. Midway through a lateral-transorbital-shunt procedure, I asked Bessie why, except for medical terms, Dr. Ben Casey wasn't speaking English. "Shush!" she said, "Wait for the commercial!"

During the commercial she told me some of the limitations of her set. "Radio shows I can get on TV also, but then I don't get a picture. Fibber McGee I get in the daytime, never in Yiddish. Benny and Berle I get in Yiddish. The doctors I can get in either language, but they are more sympathetic in Yiddish. I always like to have Dr. Ben Casey and Marcus Welby in Yiddish."

"I don't understand how you do it—how it happens," I cried. "Especially when nothing is plugged in."

"Well," she said, "I don't believe in electricity—in wires carrying power from a waterfall somewhere, but I believe in color and I believe in Ben Casey and the good work he does. I believe in Fibber McGee and his closet and I believe in Jack Benny, how stingy he is and how he tries to stay thirty-nine years old. Oh, I know no doctor could be like Marcus Welby, but I believe in it anyway. A person shouldn't have to accept anything he doesn't believe in."

"Can you get the iron and the toaster to work without plugging them in?"

"Nothing will work but this. Still, people were cleaning their houses and washing their clothes years before electricity. I clean in the old way, and Abe takes the clothes out to—"

As we spoke a black-and-white figure came on the screen. I saw it for only a second before Bessie leaped up from the couch where we sat and turned off the set with a curse. The picture did not go away immediately but went black-red like an afterimage from the sun, and slowly the figure, arm raised as though to defend or to exhort, faded soundlessly from the set. Bessie watched it with a look of bitterness I had never seen on her face in all the years I had known her. "What was that?" I asked uncomfortably.

"A commercial!" she hissed. I did not dare ask any more.

Ours is a family of large egos. We gossip because we feel our smallest news must be as fascinating to everyone else as it is to us. Deliverymen and storekeepers know every grandchild's new tooth, every symptom. Each day the family's vital signs are broadcast to everyone who will listen. This habit fooled me into thinking that we could not keep a secret. I was wrong. If you want to keep a secret, bury it in talk. Neither the family, the children, nor even my husband, Ray, knew about Bessie's arcane gift. We who shared the secret had a never-mentioned horror of reporters, psychic investigators, universities, parapsychologists, and all the other interested (self- or otherwise) persons besieging the family to test and probe and question, document, report, explore, explode, destroy. Luckily, the lights worked in the house—Bessie believed in light. They had a gas stove, and she cooked in the usual way. Thank God for small favors.

Sometimes women in my consciousness-raising group would ask me about Bessie. In the past I had used her as an example of a woman heroically above the demeaning adjustments that threaten us all. The group, still fragile and unsure, wanted Founders, Roots, History. These women saw in Bessie, or in my stories of Bessie, a "resource," as they called it, something as natural as a mineral, as usable as water. And suddenly I was frightened and silent. I said she was sick. It was a good excuse. Illness is not part of the image of the liberated woman. It reminds young people of dependence, real and sham, of limitations. Of compromise.

And then I got sick. Suddenly the sure things—health, strength, that organs would do their work silently and automatically—all these things were suddenly not sure at all. There was dizziness and weakness, sudden sweats and sudden chills. "A renal crisis" the doctor said. In essence I had begun to poison myself. I went to the hospital.

After several false starts, the treatment took effect. The weakness drew away slowly, but I was now on notice that anywhere, at any time, any one of a thousand ills could fall on me like an eagle falling upon a feeding rabbit, could take me and transform me in moments into an invalid, a person not myself, a person at the mercy of blood-washing machines, pumps, tubes, and wires. It was more than a renal crisis. It was crisis of belief exactly the opposite of Bessie's . . . where was Bessie?

"Where's Aunt Bessie? Why hasn't she come?"

"You always said you hated that in our family, everyone checking off who sent things and who came and who called and what excuses people gave—"

"I'm not doing that; I only want to see her—I need to see her."

"Cousin Grace has been here almost every day—"

"Cousin Grace is not Bessie. I can't stand one more description of

Cousin Grace's canals—she doesn't visit the sick, she haunts them. Where is Aunt Bessie?"

Had I not been weak and ill I would not have seen my mother's discomfort. Skilled cornerers make skilled prevaricators, but my mother couldn't play that game now. You can lie to people; not to machines. I was half machine. My mother was stumped. She came close to the bed. "Don't tell Ray—" she whispered. I think I must have gone very pale.

"What is it, Ma?"

"Bessie can't come to see you. She would if she could. She can't leave the house at all anymore. Bessie has stopped believing in gravity."

As soon as I was out of the hospital I went to see her. I was still weak, still separated by a great unmeasured gulf from the world, from anyone who has no serious doubts about rising whole the next morning and who tranquilly says "I will come," "I will go," as though he could make such promises.

I was shocked at the change in Bessie's house. It was autumn, and the corpses of dried leaves were banked against the sides of the steps in little heaps. Bessie would never have allowed that had something not been terribly wrong. The outside of her house had always been immaculate. In a neighborhood of two-family houses the façades, walks, steps, and doorways are a matter of intense rivalry among the housewives. I had grown up hearing Bessie mutter about "the slut" three houses down "who didn't sweep until noon, practically." Now, all down the row, the clean steps of the other houses mocked her, and I shivered.

Looking up into Bessie's parlor window, I saw that the off-white curtains were limp and dingy. I began to formulate reasons for my visit. This in itself made me nervous. Excuses had never been needed. Aunt Bessie's house had always been as free to me as my own, sometimes more so, while I was growing up and often at odds with my mother. I wanted to run up the stairs freely and eagerly as I had countless times before to give and take confidences and laughter over cake and milk. But I stopped at the leaf-strewn steps, uncertain and listening. Maybe the TV would be on—"Our Gal Sunday" as a Polish immigrant girl speaking a sweet Litvak Yiddish, or Dr. Marcus Welby, comforting in the mother tongue. There was silence. Only the accusing leaves whispered and rustled in the warm afternoon. I rang the bell and remembering again, knocked, feeling like a stranger.

I didn't hear the familiar steps. Instead, the door swung open and I saw nothing. I stood at the opening. "Aunt Bessie?"

"Come in!" a voice hissed from where I could not tell. I stepped into the dark foyer, light blinded. It was a while before I saw her.

She lay prone in the air above me, hand on the knob. When the door closed, the wind of its closing blew her up and into a lazy somersault, back and forth. She banked and turned and slowly brought herself upright to face me. Her skin was gray. "Come into the kitchen," she said. "It's better in the kitchen." With a kind of swimming stroke she breasted her way before me. She had not greeted me or looked to see if I was well. She hadn't smiled. Her eyes hadn't lit up at my presence. I sat down at the table. Bessie bobbed in the air beside me, up and down, now oblique to the right, now overbalancing to the left—never still. It embarrassed me to look and, even more, to turn my head away. I gave a quick glance around the once-familiar kitchen.

For some people it might have been a passable kitchen before the morning cleanup. For Bessie in her present condition it must have been an agony. Crumbs lay in the corners and were picked out by the afternoon sun that shone in through the dusty window. Dishes stood in the sink, and there was a film of grease on the range top. She looked around at it all with a glare of disgust. "It's a nightmare!" she said bitterly, "a nightmare!"

"Oh, Aunt Bessie!" I cried.

Two tears formed in her eyes. She put her hand up to her face and then shook her head. The tears leaped away to hang in the air in two large drops and then fell with a splat to the floor. The motion of shaking her head had brought her up out of the chair, which she had been holding onto, and over into a roll from which she righted herself after several minutes. She sighed deeply but didn't say anything. Her situation was so unreal and her misery so real I cast around for anything I could offer to bring things under our control. "Men in space—" I said, "the astronauts—those men learn to adjust. They develop all kinds of ways of making peace with their condition—" (Why had I said that? It sounded like something a rabbi would say.)

"How?" she cried back at me in a kind of bitter triumph. "Lead shoes? Weights? I've tried them all. As soon as I put anything on me, it becomes weightless, too."

"Maybe someone could come in to help—until you get the feel of things—"

"Who? Who would come in to help a bouncing woman, a floating woman, a double- and triple-flip woman, and not go blabbing it all over town! Am I crazy? Do I want crowds at the windows watching me loop-the-loop? Abe helps—he shops a little now—your mother, Minnie, Dotty, and Cousin Clara, but I can't go out at all. I'm trapped in this house, and I can't stand to stay in here and look at this—this *pigsty!*" Once again tears formed in her eyes and wouldn't roll out until she tossed her head and went head over heels in recoil.

I had nothing to give her. I was unequipped for keeping company in grief, for weeping over what couldn't be changed. My training was all for answers, kindly and helpful suggestions, practical dispositions, for tactics, marches, petitions, and demands for redress. Surely somewhere was the solution, that certain, helpful thing, that method, formula, or hint that no one had thought of before and that would seem so right when I said it.

"Maybe," I started . . .

"Do you know that when I make the bed I go up with the sheets? When I turn over in bed I turn for half an hour until I get sick, and if I'm sick enough to throw up I have to hang on or I fly away?"

"At least you don't *have* to go out. Uncle Abe does the shopping. Everyone is helping. I'll help too. You've got the radio and the TV in that wonderful color—all the shows that ever were and every movie you ever saw. Maybe you could start to make your own movies, to be creative by—"

Bessie leaned close and whispered, and the force of her whispering caused her to bob up and down. "I can't watch TV anymore, or radio. I can't because of the commercials!"

"The commercials—when I saw them on your set that day they were no different from—"

"That was before!" Bessie hissed. "It's all different now! You think the sponsor would let such a chance go by, a helpless woman trapped in the house like I am?" She looked down at me, pinched, old, aggrieved. The energy of her hissing had pushed her up and away until she lay prone in the air again, near the ceiling. I found myself remembering the authority of her tread, the vigor of her ring. It was less than a year ago that her presence everywhere was heralded with so much certainty. Now there wouldn't even be a footfall.

"Everybody hates commercials." Reasonable and lost and thinking that if only I were more reasonable I would not be so lost, I said, "They drive me mad, especially when they interrupt something. We all—"

"No! No!" And she flailed her arms in impatience. In space all Italians, Jews, and Spaniards will be punished and the hand-mute Saxons will be vindicated by the God of Newton, who hates all wasted motion. Bessie began to spin and turn. Not humbled but enraged, she cried, "Go turn on the set, Mrs. Smarty, and see for yourself!" Hopelessly I went into the parlor and turned on the unplugged set.

The picture came on immediately. Bessie's black-and-white console erupted in luscious color again. It was a movie called *Red Garters* with Rosemary Clooney. There was dancing and gaiety. There were lots of songs. No one spoke Yiddish in this one, but it was just the thing to raise the spirits—everyone was pretty or witty or graceful. The color was richer than any I had ever seen on TV. I called Aunt Bessie in to watch. Surely this couldn't hurt her. She came swimming into the parlor disconsolately, and for a while we watched the dancing and the music. Once or twice I saw her smiling a little. After about fifteen minutes there was a station break. The movie stopped abruptly, and the call letters RUACH-TV came on the screen in black-and-white. I turned to Bessie. "What station is that? I never heard of it before, and there's a picture of a shofar in the background."

"Turn it off," she said dully. A commercial or announcement of some kind began.

It had obviously been staged in the studio by rank amateurs. A slight, bent Hasidic Jew stood uncomfortably on one foot and then on the other. He took off his glasses and wiped them and then held them dangling from his hand. He could not have been an actor in costume. The clothes were too obviously his, although nothing matched—pants too short, sleeves too long, the beard bushy as though he had a chin full of gray foam. He spoke in Yiddish very slowly and haltingly, but it was a Yiddish unfamiliar to me, and the word I knew here and there gave me no clue. Bessie was floating up over me, hovering in the air. "What's he saying?" I asked, looking up at her. She sighed. "This is the sad one. At least he's better than the angry one, the one who squints."

"Yes, but what's he saying?"

She began to interpret. " 'I'm pleading with all the people,' he says, 'in the vast television audience, not to renounce the universe along with the Master of the Universe, if for some reason they find it necessary to renounce Him. I realize,' he says, 'that in every relationship a certain amount of resentment builds up over the years and that this is especially true in regard to mankind and the Master of the Universe, since the relationship is so . . . so one-sided.' He says, 'I beg you, all of you, not to stop discussing the Master of the Universe, even if you can no longer praise Him. If it be in anger or despair or even, God forbid, in ridicule, keep His Name aloud in your mouths. It is possible that certain distant suns are powered by the mention of His Name.' "

The movie began again; Bessie was crying and so was I, but I didn't want to turn off the set. When the angry one came on, the one with the squint, Bessie shook her fist at him and was pushed softly against the wall, bouncing slightly back and forth. There she stayed, answering his angry incomprehensible questions.

"You left Him!" the Rabbi shouted at last, in English. "You sent Him away, abandoned Him, abandoned your part of Him, a part that can never be replaced!"

"I stopped believing in Him, what could I do?" Bessie shouted back.

"Foolish woman, a soul goes in and out of belief a hundred times a day. Belief is too fragile to weigh a minute on. You stopped running after Him, looking for Him, struggling with Him. Even His Laws you turned from!"

"If I did, why did He take it, why did He walk away like a whipped child? Is He no stronger than a fifty-year-old woman?"

"How can His relationship with you be any stronger than you are yourself? You think He made you for the fun of it—without needing you?"

"He let it happen, that's all I know! He didn't fight back. A *mensh* fights back!"

THINGS IN THEIR
SEASON

I

They were a comfort, a retreat, a challenge, a game, a spiritual dissection, an intellectual rejoining, those Monday evenings. To scholars or intellectuals who deal in words all day, such evenings might not seem so special, but the four of us were men whose lives were practical and mundane. We felt it was a great honor that Rabbi Jacob should take the time to show us the meanings in Jephthah's vow, to discuss the Law with us, to move our Hebrew out of rote mimicry into the stage where the words had meaning and nuance. Even questions of ordinary life, things a man could read in the papers, deepened and changed their natures when Rabbi Jacob discussed them. Monday nights we would rush through dinner so as to be ready at eight. Stein and I lived closest to each other, and we took turns picking the other up and then driving over to Becker's house. Levin came from the other direction, but for some reason we preferred to meet outside and come in together. Something about favoritism, probably. We didn't want anything to spoil what we had.

Shifra, the rabbi's wife, would usher us in and take our coats. We would feel ourselves relaxing from the week's demands. An atmosphere of peace and order seemed to rise from the floor. Sometimes when we came into the rabbi's study the books of commentary and reference would be piled up so high we had to peer over them to find the rabbi behind them, but the confusion of books was a source of energy, never a chaos. He was always in the middle of the work when we came, tracking down some thought or reference, and he would look up delightedly and say, "There you are! Come in and sit down—I've just been reading what Rabbi Gemaliel says about—" and we'd be off. The dictionaries, the Midrash, the Mishnah, the Torah. Sometimes we used books on American law or sociology or science. Often we would argue the points we raised, defending enthusiastically reference versus reference, sociology versus Law, Talmud versus science. Always Rabbi's word here, reference there, kept us from rancor or sharpness. It amazed us that for all our arguing, the sense of peace never left us. I suppose that to a scholar our inquiries would have seemed childish. No one would call us fortresses of intellect. We had little education except for Rabbi Jacob, and we often got beyond ourselves, but if we missed a point or tripped up in reading, Rabbi would quote the Pirke Avot to us, the part about good hearts.

Three years. Then came a sudden, mysterious withdrawal. Rabbi Jacob announced that he was no longer able to lead the congregation. He stopped going to services altogether and stayed at home. The young people, who had always been attracted to him, were turned politely but firmly away. Shifra called us and told us that until further notice Rabbi Jacob would not be able to meet with us. She did not answer our questions. Was the rabbi sick? Was there some awful trouble in the home or with the family? Would they be leaving the community? She only repeated what she had been told to say, that Rabbi regretted having to stop the Monday-night studies, thanked us for our concern, and hoped that we would continue to meet without him.

No one could see him. Everyone who went to the house to inquire was met by Shifra, received politely, and left no wiser than he came. The "progressive" faction of the congregation was happy. It snapped up a young world-beater with a minor in sociology to take Rabbi Jacob's place temporarily and began to talk about easing the rabbi into retirement.

We too tried to adjust. We met a few times by ourselves, but without the knowledge to set our course soon foundered in petty squabbling. For months, Monday after Monday passed in sorrow. We couldn't bear to fill those evenings with anything else, and we couldn't bear to sit staring at each other. I spent more than a few of them glaring and muttering in front of the TV. Our families became impatient with us.

Then, one day, a summons: Rabbi Jacob's quiet voice on the phone. "Woodrow, do you think you could come to the house tomorrow evening, you and Ruel and Marvin and Isaac? It is Monday night, and I—"

"Of course, Rabbi!" I cried, and before I was able to ask about his health or what had happened, he thanked me, wished me good night, and hung up.

This time when Shifra welcomed us in and took our coats we were shy and ill at ease. Everything was in its usual place. She had come from the kitchen where she had been cleaning up after the evening meal. Her looks and manner were the same as ever, yet all of the familiar feel of things only increased our nervousness. When she showed us to the study the desk was bare. No books in piles, no Rabbi. Our feelings were so mixed by then that when Rabbi Jacob did come in we couldn't have said a word.

He walked around to his desk and sat down in silence. Then he looked up at us and smiled, and the room went warm. Such smiles reconcile enemies, prepare heroes, salve the soul raw from the whip of law. "Please allow me to apologize for my conduct," he said mildly. "It has been unforgivable. So taken up was I in my own search for an impossible thing, a vain thing, as it is written, that I neglected to see the worry and sorrow through which I was putting you and all my friends, but you especially. Our Monday evenings have been a great source of joy to me. It is seldom these days that a rabbi is called upon to do what the rabbinate was originally developed to do—to teach. We are used as arbiters of ceremonial detail or as social workers. Neither job is unworthy, but our Monday evenings have been an oasis to me. In treating you so shabbily I have broken many precepts of Torah that specifically enjoin against denying simple goals at the expense of impossible dreams."

"May we know," Stein asked quietly, "what has happened?"

I noticed again how still it was, how living and rich the stillness. It made a fit background for the giving and receiving of subtle thoughts and delicate differences of meaning.

"I found," Rabbi Jacob said quietly, "that I was suffering certain pains and moments of dizziness and exhaustion. I went to the doctor and had the necessary tests made, and the results showed that I am suffering from a fatal and incurable disease. I am not expected to live out the year."

Then we sat in a different silence, looking away from him and each other. It seemed a long while before Rabbi Jacob spoke again. "You know how strange a man can be—my first thought was, 'But I'm so young!' " He laughed. "Seventy-one years old and still I have not learned to be grateful for my life, but only immediately to want more. How very tolerant the Master of the Universe is! And yet—" and he looked around at all of us, trying to pull us away from our shock and sorrow, "yet, I could swear I haven't lived those years at all! I would have said thirty, perhaps, or forty, and no more than fifteen of them as a married man. I'm sure you feel this at your ages, this shrinking of time. It gets worse, you know, as time goes on, and the old compound their sin by feeling that if only they had another score of years to live, another decade even, that they would not waste *that* time, would not squander *that* richness. All the while, the Giver of All Abundance must ride by in majesty and shake His head."

He was smiling, almost laughing for that moment, and then his face clouded. "In my venture into ingratitude I begat many sins. I have found this to be true, that one sin begets a dozen others. I became impatient, jealous of the time I had left. I wanted to study Torah, I thought, to perfect that intimate conversation with the sages before I left the world. I thought that if I withdrew from the silly details of daily life—the soothing of sisterhood secretaries, the mollifying of board members, even of the necessity of correcting your translation errors—that if I shook off all these weights I would be free to reach toward great truths, to plumb the depths of Talmudic wisdom, to . . . *shine*."

Beside me, Levin was weeping quietly. I, shocked into the rawest reaction of selfishness, heard my mind saying to itself over and over, "What will I do on Mondays? What will I do when I read the Bible and confront those coils of contradiction? How will I find the meaning in all the places where there seems to be no meaning?"

"It is said," Rabbi Jacob murmured, "that the Lord withdraws himself. He leaves a gaping vacuum inside each man, and the more the man is conscious of the vacuum, the larger it seems. Our sages tell us He does this so that the man will have to grow out into that space, will have to expand in seeking Him and will come at last to be a finished creation by finishing himself. The gift is that we are unfinished. The sixth day is not yet over for us. He did not wish to keep from us the greatest joy, the joy of creating something—not only civilization, but ourselves. It makes Him and us colleagues in the work. He needs a more free and equal colleague—so He withdraws. I withdrew, but I am not the Lord, and therefore the space I left, the vacuum I formed, yawned around me and nearly swallowed me up. Like the miser with money, I put time before the Lord, breaking the second commandment and therefore also the first. I was almost lost, before my Shifra, as only a wife can, brought me to my senses and made me see how close to the rim of apostasy and chaos I was. Come, take down the Midrash index—there is still time tonight. I want us to study together as long as we can—weeks, months, maybe a year, and if I am impatient, forgive me. I am more conscious now of Time flowing away."

We studied. At first it was stilted and self-conscious, but soon we were ourselves—the true self always reappears—stubborn Stein, plodding Becker, scattered Levin, and myself (What is my weakness? I don't know). It was only later when we were standing together outside Rabbi Jacob's door that we looked at each other and felt tears well in our eyes in the icy night.

II

I had a dream. I was at Rabbi Jacob's desk, behind a wall of books. Beside me, various tractates of Talmud marked here and there for reference were stacked. Opening one, I read in Hebrew: "Time is money." It was in the center portion where the Torah passage is. To the side, in additional commentary, it said, "Possession is nine points of the law." On the other side there were only numbers and letters. I did not understand and turned the book back to its title. Then I saw that what I was studying was not Talmud at all, but one of the mystical books of the Cabbala, which had somehow gotten in with the Talmudic work. To understand I would have to go deep into visionary associations and numerology. I looked at the numbers and letters again: שׁ אִים בּ ים יׄם 1½‪ 1בְּ1½ 10בַּ 3. What could that mean? The portion referred back to the original material. Time is money. Perhaps I should be thinking about possession of Time as though it were money, about Time and the law.

And suddenly I had it, as it comes sometimes in dreams, by revelation, and I looked again at the numbers and letters and at the sudden clear sense they made. What if governments had found a way to tax Time? They tax money, and Time is infinitely more valuable than money. We say we "spend" Time, and it disappears like money, yet we all know that after the years have gone they do not seem like real years, each a year long. The weeks and months slip by almost before we can count them.

The letters and numbers before me were a formula, the formula by which the governments figure their taxation. I got some paper and wrote it all out: שׁ אִים בּ ים ים 1½‪ 1בְּ1½ 10בַּ 3. In English it translates as 3 in 10 and 1½ in 1 and 1½ day in day in man—per man: 3 years out of every decade plus 1½ months per . . . per year, plus 1½ weeks . . . no, hours, per day per man. Ish, not Adam—not a common man, but a mature man, grown and carrying a heavy portion of the world's weight. The Cabbala and Talmudic texts were open and spread-eagled in punishment before me when I finished my figuring.

There is a specific injunction against spread-eagling books, but I somehow felt I had broken free of ordinary Law and commandment. Ish was suffering and Adam would free him.

Rabbi Jacob came in wearing tallis and tefillin. How old he looked, how taxed. He had been levied upwards of thirty years, had lost them from study, from work, from life, from us.

"Come," he said, "the maariv service is beginning. Let us go in to prayer."

"I'm not going to pray anymore," I answered. "I'm going to the place where they have it stored. I am going to rifle the storehouse and come back with your Time."

I woke lighthearted and laughing. I could hardly wait to tell Stein and Becker and Levin the funny story of my dream. Now, I thought, when I wait on line at any government bureau I can complain of double taxation. And what a secret, the secret of all that Time stored somewhere! Who could be in charge of collections, of storage? The commodity was so much more valuable than gold or radium—who could be trusted with such a thing? The guards would have to be people who thought they were guarding something else. And the classification of such a secret? X^2, of course! I laughed through my shaving; I was jaunty at breakfast for the first time in months. X^2, Secret of Secrets. Maybe that wouldn't be so bad. The more classified a secret is, the easier it is to get people to give it out since they themselves are not sure who is in on it.

A tax on time. Time collectors. Time storage. In what, boxes? Why not, I wondered, spin out the joke a little for Becker and Stein and Levin, who needed to laugh and be lighthearted, too? I wrote a letter.

FROM: Z'man Container Corporation
TO: CIA Washington, D.C. Maximum Classification—
        Top Secret
RE: Your most-valuable nonsolid resource

Dear Sirs: We have been subcontracted to supply a number of boxes and containers to your most-classified installations in rural areas. These boxes are to measure and hold our most-valuable nonsolid commodity. We have had great difficulty contacting the liaison personnel in charge of the contract. Please advise.

To my surprise it was answered.

FROM: CSLS 31 Treasury Department, Washington, D.C.
TO: Z'man Container Corporation

Dear Sirs: The Department CC 135 has been moved to the Disbursement Division of the Treasury Department, subsection Billing and Audit. In future please address inquiries to Mr. John Rulliger of that Department.

I wrote again.

FROM: Z'man Container Corporation
TO: Mr. John Rulliger, CC 135 Treasury Department,
          Washington, D.C.
RE: Subcontract of essential materials

Dear Sirs: We are sorry to inconvenience you, but we have had great difficulty contacting the liaison personnel in charge of the subcontract of the boxes and containers you contracted for to be sent to your classified installations in rural areas. These boxes are to measure and hold our most-valuable nonsolid resource/commodity. Time is getting short, and if we are to fulfill our responsibility we need the necessary information regarding size, weight, number, etc.

FROM: J. Rulliger, CC 135 Treasury Department,
        Washington, D.C.

TO: Z'man Container Corporation

Dear Sirs: We did not know that Ferris Container had subcontracted any of its work for us. However, we are aware that
there has been a reorganization at Ferris, and possibly in the
confusion of changes in the middle echelons, contact has been
lost. Liaison is carried out by the X 18 J computer at Linch,
Wyoming. You can address all materials to this terminal through
the regular number.

In attempting to share my joke with Becker, Levin, and Stein, I had
become a professional comedian, and I saw the difference immediately. By trade, I'm a tailor. I work at Martin's Menswear doing
alterations. When I hear a funny story I like to pass it along to one of
the men on the floor or to a customer being measured. But arranging a
joke, building it, planning it, and then calling people away from other
things to come and laugh is quite different and infinitely harder.
"What's the trouble?" Stein asked. "You sounded so odd over the
phone—it's not something about the rabbi, is it? You didn't hear
anything—"

"No, no!" (What a way to start a funny story!) "Something happened to me, something that made me feel so much better I thought
I'd ask you to come over and hear about it, that's all."

They looked at each other and I looked at them. They seemed so
stodgy and slow, sitting in the sunny part of the living room. The heart
for telling the joke left me, but I had to go through with it all the same
or send them home with nothing. So I began. I told them the dream in
all its details, about the government's having taxed Time. Then, the
capper. I showed them the letters. They sat and stared at me. "There's
more to it," I said. "Once you see the thing this way there are all kinds
of themes in it—like a Talmud portion—little diversions. This morning I was thinking, well, it must be a graduated tax. As a man gets

richer in Time, that is, older, the amount must increase geometrically. That's why a year seems so long to a child. He is not taxed. The year then is actually one year long, whereas for Rabbi Jacob—well, according to my calculations it might be as much as seven years out of every decade." Three stares and dead silence.

I admit I was irritated with their slowness, but I began to think I could see what was behind it. When one studies Jewish Law for any time at all, he realizes that almost nothing is impossible. Damage cases involving three-legged cows owned by underage alcoholics are dealt with without so much as a pause in the rhythm of the chant. Every possibility is weighed and considered. Think your wildest thought—some bearded old sage in Pumbeditha has thought of it before you, and far from banishing it to a passing shrug, has handed it around to the other sages for discussion. Talmudic disputation is by its nature finite and very literal. The problems it poses and wrestles with are problems of living, never of belief. Could it be that these men were so earthbound, so literal, that they were unable to take a Talmudic word or two and blow them away into moonbeam shavings just to watch them glitter on the wind? I think I sighed.

"You said in your letter rural installations," Levin said ponderously. "How do you know that it's Time they keep there, and not some mineral or other?"

"I said installations, plural, and you notice they didn't balk at that. I've given it thought. The Time would have to be kept in small amounts in out-of-the-way places, because if there was any leakage or accident they wouldn't want people around who could experience changes in their perception. Time is heavier than air, but only slightly, and thus needs to be stored—"

"Heavier than air—" Becker interrupted. "How can you tell that?"

"By observation. If it were lighter it would rise in the air and the birds and people in the mountains would all be longer-lived, while people in the valleys would all die young. If Time were the same weight the birds would live at the same rate as we. Of course, if Time were much heavier it would concentrate in all the low places and couldn't be moved except by great winds. But Time *feels* light—when a person is at peace, resting, it is as light and light-catching as a dandelion wisp blown by a child."

"Try and get a good night's sleep when you're worried," Stein cried.

"I'm sure it slows at night. That must be because it is cooled. Cooled Time, like cooled air, must travel at a slower rate. This would explain why birds live such short lives—their body temperatures are higher than ours, higher than the long-lived crocodile and the slow turtle. The storage places would have to be in remote areas, probably cool areas too, and the Time would be refrigerated or perhaps frozen, not to protect it against spoilage, but to slow it, to preserve it in its present form for as long as possible."

"What do you mean by 'present form'?"

This was the most recent part of my joke, the physics part. I had laughed all morning. "We've been told that the universe is a closed system, that air and water are not gained or lost but only changed to be recirculated in some other form—now solid, now liquid, now gas. If no other property in the whole physical system is gained or lost, how can it be different with Time? What seems to be a loss of Time, the spending of Time, must be only a change. The government isn't interested in eternity. If it were, it would practice deeper virtues. It is interested in Time, in this present form."

"You're aiming toward something," Becker said. "What are you after? What's all this about?"

"It's about moonbeam shavings!" I cried. "About dandelion fluff!" And suddenly I knew it wasn't at all. "It's about Rabbi Jacob dying," I said, "before I am ready for it. There is Time. It exists. People use it, spend it, count it, waste it, ignore it, diminish it. I want to steal it, to go where it is stored and steal it, and then I want to shut Rabbi Jacob up in a roomful of it until he breathes it in, receives it through his pores, until it gathers in his clothes and lies with the lint at the bottom of his pockets. I want to cloud him with Time."

"It's a sin," Stein murmured, "stealing anything, and so consciously done—stealing Time would be a sin."

"A computer," Becker said, "the letter mentions a computer. They scare me. What do we know about computers?"

"A computer will give us our chance," I said, "our perfect chance. I saw on TV a show about—"

"If we can find a way to keep Rabbi Jacob, I would risk a lot," Becker said, "a lot."

We knew he was speaking of an idea we had discussed briefly with the rabbi. Some medieval Jewish mystics held that the acts of men have widespread effects in the heavenly realms as well as in the physical world. Perhaps a lie extinguishes a star. When a man curses the Lord, Venus pales for a moment; a woman's gratitude gives an aspen root the power to split a rock. "With this time," Levin murmured, "our studies would widen us. We would be able to do acts of courage and to learn deeper justice . . . " He turned to us. "You know what happens when Rabbi Jacob talks about the gifts of some people to survive and endure. Doesn't it make your soul sing? Remember when he discussed the implications of the double helix and the communication of dolphins? Imagine a lifetime spent learning such things, opening outward with the Law and all the sciences and all the new things to come!"

"It's a sin," Stein said again. Becker looked from one of them to the other.

"I would steal for Rabbi Jacob," Levin said quietly. "I have been thinking this over, and what it comes down to is that *if* the substance in those installations is really Time and this Time can be breathed or injected or rubbed into Rabbi Jacob somehow, I would wish to do it unless—"

"It's a *sin*!" Stein cried. "Don't you understand? Of the two classes of sin it is the worse, since it acts against no particular man, it acts against God, and only God can forgive it."

"If we get caught," Becker said, "God will be the least of our worries."

"I wrote those letters playing, but the game isn't over. I want to play some more. I need to play, because if I don't I will be thinking about a pitiful handful of Monday nights, about the unfairness of it all, and I will fall into heresy. Last week I was reading a new collection of Talmud commentary and I came across what the law calls 'the evil impulse.' The sages tell us to fight this evil impulse with all the power at our command, and when there is no more with which to fight, nothing more with which to subdue the evil impulse, to dress in black and go to the sin and sin it."

"And then to endure the punishment that comes from it, I think," Levin said quietly. "But whether this is a sin or just a game, I don't know. I only know I want to go on playing it, or sinning it, whichever it is."

"Thank you," I said.

"You want us to help you, don't you?" Becker asked. "You are asking us to help, but if we deny our help you will do it all alone, won't you?"

"Yes."

"We would have to learn more—much more," Becker said, "about Time and . . . about the crime." We found ourselves laughing, but only I was laughing with relief.

It was late. We planned another meeting to give everyone time to think. The greatest danger at that moment was in seeing Rabbi Jacob for our Monday meeting. Surely a dozen ethical issues had been raised, and our concerns were bound to be reflected in the kinds of questions we brought to the Monday session. Fortunately, Rabbi's "withdrawal" had given him a backlog of things he had thought of to discuss with us, and we spent the following Monday ploughing the stars over the question of withdrawal from the community and the places in the Talmud that enjoin against it. During the week I did some more work.

I called the adult-education people at the junior college and asked them about courses in computer programming. They said a night class was being offered. I called the man who was teaching the class and told him I might be interested in taking it, but that I needed to consult with him first. I had, perhaps, the wrong expectations in what I could get from such a course. We agreed to meet at the school. After a brief demonstration of a small model he used for the class, he asked me what I did. I told him I was in business. It hurt me to lie directly like that, face-to-face. It made me feel even worse to know that this was only the first lie, one of a number—that there would soon be so many lies that I would lose count of them.

"In five years, no businessman will be without a computer for his business and private use," the teacher said. "Computers are being used to monitor all kinds of things—food supplies, transportation patterns—even pollution."

"Pollution?" I asked politely.

"Take a river," he said, warming to his work. "A river passing factories and cities and towns on its way to the sea. Here sodium and phosphorus enter, here sewage; here the effluent is cleaned before it is put into the river, here a feedlot leaches nitrogen and ammonia. Certain chemicals react on one another to form entirely new compounds. Properly programmed, a computer is able to tell exactly what the components of that river will be at any location."

"It doesn't only go *into* the river," I said, feeling strange, "it comes *out,* too—it must be drawn *out* of the river at one place or another . . . for *use.*" Something was beginning to dawn on me.

"Yes, of course," he said, "but the whole point is that—"

"Time is a river," I said. "One often hears it spoken of in that way." I was smiling. The teacher gave me a strange look. As he finished his talk I listened as hard as I could, but my mind was busy with its own figuring. Concentrating on the process by which Time had been taken away, I saw that I had never understood the possibility of its being put back, *used.* They couldn't simply be storing it; they must be using little amounts of it like the gold at Fort Knox, moving it, shipping it, delivering it to people for use. For *use.*

I could see at the next meeting that Stein was still worried about the nature of the sin. I had thought when I saw them next that I would try to put a pleasing face on things when I explained the problem. After all, if the material monitored by the computer at Linch was Time, it was our Time, time that had been taken from us without our knowledge or approval; it belonged to us. We would be reclaiming it. When I saw Stein I knew that such evasions of the truth were useless and that to lie like that would be demeaning to me and to him and to all of us, and to the act we meant to do, whatever that would be. I had prepared a little speech about why Rabbi Jacob needed to stay alive to help us gain wisdom and knowledge of the law. The life of every wise and good man, I was going to say, embarrasses evil, warms the cold places of experience, piles stones on the graves of tyrants. As I looked at Stein and Levin and Becker, I knew that I had to be clear and to evade nothing. "What if it is Time, stored in ten or fifty or a hundred places around the country? Before I ask you to come with me, we will make certain it *is* Time and not something else. We must work quickly because the container corporation people and the government and the computer people may get together and then we'll be sunk. I'm asking for your help, although I know it is a sin. I plan, however, to risk as little as possible. There will be no breaking of any commandment for which death was ordained by ancient Law and no profanation of the Name of God. I have just put in ten hours in front of the TV set watching crime shows so that I could learn the proper way to commit a crime and could see some criminal skills being practiced. None of those crimes were right for us. All of those criminals profaned the Name of God—they would make a good man doubt God's sanity. Our crime, if you consent to help me, must be a crime without violence. No one must be hurt, no one must be caused to doubt God's sanity. I saw a scene on TV in which a criminal pretended to be hurt and then attacked the man who came to help him. What a terrible thing!"

"I remember Rabbi Jacob's discussion of the evil that drives good men to sin in response to it," Becker said. "My problem there is in the definition—"

"What you're saying," Stein interrupted, looking at me, "is that you want a crimeless crime by invisible men who steal without the victims knowing it."

I nodded. "Perfect," I said. "That is precisely what I want."

Levin threw up his hands. "All right. Let us assume that it is Time we are stealing, Time stolen from us all, from our sleep, our studies, our trips with our grandchildren to the circus, Time stored in bags or boxes or tiny vials like the ones doctors give shots from. How are we to steal it?"

"The government collects it, but even something as compressable as Time imposes demands of various kinds—pressure, perhaps. The economics of the thing, psychological as well as financial, demand that it sometimes be used, taken out of storage and opened up somewhere to be released slowly . . ."

"For instance?" Becker said, looking dubious.

"If our wheat harvest has been slowed by bad weather, crop-duster planes could fly over the Midwest spraying Time. The stock market needs a rally of confidence. There would be a need to release small amounts of Time in certain key places. Let us ask the question Where is the advantage of a greater number of hours, days, weeks? There is a computer at Linch, Wyoming, that monitors all this, frees the Time, allocates it, counts and measures it. The place at Linch might be a storage bank also; it is rural, quiet, central, and cool. Just the place for a storehouse."

"You mean we have to go there with guns and rob the place?" Stein said, still offended and making the worst of it.

"We have to make the computer free this Time to us. We have to make the keepers of the Time bring it to us in the usual way. First, I think we must look over the Ferris Container Corporation which is located in Pontiac, Michigan. No, pardon me. First, we must decide if you want to commit yourselves to this project."

"Sin," Stein said.

"Sin," I agreed.

There was silence. I saw Stein move his eyes from me to the things in the room. I heard Levin moving in his chair, sighing. Becker sat still. After a while he said quietly, "What you say is true about it being a sin. You know the story of Bontshe Shweig? I always figured I was a little like Bontshe, living a silent life not because I was a hero but because I was too stupid to know how to yell. The angels laughed at Bontshe. I would rather have the angels curse me than laugh at me. It's for Rabbi Jacob that we would be doing this. When you said that thing about the wheat crop I saw Rabbi Jacob standing there in the wheat field, too. If Time falls on the wheat fields surely it falls on the grasshoppers and the things that plague the wheat. Why not on him?"

"We haven't even gone once through the Torah," Levin sa~
would need a few years even to begin to learn how to study by ~
selves, how to find our way through the hard parts—"

"What if they caught us?" Stein said. "They couldn't try us because of the secret. They would have to kill us."

"Really?" Becker whispered.

"I don't believe in any of this," Levin said. "I don't think Time is
stored. I think it's gone. If it is stored I don't think we can get a
computer to give it to us. I don't believe we are clever enough to get
away with anything, and I want to go on record right now as being a
complete and unalterable nonbeliever in the whole thing."

"You're not coming along then?"

"Who said that? Of course I'm coming. I couldn't stand being at
home while you three are making fools of yourselves in Pontiac, Michigan, or Linch, Wyoming. When you leave here the average level of
intelligence will rise six points. I wouldn't be able to live in so lofty an
atmosphere!"

III

We said we were from Israel. After sending an introductory letter on
stationery that Stein had had printed, we called the public-relations
man at Ferris Container. We had elected Becker to "head the delega-
tion" because he made the most convincing Israeli. We decided that
Israel would have a far more primitive setup than whatever the Ferris
people showed us. We would play to their patriotism a little and might
mask the fact that as managers of the largest container company in
Israel we did not have a clue as to how containers were produced.

The men of Z'man Container Corporation were given far more
than the usual tour. Our wonder at the splendors of American technology was repaid in full. They couldn't show us enough. And it *was*

wonderful. I don't know what I expected, but it certainly wasn't the variety and complexity of boxes and containers—plastic, paper, metal, coated and plain, folded, extruded, molded in a bewildering array of sizes, shapes, and special linings. Most of the runs were charted and monitored by the computers that took up two big rooms in the heart of the plant. Mr. Onthank, the P.R. man who showed us around, discussed the problems of synchronizing the arrival of raw material with the needs of special runs and the problems of remaining flexible, ready to redesign and retool at the drop of a hat, for the special needs of client corporations. When asked politely how various problems were handled in Israel, Becker relied on frank generalities. "Of course, in our country, we do not have the needs that you do—our rates of production are lower. We use computers also, but we have the problem to change now from less to more variety and also to increase technology. It is why we visit all over your country different companies, big and small."

"Well, we aren't the biggest by a long shot," Onthank said. "We prefer a wide range of contracts from middle-sized companies, chicken farms to scientific supply houses."

"And of course, the government," Becker said. My heart began to beat faster.

"I suppose we might do some government work, but the amount is negligible."

"The importance is great, though," Becker persisted. "We were already visiting to Linch, to the facility there."

"Linch?" Onthank said. My throat was dry and stuck together. Had I had a club I would have murdered Becker with it. This was supposed to have been a sightseeing visit.

"Linch, Wyoming," Becker said. "We have also the same problems in Israel, only with slighter numbers so the rates must be higher."

"Frankly, I don't know of anything at all we have in Wyoming," Onthank said. "Are you sure you don't have us confused with another firm?"

"Definitely not," Becker said. "It is the reason that we are now visiting this company. There is, in future distant, a plan to deposit, I think, in various countries, and to be standardized in equipment is necessary. Just to begin, of course. Actual plans later, much later."

Becker was not a great actor. What he was saying terrified me, and I was no less terrified by the way his accent and diction thickened and thinned, now a slight modification of English, now an almost indecipherable sentence or two. I was expecting Onthank to notice the discrepancy at any moment, but he seemed unaware of it. As we passed the administration offices on our tour, Onthank excused himself and went into one of the offices, leaving us gratefully alone in the hall. Levin seized the chance. "Goddamnit, Becker!" he muttered. "What are you doing? We're supposed to be looking, that's all! You've spilled the beans, and Onthank is in there calling the Treasury Department this minute!"

"Which may remember Z'man Containers," I said, "but as an American, not an Israeli firm."

"We could still leave—just walk away," Stein said, "and not get caught."

"We haven't broken any laws yet," Becker said with surprising placidity. "The Linch business was information given to us by the Treasury people themselves. We came here to look but also to find out, if we could, what there is to find out. It's the machines, the computers that frighten me, not the people. We are only talking to people."

"How much do they really know?" Levin said. "You yourself said no one could be trusted with the secret."

"I also said that the clever way would not be to pretend the facilities didn't exist but that they were being used for something else —industrial gases of some kind . . ."

Mr. Onthank came out of the office and with him was another man. We did not breathe. "This is Mr. Jurjevitch," he said. "Mr. Jurjevitch knows more than I do about the Linch facilities. I'm going to leave you in his capable hands for the remainder of the tour. He has a wider knowledge of that area of our operation." We could see that he was miffed. He had probably ducked into a VP's office to ask about Linch and had the whole thing whipped out of his hands before he knew it.

Mr. Jurjevitch knew all about Linch. He assumed that we did, too.

Occasionally Stein would say the first three lines of Psalm 114 in Hebrew and I would answer with the second three so that we would seem to be conferring. Becker spoke again of the necessity to standardize equipment. "You will go of course soon on metric system," Becker said to Jurjevitch, "and will the changes be great?"

"Oh, for the Greenwich Project we've been on metric since the beginning. There won't be many problems, gentlemen, except of course for the pressure valves at the bottom. The basic packaging for the product could be a two-kilo freezer box."

"Interesting." We nodded to each other.

"Oh, we must not forget," I said, "when the negotiations go through we will have what they call liaison men. I am such a man for our company, and before we have left for U.S. I was to get some names of your men to meet here, but the date was pushed ahead because of some government thing and we never got the names, and now we are moving too fast to have the information sent to us—"

Jurjevitch smiled. "I suppose all governments are the same in the way they get things screwed up—uh—confused. You will probably be dealing with Louis Merrem and Frank Dahm here. Louis is in Kansas City at the moment, but I'm sure I could get hold of Frank—"

"Oh, no, please," I insisted. "There will be other visits when plans are firmer, and we do not wish to embarrass ourselves or our country that things were not done correctly." He nodded, understandingly. A nice man.

When we were at last out of the plant I was sticky and uncomfortable. I felt rank with the sweats that had started on me and dried and started again whenever things got tense. We stood in the parking lot around our rental car and caught our breath. "I want to close this as soon as possible," I said. "Z'man Containers will write to Ferris in a week or two, and pleading national emergency and the scope of operations, will tell them with deep regret that the plans for internationalization of the resources 'must be postponed for the present.' "

"Why bother? It would be another piece of evidence, another letter in a file."

"Yes, but it would close the file and then no one would need to ask questions. If anyone remarked to the Treasury Department people about international plans, they too would probably say 'not at present.' Things fall through—a closed file."

"I took all their promotional material," Levin said. "I also copied the first numbers I saw on their computer printouts. I also got some of their stationery. I thought we might need it."

"I never knew I could do what I did!" Becker cried, "acting that way—I almost talked myself into believing there was a Z'man Container Corporation in Israel and that I worked there. Stein was wonderful, too, the way he looked and nodded and then said things to us in Hebrew."

"I used Psalm One-fourteen because it had lots of names and places and no hallelujahs or amens in it."

I looked at us standing there close together. How breathless and triumphant and excited we were! How we were enjoying our lies and thievery! I never would have believed it, and I hadn't the heart to point it out to them. The Laws prohibit these things because they are evil and exciting. If lies and deception bring color to the cheek and a sparkle to the eye, incest and murder must be a taste one soon savors like wine. I shivered and could not speak for a minute.

FROM: Ferris Container Corporation CSLS 31 1x1x 901
TO: Cix 531 BULC 175302, Linch, Wyoming
RE: Greenwich Project

Dear Sirs: Due to a fire in northern New York storage facility, please send an 8-box shipment to the boardroom of the First National Bank, Tarrytown, N.Y. Date to follow.

FROM: Z'man Container Corporation
TO: Ferris Container Corporation

Dear Mr. Dahm: During our conversation with Mr. Jurjevitch regarding internationalization of the Greenwich Project CSLS 31 standardization was mentioned. Since we do not know what the valves on your units are like, would you please send us the requisition material for 8 of these units. It is not necessary to send us the units themselves, as negotiations are not to such a point. Please send this material to Mr. Yitzchak Levin, Page Hotel, Tarrytown, N.Y. Please send these as quickly as possible as we are to leave in three days for return to Israel. Please speak also to Mr. Jurjevitch and Mr. Onthank with special good wishes for their hospitality of us when we visited your plant. Now as American government's guests we are touring installations at northern New York and admiring American development and also friendliness for which you do not have reputation abroad but it is truly so. Sincerely,

"You're laying it on too thick," Levin said.

"It sounds like me, and that's what we want," Becker said. "What I don't know is why we need it in the first place."

"It's an assumption of English usage," I answered. "We will have a requisition for *boxes*. The delivery people will have a shipment of *boxes*. When we say *boxes* in English we assume we include the contents of the boxes."

"I'm going to jail for linguistics," Becker said.

"Semantics," I corrected him.

"I can't get the identity cards right," Stein complained. "They'll be embossed and have the seal and all that, but something is missing."

For some reason, Stein's fussiness about his part of the project made me impatient.

"What's the matter, is the eagle drooping? Who is going to peer into its eyes to see if they sparkle!"

"The seal has no eagle. Stars, balance, key. No eagle. We need an ID card that will be convincing, a card with some *character* to it! You of all people should understand," he cried. "You and Levin. You wouldn't let a puckered seam come out of your machine uncorrected. Levin couldn't walk away from a mortised joint that didn't meet. You read the words on a page—I look at the printing. A man has a certain pride in his work even if he doesn't sign it. I'm a printer. This work is mine."

Becker shrugged and looked heavenward, but I looked at Stein and understood what he was saying. We had found out secrets, given ourselves false identities, lied. It was deep water we were in. We might be caught, imprisoned, even shot as spies, and if we had to stand in some sunny afternoon street in handcuffs under the drawn guns of police, at least the phony cards we had flashed should show the careful craft of a good printer.

We had made the arrangements as well as we could. "The boardroom" sounded impressive, but it was my bank, and the bank let any of its depositors reserve it at certain times. We had reserved a Thursday afternoon a week ahead of time. We then sent a telegram to Linch ordering our eight units to be delivered to us at the boardroom on Thursday. The requisition forms from Mr. Dahm at Ferris came the next day.

By this time we figured we had used every manner of interstate communication to defraud except carrier pigeon. We had falsified documents and would impersonate an arm of the government, a small but select arm. Stein, I could see, was studying us for other signs of criminality—the advancing cynicism and self-centeredness that begin to shadow the criminal personality until it is so darkened that its original lines can no longer be perceived. It is true that Becker had taken to calling me "buddy," and he also laughed more than usual. I, being frightened much of the Time, had trouble sleeping, and this began to show in my work. Also, our sessions with Rabbi Jacob had become occasions for hiding rather than seeking, for expounding "safe" Law—law that did not touch us. Sometimes I saw a quizzical look cross Rabbi Jacob's face. I began to feel a profound pity for those who have to practice duplicity as a way of life—spies, saints, and sex criminals.

Linch replied. Nine-tenths of the Teletype message we received at the bank was coded, but we did see the words *8 units, confirmed Thursday*, and *Tarrytown.*

What does a Treasury man look like? We were in a place where there was money; we were wearing suits and ties and we had Stein's good-looking cards in our wallets. Levin, a widower, had volunteered to clean out his freezer compartment, although I had turned him down for the present. The danger should be mine, at least until we could find out how the Time worked. We had brought an ice chest with us, and there was nothing else to do but sit in the boardroom and wait and wonder what mannerism or word or silence or number, said or unsaid, would give us away. The Germans caught a spy during World War II because he changed his fork to the right hand when he ate—the American way. Beatings followed. Tortures. Confessions. Death. I stared at Becker, Levin, Stein. They stared at me. We knew that if we were caught we would run for the treeless refuge of cowardice, all the traditional whining that started when God asked Adam and Eve whose teeth marks were in the apple core lying at His feet: "I followed *him.* It was *his* idea." "I was misguided." "I didn't know the real plan." We were paying no taxes at all on the time we spent waiting. Each minute was a full sixty seconds, each hour a full sixty minutes. We weren't used to untaxed time. It felt like forever.

At 4:30 there was a knock at the door. It suddenly occurred to me that none of us was young and that a heart attack would not be beyond the realm of possibility for any of us. Levin got up and went to the door. The two men standing there looked like ordinary uniformed delivery-men. We stood up and showed our cards and the requisition: eight boxes CSLS 31. They scarcely looked at them. "Where are your carriers?" one of the men said. Time tore apart again, stopping. It seemed as though I couldn't understand the words anymore. I stood where I was. Then Becker swept forward. "Didn't *you* bring any? We thought *you* were supposed to supply them—"

"Christ!" the elder of the two said. "Another screw-up. We've got six other shipments to deliver by tomorrow, and five of them are at the other end of the state. Now you say you don't have any carriers. We can't give you the ones we have. You'll have to carry the boxes by hand. I suppose you've never transported without carriers, have you?"

"No," I said wanly, "never." He shook his head disgustedly. "Carry them slow and keep them cool. No jogging. This stuff, whatever it is, is very unstable. You'll have to loosen the pressure valves very slightly, and there will be a very small leakage—if you don't, you're risking a terrible explosion. I'd wait until after dark if I were you—the stuff is more stable then. And next time requisition the carriers too. Why in hell they don't supply the carriers on the unit requisitions, I'll never know. Take care of those things—" They unlocked a big wheeled box and removed an insulated case and from it took eight two-kilo plastic boxes, set them before us on the table, and left.

The boxes were too heavy to put in the ice chest. We had done all our worrying about size and had never thought about compression and weight. We put four of the boxes in the chest. When the chest was in the car we would probably be able to put the others in. The problem was getting the boxes out of the building and across the parking lot to the car. As I watched I saw the four remaining boxes begin to swell ever so slightly. I reached over and loosened the little plastic screw valve the smallest turn. There was a very slight hiss. "We've got to hurry," I said. Stein and I took two boxes each, Becker and Levin carried the chest between them. There was ice in it, and it was so heavy that they had to lift it from the bottom. I told Becker and Levin to wait until we had gone and not to follow us too closely. If our Time exploded we did not want the shock of the explosion to set off their Time too. The boardroom was on the sixth floor. We were in agony while the elevator went down and came up again. "Listen," Stein said to me while the untaxed moments dragged by, "we have eight boxes. Right? That's years, decades, centuries, maybe. My sister is in the hospital with a cancer now twice operated on. What if I took one box to her—just one—and I could dole it out to the rest of the family—just little bits of it, just enough to—"

"This is Time we're stealing," I said as gently as I could, "not happiness. Your sister would be having nothing but more Time in agony. Is that the blessing you want to give her?"

Talmudic writing always stresses mildness and now I know why. I often wondered why the Fathers never showed a sage hopping mad, even in the face of evil or stupidity. When a mild man says no, there is no arguing with it. Stein had begun to weep quietly, but the way was unalterably barred. When the elevator came we got on followed by Levin and Becker, who said they could wait no longer. We rode down in silence.

The lobby of the bank was almost empty and the street seemed comparatively bare. "Look!" Levin whispered behind me, "there's hardly anyone here. It's a miracle in this rush-hour Time, everything dead like this—I swear, it's a sign—"

"Please!" Stein hissed at him. "Don't blaspheme in the National Bank. God may allow us to live in spite of what we're doing, but that's no sign of His approval. That He spares the guilty and allows the innocent to be enslaved, burned in ovens—"

He stopped walking and I stopped too and looked at him. He began to stammer. "I . . . I . . . Why am I saying such things now? Why am I thinking such things?"

My heart went out to him. I too could feel a sorrow, a heaviness welling up in me that I could neither explain nor put aside. We continued through the lobby of the bank, and no one looked at us. I felt myself beginning to drown in despair. Behind me Levin sighed, a sound that ended in a groan of anguish. "Over our heads the ashes of our fathers are still floating gently down, and by our sides our children grow up not knowing, not wanting to know, what those fathers died believing. In the middle I come, trying to be happy, bereft of my father and divorced from my children—"

We picked out the car on the other side of the parking lot and began to walk toward it. In our despair we seemed to be crawling in slow motion toward a goal a mile away. "This city is like a wilderness," Becker said simply, "a wild place where people act as mindlessly as ants or as savagely as animals."

"And my sister's soul—will it walk in this nothingness!" Stein cried.

"Wait!" I shouted at them, and they stopped. The boxes in my hands were beginning to swell dangerously. Had I not shouted I think the men would have bolted and run screaming into the street, each one alone, howling his despair like a dying animal. The vision had been mine and the leadership, too, and they remembered in Time what they had almost forgotten—who we were stealing for and why. "Now we know," I said over my own anguish, "that what we have been stealing is really Time and nothing else. With the valves open the tiniest crack and the pressure building we are becoming victims of this Time!" They had stopped again and were staring at me. "Can't you see, it's the Time we've been carrying, the Time that's making us half crazy with despair!"

"My God!" Levin said. "And we were greedy over it!"

"Let's go quickly before we suffocate under it, before our bones are broken and our spirits crushed."

"Why *despair*?" Stein asked. "The Time we are carrying should have as much joy as anguish—more, really. America is a fortunate country."

"It's not *experience* we're carrying, it's only *Time*," I said, "raw Time. All of us lie before it like sacrifices on an altar. We have to fight or we'll go mad!"

"Easily said," Levin moaned, "but how is it done? It's crushing me. I can hardly stand up!"

"How have Jews always fought Time and despair? With civilization—with Law."

I began to chant. I made no conscious choice. It was, I suddenly realized, the passage we had been looking at last Time at Rabbi Jacob's. It was a passage regarding the determination of leprosy. I saw Stein begin to open his mouth to ask me why I had chosen this passage and not some exalted verse that bloomed poetry and celebrated divine mercy or justice. I went on, changing to another passage, which I realized to my chagrin concerned menstruant women. "What are you doing?" Becker cried, and then I realized that I had pieced these texts together because they concerned ritual uncleanness—perhaps a metaphor for our own uncleanness before the world and the Lord. I was about to explain until I looked around at the three of them and saw that their faces had relaxed and then realized that I, too, no longer felt the keen edge of anguish.

We began to walk once again, more slowly. The boxes were swelling in the centers, and although we were confident now that we wouldn't die of Time, we began to worry about an explosion. Looking behind me for an instant I saw that Becker and Levin were deadly pale. "Thank God for the Law," Stein whispered. "Why do we imagine we suffer more despair than our fathers?" He was smiling wanly.

We were at the car. It was Becker's, a rust-pocked old DeSoto. We had taken it because it was the biggest car we had. With the ice chest supported on the floor of the trunk, we lay the other two boxes on top of the cover to hold it down. By now they were in pretty bad shape. If we opened the valves a little to release the pressure we would probably not be strong enough to withstand the power of the released Time. If we left them as they were we risked an explosion that would surely blast us to pieces.

The sun was setting. I felt the sudden coolness in the absence of shadows. The car was still warm from the day. The boxes would never stand that heat. I wanted to break down and cry—the cycle of tension and release was making me ill. I needed a quiet Time to heal. Time.

We released the valves again very slightly. There was only the faintest hiss, and the swelling in the boxes did not go down as much as I had hoped. We got into the car carefully and drove it toward the north side of town, absurdly glad that we lived on that north side, the cool north.

"You know," Stein said, "I was thinking about Hitler before—"

"Never mind," I said. "It's only the Time, leaking."

"No, I wasn't despairing, or not entirely. It occurred to me that he has become connected with us, so much a part of our history—sometimes I forget he wasn't a Jew."

"It was a favor God did us," Levin said. I laughed.

"How he would have hated that," I said, "to have his name remembered by us alone, forgotten by all the happy, healthy young Aryans, to remain forever the wolf in a Jew's nightmare."

"I wonder if he will ever become the kind of comfortable and homely enemy that Pharaoh is or Haman—the gregar-voice of celebrating children, domesticated and reduced—the salt to a Passover egg."

"He'll have to fade for a century or two and come into our history more humbly. We don't celebrate inchoate evil. The devil has never been invited to our feasts."

"Too often he has been just outside the door."

"God, we'll have to be so careful with this Time!" Becker said. "It seizes on the slightest weakness. There are people who grow old doubting God's mercy because of—"

"One more word," I said, "and I will chant the law of menstruant women again."

"God forbid!" Becker cried, and we laughed and healed ourselves.

I had told Ruthie to clean out the bottom of our freezer. Until we could learn how to use the Time it would have to stay with me. I had told her the boxes held antelope blood for my boss's blood sausage. A kosher homemaker, she would never touch them, and when I wrapped them in heavy plastic she would see the move as a reasonable way of keeping the contents of our freezer from ritual contamination. Amen. If we could only get the boxes home before they all exploded . . .

IV

It is Monday night. We are sitting at Rabbi Jacob's table, two cups of tea into the discussion. Maimonides, on charity. It has gone back and forth several times with those in full agreement (Becker and Stein) having to concede now and then to arguments from Levin and me.

Levin's point is that completely anonymous charity has a way of becoming a cold, impersonal exercise for both the giver and receiver. My point is that my giving of charity anonymously and in secret precludes others from following my example, especially my delight at seeing a neat bit of giving well received. Becker pounds the table when he is excited, and in the glasses the little crystals jump.

To the right of each man there is a small glass of what looks like ice water, yet no one drinks it. We drink the hot tea, rich with sugar and lemon. Sometimes one of us will make a waving gesture over his water glass. To the outsider it would look as though we are waving a fly away impatiently. It is a rude-looking gesture, and the stranger would be amazed to see that it is additionally rude, since all the flicks are made in one direction, toward Rabbi Jacob. He has told us that it will not help, that waving the very slowly dissolving Time toward him will probably not cause him to live any longer, but you saw him last week at the services. Didn't he look younger, stronger, happier? Didn't it gladden you somehow just to see him standing there smiling? Didn't you hear the fall of a stone on the tyrant's grave?

THEY LIVE

Four Hundred Twenty-one. It was the right address. Surprising. Not a cellar in a sleazy tourist trap, not a weathered shack in the scrub palmetto outside of town. This was a lovely old-fashioned house in the historic section of the city. Through the trees she could see Matanzas Bay. The street was green and quiet. Flowering trees perfumed the neat front lawns, and at 421 a splendid vine grew up a trellis shading the front of the house. The vine had little starlike flowers growing among the green leaves. This couldn't be the place. For a moment Kay was on the point of telling the driver to take her back to the hotel when a plump middle-aged woman came from the back of the house. The woman had obviously been gardening. She had on a pair of denim pants and an old straw hat to keep the sun off. She came toward them purposefully without shyness and stopped at the open window of the cab. "I heard a car stop and thought it must be you. You are Kay Tracy, aren't you? I'm Marjorie Maas."

They went up the walk, Mrs. Maas chatting comfortably. If she had been surprised by the house, Kay was confounded by Mrs. Maas herself. The woman exuded the homey poise Kay associated with garden-club presidents. "Let's go around to the back," Mrs. Maas said. "There's a quiet place where we can talk. Some people are very shy the first time and feel more comfortable being outside. Possibility of escape, I suppose."

"You mean people come here more than once?"

"Oh, yes, some people change their minds entirely; some think of new details to modify their plans. I don't believe in being rigid about these things, do you? People do change, and they should be comfortable with any plan they make."

The back garden looked out on the bay. Vines and shrubbery formed natural fences between the houses. There was a restful silence, the silence of shade and deep grass. Under one of the larger trees, two wrought-iron garden chairs and a small round table, painted white, stood waiting. Mrs. Maas motioned to Kay to choose one of the chairs. It was a gesture of old-fashioned courtesy made almost primly. Kay sat down, Mrs. Maas followed. Kay found herself calmer than she thought she would be. "What a charming place," she said. "What a wonderful place this is."

"You're surprised, I think." Mrs. Maas smiled. "Most people expect to come to some grubby hotel on a squalid street and meet an unpleasant drink-sodden old party. I do my work well, and it is quite lucrative. I enjoy living well. The neighborhood is congenial—retired people, mostly, quiet and well-mannered. When I need to employ any help, I do so from a small group of dependable and trusted colleagues." She turned, smiling politely, to Kay. "Now, which is it to be, murder or suicide?"

Kay was left speechless for a time. She had not thought of confronting the word aloud. "I . . . I didn't know you . . . uh . . . arranged murders," she said.

Mrs. Maas smiled slightly. "The people who come for murders wonder that I arrange suicides also. From my point of view, of course, the problems are the same. So, that is what you need, then, a suicide?" Kay nodded. She was still unable to say the word. "I should apologize, I know," Mrs. Maas said, "but I never could abide those silly euphemisms . . . 'doing away with,' 'dispatching.' You know, in English law there is a crime characterized as 'interfering with,' and it includes murder. Both murder and suicide are quite serious matters, and I think they should be faced frankly. Very few of the people who come to me do so on impulse. The people I see are consumed with their thoughts, prisoners of an unpleasant passion, ways and means of killing. They know little about the human body, their own or anyone else's, and so they often botch things horribly."

"I want to die," Kay said slowly, "but when I think of poison or guns or throwing myself off a building, it's so . . . so ugly."

"Of course it's ugly," Mrs. Maas said, "and a fastidious woman recoils at the thought of such a horror. Yet, I think we ought to be quite sure, both of us, what purpose this suicide is to serve."

"Purpose? . . . Well, my death—"

"Quite so, that is one purpose, but usually there are more. A certain suicide I once arranged was for a beautiful young woman whose husband treated her like a kind of geisha, a living ornament in his home. He was an architect and often entertained prospective clients there. He had chosen his wife to go with the house. He saw a harmonizing form in her, Classic Modern, but he wanted no strong feeling that was incompatible with his style of art. She had herself blown up in her jewel box of a boudoir, and she led him to the mess with a gold ribbon and a marvelous note. Reality dripped from the ceiling, yet she was as fastidious as you are, I think. She spent hours choosing a proper outfit that day, and we discussed that, although I hadn't nearly her flair for clothes. I'm sure you've realized that suicide is the ultimate 'one-up,' as it were, the accusation that brooks no defense, the argument won at last. That is why it is so fashionable and so forbidden in most places."

"I thought society was against suicide because of some moral consideration—the value of suffering, or at least what it calls 'the preciousness of human life.' "

"If that were so, would we wage wars at a thousand times the cost in human life? And who doesn't make war? Only tiny tribes too poor to afford it or those, like the Swiss, who do better to profit from the wars of others. I know I shouldn't theorize on this matter. I have no training in logic or statistics, and it is unfair to judge by my clientele—they aren't typical at all, being wealthy and well educated. Most of my clients hold graduate degrees, and all but three have been college graduates. Those three were self-made men of great wealth."

"They came to arrange murders, didn't they?"

"Two did, but after we talked they changed their minds and chose suicide. They had to learn what you know instinctively, that murder gives its victim the kind of power that suicide gives *its* victim—the power of that echoing last word."

"I don't want to get even with anyone. My husband is a fine man—considerate, kind, a good provider—everything a husband should be; my children are lovely. I have all the things I want. I feel empty and tired, that's all. I'm bored with my life and with life in general, and I want to be rid of it."

"I suppose I'd better get a few notes on you—oh, don't worry. I work with great confidentiality, and while I have spoken to you freely of other clients, I have not mentioned times, places, or names. I'll just go and get my book."

Mrs. Maas rose and began to walk to the back door of the house. At the beginning or their conversation Kay had fixed her age at about fifty, but she had such an old-fashioned manner that she now seemed much older, although she moved well and her face was unwrinkled. She had taken off her sun hat when they sat down under the tree and Kay saw that her hair was graying, but not spare or wispy. Something in her speech or the way she held her body or her hands evoked the words *ladylike* and *proper*. A nineteenth-century orderliness and formality was present in the garden also, as Kay looked around at it. There was a weeping willow and a cypress, the inevitable trees of the Victorian garden, their disarray so consciously introduced and so carefully pruned and controlled that Kay found herself smiling. As a modern woman she liked to think she was above the conventional suppositions about propriety and good manners; she saw through their fragile comforts. Most planned harmony and restfulness—banks and doctors' offices—depressed and annoyed her, but this garden, for all its earnest and conscientiously spiritual quality, refreshed and amused her. She was not surprised when a moment later the bells of the churches in the center of the city began to ring. She stretched in her chair. On bell-sounding Sundays, on the bee-droning lawn, sun-dappled under the great trees where there must, later in the afternoon, be grandchildren, cookies, and lemonade, murders were made. Slow deaths and quick deaths, explained and silent, for money or love or hate, or, most sorrowfully, as in her case, a soul-destroying boredom. The back door opened and Mrs. Maas returned holding a long, old-style ledger. She moved efficiently across the lawn. Kay had a feeling of no wasted motion. "I stopped to put the kettle on to boil," Mrs. Maas said, "in case you would like some coffee or tea."

She sat down and opened the book, turning past pages of a small, neat script. "If you don't want your name to appear, I have a code word that can be used, or you might wish to give yourself a name the way they do on those new citizens-band radios. When I first heard of them, I thought how seldom the average person has a chance to characterize himself. I'm sure that is part of their appeal."

"It doesn't really matter, I guess," Kay said. "You could call me Terminal Case."

"All my clients are terminal cases, in one way or another," Mrs. Maas said. "Are you saying that you have a terminal disease and that you wish to take your life quickly and painlessly before it is taken slowly and painfully?"

"No, I'm in excellent health."

"Oh, good!" Mrs. Maas nodded. "Really good health is rather rare, you know. These days I feel it is at least partial evidence of a good character. You mentioned you have a husband and children . . ."

"Why do you need to know about them? My husband and children have nothing to do with this."

"Look here, I am not in the business of shattering children. If there are youngsters in the house I will want to know it. I will need to know their comings and goings—when they are out and to what lessons and to which schools and who their friends are. We must arrange it so that you will not be found by your children. Perhaps we will decide not to use your house at all. The wounding of your children is inevitable.

That they may be wounded as little as possible is one thing on which I am adamant. Even if you don't wish to use your death against your husband I suggest that I know the details of his schedule as well."

"I don't want to be *found* at all—I want to be lost, to disappear."

"What is your address?" Mrs. Maas asked. Feeling thrown off balance, Kay gave it. "And how long have you lived there?"

"About three years."

"And where before?"

"It's all very cliché," Kay said, "upwardly mobile, suburban life-style, upper-middle class. Nora, Karenina, Madame Bovary, a hundred other heroines of fiction—"

"You see yourself as a heroine then?" Mrs. Maas smiled. "Interesting in a potential suicide."

"I meant principal character, that's all."

"It comes to the same thing. The people who come as murderers are very much the stars of their own epics, as it were. With suicides there is usually a lack of star quality. Some of them aren't even supporting players in their own lives. Madame Bovary . . . I certainly hope you are not deeply in debt. In my business one cannot go to the law for payment if there is a default, and therefore I like to do business in cash, or at least by cashier's check. You understand—I have had some very sorry experiences. When I started out in this business people took terrible advantage."

"I brought some cash . . . I think it ought to be enough. I haven't asked how much you charge."

"The initial consultation is one hundred dollars. This is a consultation. Here we decide times, means, et cetera. If you should need other meetings they will be thirty-five dollars each, but the time then, as it is now, is flexible—we will take all the time we need, although at three I am expecting my son and daughter-in-law and my grandchildren." Kay smiled.

"Why did you smile just then?"

"About the grandchildren—I knew you had grandchildren, that's all, and that they probably came on Sunday afternoons."

"Does the thought of that routine bother you?"

"It's my own routine that bothers me."

"We will need to study that later. I was telling you about my fees. The flat murder-suicide rate is seven hundred fifty dollars, and that includes drugs, tools, et cetera—any equipment we might need. The rates go up for special kinds of murder or suicide. A suicide that looks like an accident, for example, is fifteen hundred dollars. That is, if a claim for insurance is filed and the case has to be examined by an adjuster. The case I spoke of before, the suicide for vengeance, is twelve hundred fifty dollars. We had to orchestrate the entire family's movements for days so that the husband got the full effect of the wife's act and yet her parents and the children and their friends were spared as much as possible."

"What do you expect the charges to be in my case?"

"Yes, let's get down to exactly what kind of plan you want."

"I don't want anything messy or hateful, I just want to be eliminated, extinguished, blown out like a candle."

"That is quite a poetic statement, but unfortunately you weigh some hundred forty pounds. You take up space between five and six feet in length, seventeen inches in width, and a foot of thickness. You can not be 'extinguished' so simply. Tell me this—are you angry at God?"

"What?"

"Are you angry at God? I'm not trying to be impertinent, but your expression just then reminded me of another client, a very modest-seeming woman, downcast eyes, long sleeves. She wore her hair back like yours. She expressed nothing but love for her husband and children and yet she was planning a suicide. We talked of this method and that and she wasn't pleased with any of them. She too kept saying that she simply wanted to end it—she used that phrase, *end it*. I finally thought to ask her *where* she wanted to die, and she said at the communion rail of the cathedral at Lourdes. Then it all came out. I have never seen a person so angry at God, such a deep and convinced believer."

"Did you comply with her wishes?"

"She also wanted a private death, in solitude. Privacy and Lourdes were incompatible. We settled on a shrine of less notoriety."

"And you carried out her wishes?"

"As a matter of fact, in that case, no. She contracted a fatal disease, made up her quarrel (no one could have kept those two apart for any length of time), and spent her last days doing therapy for families of terminal patients. She wrangled from her God every last possible minute."

"You sound as though you admire her."

"I suppose I should—as a life model she is admirable. As a living person I found her manner unpleasantly abrasive. She prided herself on her tactlessness, which she called directness. Also, I lost my fee, which one does in business, but not usually with such a display of pious arrogance. At my age, one finds consistency a cardinal blessing."

Kay became aware that she was obscurely irritated. Mrs. Maas might have been reminiscing about her friends in junior college. The carefully modulated voice never lost its cheerful lilt; there was a finishing school quality to it (a lady never raises her voice) that Kay began to dislike intensely. Mrs. Maas had put her hands on her knees and said, "Well, let's get on with your plan—" when the kettle began to whistle in the kitchen. The idea of coffee, which had seemed so quieting and civilized before, seemed now only to further Kay's annoyance. At the same moment a large blond youth shambled into view from the side of the house. His hair was long but frizzy, so that it looked like a nest around his head. He wore a beard, jeans, and a dirty T-shirt.

"Hey, uh, Mrs. Maas—"

She had gotten up to go for the coffee and Kay saw her freeze in mid-stride. Even from the back, the lines of her soft blouse changed as the body beneath it went rigid with disapproval. "Ronald," she said icily, "you are to leave this house at once. If you ever come here again without an appointment I will consider our relationship terminated and I will take steps to see that you annoy me no further. Do I make myself clear?"

"Well, hey, see, I got this idea—"

"Do I make myself clear!" The boy reddened, then turned, muttering and left.

"Really!" Mrs. Maas declared as Kay held the screen door open for the tea tray. "One hardly knows how young people are being reared these days. He hasn't got a job, he has no money, and he wants me to kill his mother for some hypothetical family fortune. He's been trying to interest me in a share in this windfall if I will kill the only person on earth who sees him as a human being. It's ludicrous! You look shocked. Of course, I keep the problems of my clients confidential, but as he is not now a client, never was, and I assure you, never will be, I don't feel bound to respect his confidence."

"It wasn't that, it was . . . well, a boy wanting to kill his own mother . . ."

"*You* want to kill someone's mother," Mrs. Maas said. Kay consciously decided not to acknowledge the remark.

"Would you have done it, killed the woman . . . I mean, if he'd had the money?"

"Probably not," Mrs. Maas murmured as she poured boiling water into a filter arrangement on Kay's cup. Her voice had gone back to its genteel, Victorian tone. Kay recognized it as the voice of all the kindergarten teachers she had ever known. "People of his sort are so unstable, it's hard to find out what they really want, and death is a permanent condition. They're unused to anything permanent; they don't understand permanence."

"But to . . . to *murder* someone . . ."

"*You* want to murder someone, why do you fight that difference?"

"But she is innocent—she may not want to die, may not even know . . ."

"That overgrown baby no doubt has plans to do something to his mother's car so that she will go out in traffic and very possibly destroy someone else, perhaps many other people. The Graham boy blew his mother up in an airplane, and while that's harder now, trains and buses are not given such security. *My* killings involve no one else. People aren't maimed, pushed out of windows, or, except where the client wishes and is a suicide, blown up in garages. The person *you* wish to murder is horrified by that sort of death—"

"You're trying to talk me out of this, aren't you, to make me feel guilty for the emptiness of my life, to—" In the middle of her anger, Kay had a sudden, chilling vision. That boy, who had seen her, who would know her as a client, might be waiting even now for her to leave, might think to follow her for—extortion or blackmail—his violence gliding like a snake's stare from one target to another. "He *saw* me! That boy saw me here. He *knows*. A person like that could . . would . . ."

Mrs. Maas leaned back comfortably and laughed. Her laughter, like her voice, was genteel and carefully modulated. "Good heavens, you couldn't be safer! That poor mooncalf is so self-involved I doubt if he even registered your presence here. He is twenty-one years old. It is inconceivable to him that people older than he could know despair. In his arrogance he cannot imagine that someone resembling his mother could suffer. If he saw you at all it would be as a stock figure from the garden club or the ladies aid. Our wrinkles and gray hair are perfect disguises that the young never penetrate. The putative murderess of your children's mother is as safe as the national bank."

"I want you to stop doing that, to stop calling me a murderer—to stop putting me in a class with bomb throwers and criminals!"

"Forgive me for being indelicate, but suicide is a crime—the only crime that, if successful, guarantees that the perpetrator will not be punished for it. This makes it the most serious crime of all."

"I'm not like that miserable boy, and I'm not a mobster. I came here to end an intolerable situation in as graceful a way as possible. Why don't you see that?"

"How very red your face is," Mrs. Maas remarked. "I wonder what is causing you to be so angry."

"Are you going to help me with this thing or not!"

"I will try to help you as soon as I find out what kind of death you want."

"I want to die with dignity, to end this endless life of mine without the tawdriness or agony of a common suicide. I am willing to pay for this, even your outrageous fee, but I am not willing to suffer indignities and humiliations!" Kay was trembling with rage. She did not know when she had been so angry. The very posture of Mrs. Maas sitting opposite her, balancing the teacup carefully, legs together like some debutante, increased the rage until she thought she must strike that self-satisfied woman, smash the porcelain cup to shards, bloody the nose on that smug face. For a moment she was too angry to speak, and then it occurred to her that she had been defending her own position long enough. Surely this placid killer had something to answer for.

"I know why I want to die—because my life is empty and meaningless. Why do *you* murder? What makes *you* sit there so secure and confident and so damn superior to all of it!"

"Because my life is neither empty nor meaningless," Mrs. Maas said quietly. "But your interest in my motives surprises me. Few of the people I deal with are able to see beyond their situations sufficiently to question why I murder—unless you are questioning me purely as a matter of attack and defense."

"It took me over a year to come to the point of writing to you for an interview. I had your address, for which I paid—well, I won't go into how much, but it was a good deal. I kept it with me in my purse, changing it when I changed purses, and I'd look at it and then put it away. One year—tortured by possibilities before I wrote—and now I'm here trying to plan the last thing I will ever plan in my life. I have the fee, I'm willing to do the necessary work, and you seem to be purposely throwing up barriers, asking me antagonizing questions with a kind of prissy superiority that I can't stand. Yes, I think I deserve to know more of your reasons—of who you are."

"—My credentials, as it were. About the prissiness, I must apologize. It is strictly a matter of upbringing—the training of another day and from a culture which is no more. I think you deserve an answer—an explanation of who I am and why I work this way. To begin with, I was born in Holland in 1931. My parents were Dutch Jews. One doesn't think of this combination of influences as conducive to a mystical temperament, but in the case of my parents, the mystical strain was highly developed. To the Jews, you know, the idea of Satan as a fallen angel is foreign. Their monotheism is too total—it is in the New

Testament where Satan is presented as the devil. In Job, for example, Satan relates to God as to a lesser colleague. In my parents' view, and the view of many Jews, Satan was and still is God's foremost servant, that Other, that necessary negative pole that charges the universe—I speak metaphorically, of course."

"What has this to do with—"

"I'm coming to that. Of course, none of these things was presented to me philosophically when I was a child, but one sees and hears and absorbs more than one realizes of deeper ideas. One learns unconsciously a subtle, pervasive response to the world and a definition of reality even in the early years."

"Yes, yes, but what—"

"I know my manner upsets you, but I wish to be allowed to proceed at my own rate."

"Yes—all right—"

"The Germans came in 1940—a weekend in May. It was a lovely weekend with warm weather, which I realize now my parents must not have noticed in their anguish. I said they were mystics. I should also have said that they imbued me with some of this quality. To the mystic the world is hung with symbols, metaphors, and ceremonies carrying deeper meanings. What a pity I did not read my parents' deeper meanings correctly!

"That Friday my father, surprisingly, stayed home from work. As it was lovely, he suggested a trip into the country, crossing into Belgium for a picnic. Although my mother complied and went quickly to pack a lunch for us, my parents seemed impatient, and several times they exchanged what I thought were angry looks. We were borrowing Uncle and Aunty's car, not having one of our own, and the first truly grim note of the day was a fight among them all. My father wanted Uncle and Aunty to come with us on the picnic, and they would not. My mother kept saying, 'Just close the door—just close the door and come.' She even held out her arms to them, but they would not. Then my father called them stupid and blind and my mother started to cry. I was amazed and upset by my always-kind father's violent and crude behavior and that he had made Mother cry. Uncle and Aunty were our closest relatives, our dearest friends, but my father cursed them and drove away.

"As we went across into Belgium my father suggested that we should sing some songs, so we did, but when my mother began to cry again because of his rudeness, he ordered her to stop. He spoke quietly: 'No more tears,' he said. 'I command it.' Then, most strange of all, he suggested that we should drink wine as we rode. I saw that they had brought four or five bottles with them. They drank and made me drink also. By this time we were well into Flanders, going near the coast on small country roads, drinking wine and singing. My father stopped the car then and told me to get out. He lifted up the front seat of the car and began to pull the stuffing out of it in the middle until there was a space made, like a hollow, and with a wire cutter he cut the springs there so that there was a hole, a small hole made. He told me to get into it, to curl up in that hole and to be silent, silent no matter what happened. He spoke without tenderness, without love. He spoke harshly, quickly, but giving weight to each word. 'And now, be silent,' he said, and commanded me with his eyes.

"They put the seat down on top of me so that I lay doubled up, my head pressed against the wooden bottom of the seat. And they began to laugh and drink again. Whenever the car hit a bump the spring ends bit into me. Once I screamed and my father cursed me. His violence terrified and appalled me. The worse my sufferings became, the harder my parents laughed. At some place they stopped and were explaining the picnic to some men. They seemed drunk, irrational, beyond control. I could not relate these savages to my own gentle parents. It was as though devils had entered them, had taken their souls. They only looked and sounded like my scholarly father and my gentle mother. They were offering the men wine, too, laughing and shouting, 'Come with us! Take a couple of hours off. We'll be back in a few hours and nobody the wiser. We have to get home early this evening to take the damn landlord his rent money.' "

"I don't understand," Kay said. "Why did they do all that?"

"I did not understand either. I did not understand when blood began to come from my leg, which had been pierced by the spring—

my father dared not cut more, you see, more would have shown—but I did not know then what they were doing, even when they began to laugh about me. 'We left the brat at home,' my father told the men, and my mother laughed. They both laughed. I did not forgive them that for years, though I was to know soon after why they had done it. I did not forgive them until I myself was a mother. Since then I have spent some time musing on the desperate strength given to the gentle, to cornered animals. The men laughed too and drank, and after a time we went on, but I was beginning to become ill. The cramped position was making me suffer from lack of air. I felt as though I was going to die at any minute. Then, after what seemed an eternity the car stopped and my father raised the seat and pulled me out.

"We had crossed the French border, you see. Had they not hidden me, had they not posed as half-drunk picnickers leaving everything behind, including all their possessions and a 'brat,' they would never have been allowed to leave the country, to cross that border. The blind hedonism of the middle-class European played into the stereotyped idea of the border guards, who, although the border was not yet closed, would have detained anyone who looked as though he might be taking valuables out of the country.

"It was explained to me, in my father's scholarly way, that night in France, but I was unable to get beyond the actuality of the torture. They had hurt me and laughed about it, ridden singing through the green May weather while I struggled to breathe, while I bled and suffered for no reason; they had joked about me to strangers while I lay dying."

"Are you saying that your trauma in childhood made you turn to this?"

"No, I am speaking about the relationship between God and Satan."

"Well, go on then."

"None of us dreamed that France would not hold, that already it was full of defeat and corruption. France seemed the only way out for us, and many of its people did what people do in any war—they profited for as long as they could. We were ruinously overcharged for everything. The car was stolen while my parents were trying to make arrangements to sell it for passage to the Americas or England. The outcome of this was that my parents traveled more slowly than the German armies. The Dutch passport made them suitable victims for the buyers and sellers of people. They were betrayed and sent back to what I do not know."

"And you?"

"I was the recipient of the last money my parents had, and how bitterly I resented it then. They sold me, or so I thought. They left me in a French convent orphanage for blind children. My name was changed, and I was told never to use my former name and never to mention my former life. I was given a pair of shaded glasses and was told to wear them always. The glasses rendered me almost blind. God and Satan, you see."

"I see what you're trying to do. You want to show me 'real' suffering, 'real' pain, to tell me that I have no reason for what I'm doing, that I don't deserve to commit suicide!"

"My dear woman, do I seem so foolish or so arrogant as that? I am answering a question you asked of me—why I do as I do. Do you imagine that I am recommending the virtues of such an experience to you?"

"I'm sorry, I was being defensive, I know."

"And for no reason, I assure you. I am not comparing our sorrows or belittling the spiritual anguish through which you are going. Perhaps I have been mistaken in answering your question—it is possible that you did not wish to know this of me, but something quite different—something which I am unable to answer."

"I have half the story, I may as well have the rest."

"I learned English at the convent and many other things. Satan, to those Religious, is seen in quite a different way and has other purposes than the Satan of the Jews. I must also say that I believe the formal quality of my manner is a product of those years. At first I was hidden among the other orphans, but the natural mysticism of my background soon appeared and the sisters began to deal with me in a way subtly different from other children. That, and the fact that I was not blind put me in a special relationship to the life of the convent and the school. After the war I learned that none of my family had survived. I stayed on at the convent, and when I was seventeen, Mother Rose, the Mother Superior, a woman of great gifts, asked me if I did not wish to enter the religious life. I was at that time, as now, a mystic without God. Convent life had the order and silence necessary to heal me, the predictability and formality I preferred. I loved that withdrawal from the world, and for three years I seriously considered baptism and the taking of vows. Had it not been for Mother Rose I would have stayed, I think. It would have been a monumental sin. It was the life I wanted, you see, not the God. The altar was empty for me, the Host a wafer and no more.

"I left the convent in 1950 and sought out the Jewish community. Their ways were equally foreign to me after all those years. I felt as I went into the world that there must be some special expression, some mission or extraordinary truth for me to follow. Many survivors feel this, I am told. It is a response to the anguish and guilt of being saved when those wiser and more deserving are not."

"Why do I keep feeling your disapproval? Now you're talking about special destiny, purpose, and survival. Fine, if you have all those things. I don't. It's why I want to die. You have purpose even as a murderer. At night you can count the unhappy victims of the day well dispatched. It's the difference between us. I simply want to be one of those victims. What's stopping you? You're supposed to be an expert; why are you hesitating?"

"Killing is my expertise, I admit, but a thoughtless killing offends me. I am also an expert, as I have just told you, in empty altars, and the problems there are sometimes less easy of solution. Something tells me that you feel this deadness in your life because you feel deprived of true company, real people, real acts and meaning in a world where God is dead. The mask of boredom and accidie has been penetrated to show the rage that you have striven so hard to keep from feeling."

"God is not dead, He never lived at all. You said so yourself. God is an idea, and the idea is irrelevant, totally irrelevant!"

"I beg to differ with you. For those in your world God died immediately after the last rites were said over Satan, His first and foremost angel, the necessary friction against which the universe moves. In this matter, you see, I believe my parents' people to be correct. I never believed God to be dead, only invisible to *me*. There is a world of difference between our ways of belief."

"Did it never occur to you that when I say irrelevant, I mean it in every way—His nonexistence is not worth discussing."

"Then the question comes back to why you consider life not worthy of your fullest investment. That question is not irrelevant, and so the question of the existence of good and evil is not irrelevant, and thus the question of God is not irrelevant, because He and His good do exist, and they must, because His first and most necessary angel lives. You have ignored evil, continuing a mistake that could have been corrected by a single look at the terrorism, brutality, and torture in the world. I serve the servant because I can see him. I cannot see the Master, but I know He is still in residence because the servant is busy in the house."

"You are mad," Kay said.

Still smiling slightly, Mrs. Maas leaned forward and freed a gold locket she wore around her neck. She pulled it up by its chain and then opened it and turned it in her hand, leaning forward to show it to Kay. Inside the thin gold shell was a champlevé portrait in exquisite detail: night-black Satan, his wings half furled, his tail snaking around him, stood overlooking the world. He was poised on a rock as though he had just lighted there for an instant, and behind him was the iridescent robin's-egg blue of the enamel sky. Mrs. Maas smiled gently at the portrait. "They live," she said. "They live."

THE JAWS OF
THE DOG

They were afraid of being robbed—of life, of limb, of property, of money, of dignity, of chastity, of their places, their future, and their choices. They were afraid of local muggers, of new immigrants, of violence itself, and of the city's anarchy. When my sister Ruth visited them they would tell her about new communities in which people lived walled away from all outsiders, places where the borders were patrolled by uniformed men with attack dogs, places where bicycling children had to pass through checkpoints and be identified by men with guns.

When I came I would ring the harsh-sounding bell in a coded sequence and wait for the bolts to be pulled, the chains undone, the locks turned one after another. Before the last bar was slid away they would cry to me in their high voices, "Is that you? Are you all right?" and they had told me if I were at gunpoint—being used to gain entrance—to give another name, as though in their panic they would hear another name and be able to respond in some way. When I did come in they would make tea for me and tell me in awed, sibilant voices about the morning's murders in the newspapers and last night's horrors on TV.

And I could not help them. They had refused to leave the old neighborhood, which was rapidly decaying and through which they ventured only rarely now, armed with whistles and clutching one another in fear. When I brought them home for weekend visits they said they felt imprisoned in an area where nothing was in walking distance. My children are careless and noisy and never more so than when the two old aunts were there. I took them to museums and concerts hoping to offer them some kind of spiritual freedom in the world of art and beauty, but the serene Bellini and the twilit Leonardo were no match for the constant, worldwide, moment-to-moment anguish of the six-o'clock news.

They knew everything, every ghastly murder of a helpless old woman by a junkie for a fix, every killing for thrills or sadism, every kidnapping, every rape. Coming from the art show, the concert, the witty movie, they would ask me in for tea again and a bit of the dry cake they made only rarely now, and they could scarcely endure my presence for the half an hour I took from the evening news or the last part of the paper.

The family praised me. The cousins, who lived out of town, called me often and told me how grateful they were that I was looking after their mother and poor Aunt Gusta. I told them they had nothing with which to reproach themselves and hung up bereft because I loved the old ladies for the people they had been and I was losing them to an enemy far worse than age or illness.

"Move!" I cried as we walked to their apartment through the haunted street. "You said you needed the synagogue and the neighborhood. The neighborhood is gone, and you are afraid to go to the synagogue at all. There are places across town where—"

"You didn't read what happened there, across town in Greenhill?" Aunt Rose cried. "A woman was raped and murdered there, in broad daylight."

"In broad daylight," Aunt Gusta said antiphonally, "people are held up."

"There has always been violence in the world," I admitted, "but I don't see why you both should want to stay here and preside over the death of this neighborhood house by house. It's making you morbid and sick. Look at you. You used to go to luncheons three times a week here and there to raise money. Was it epilepsy, asthma, TB? You were on the problem like a flash, and now you never leave the house. Please—think of the family—"

Five years ago, four, three, they would have shut me up with a look or a word. Now they took my well-meant meddling like whipped children.

"They made me hate myself," I said to Ruth. "I dragged out everything but the American flag, and all I ended up with was the shame of having failed them and of doing it so rudely."

Ruth has most of the modern wisdom in our family. She has been through TA and encounter therapy and est. She has been to Esalen. She has been Rolfed. She is handling her second divorce well and is "growing."

"Miriam, they are going to have to be responsible for their own lives!" she said, and I knew this was true. "They are going to pick up and move or stay where they are and die of fear, but your nursemaiding them isn't helping—it's keeping them in a sick, dependent role." And I knew that this too was true. "They're getting a payoff for being sick and morbid, and I can't help thinking you are too—some kind of a reward for being their nurse." I knew this also was true and that it was irrelevant.

"Ruth, you are seven years younger than I am, and that makes a difference when you're a kid. You don't remember them the way I do, and you have a lot less to thank them for. Neither of us has ever been sick and old and fragile and scared."

"They are making themselves all those things!"

"Maybe so, but what you're saying is that no human being is capable of helping another. Don't you see how barbaric and sterile and cheerless that is? It means we'll all have to get guns and go armed . . ."

Armed. Aunt Gusta with a violin case, Aunt Rose with a Saturday-night special taped to her thigh. At a sound the case is whipped open, the tape pulled away, the sawed-off shotgun spraying lead. I laughed to myself. But *armed* . . .

I decided to consult someone. The talk with Ruth had been painful, but it had shown me that I did want help from outside, from someone wiser than Ruth and more practical than I. Our congregation's old rabbi, Rabbi Jacob, had retired. The new man gave me Ruth-like advice and talked about a retirement village for senior citizens. I remembered Professor Orwig then.

I had heard him speak at a drug seminar for the parents of high-school children. He was a professor of comparative religion, and he had a son in one of my son's classes at school. He had spoken with intelligence and compassion about cultural aspects of the drug problem, and about other problems as well. When I called him, asking for an appointment, I was unsure as to whether or not he was the right man to see. I told him this and that I couldn't describe my problem over the phone. He sounded intrigued by what little I could say and gave me an appointment with encouraging readiness.

"I don't know if your discipline is the correct one for the problem I have," I said. "The problem isn't medical or psychiatric or even architectural. It's a spiritual thing, but the modern spiritual answers are too stony and dry for me, and the older answers—that God wills such suffering, are intolerable to me and to my aunts."

"What answers do you want to talk about?"

"The word I thought about was armor, a protection beyond the normal assurances that no longer work. We are Jews, but I want to talk about something supernatural."

He smiled, and then sat back in his desk chair, rocking it gently. I was relieved. I had been half expecting ridicule from him or condescension, but he was obviously giving my problem his serious consideration. When he spoke it was slowly and with care. "I am not Jewish myself, but I admire the faith and the people. Of all the older religions, Judaism has allowed itself the fewest ways around the slowness connected with the mercy of God."

"I don't understand."

"Catholics can slip easily into an older way of curing fear, only a few generations ago there were the easy anodynes—vials of holy water, blessed medals, prayers to particular saints. A demiworld of special powers opens to the Moslem. Worldwide, of course, there's witchcraft. The Jews practiced that self-protection in a very rudimentary and sporadic way in the Middle Ages with the Cabbala, but it never, even during these dark times, achieved any real place in Jewish life. Your monotheism is very strong. I find it admirable."

"It is," I said, "but there is a saying in Yiddish: God will help me, but oh, that He helps me until He helps me!"

"Not only are you resolute in denying yourselves the power of evil, but theologically speaking, there is no advantage to the Jew in dying, no promises of or for the afterlife, no lots staked out in Heaven."

"No."

"Have you thought of training your aunts in the use of *real* weapons—self-defense classes?—"

"Perhaps ten years ago I could have. Now—I think they are too frightened to listen and too brittle to throw attackers over their shoulders."

"The attackers have grown too many and too strong, haven't they?"

"Yes, they are fear-blown giants, all of them. It's one reason why I wouldn't trust my aunts with guns, besides the real worry of something actually happening and the guns being taken away and used against them or stolen and used for other horrors for which we would then be partly responsible."

"Ethical monotheists," he said. "Admirable."

"Frightened women," I said. "And the world gone that surrounded them with work to do. The truth is, I think, that even in the old country, we had the problem. The enemies were more real, that's all. I need a cure."

"We'd have only the flimsiest structure to build on."

"Like what?"

"Do they have a mezuzah on the doorpost?"

"No, they are both too modern, too rational."

I laughed and so did he. "Get them one," he said.

"I'll do it today."

"Have them touch it entering and leaving. Make them do it for your sake if nothing else."

"There are special rules for putting it up—"

"Good. Follow them to the letter. I have a lot of studying to do if I'm to help you in this way—if you are sure this is the way you wish to take."

"It's the only way I can think of that has a chance of working without making 'senile citizens' of them."

"I'm subverting you, you know that."

"They have been subverted already. According to our rabbis, if they had followed the commandments and lived up to the precepts, they would fear no one but the Lord. To be fearful is, you know, sort of idolatry."

"Admirable," he said.

"For Titans," I said.

I got the mezuzah and made Aunt Rose put it up while Aunt Gusta read the "Order Concerning Placing Mezuzah," step by step. The procedure took all afternoon, but in spite of their feeble objections, I think they were moved by the gift, and they did not refuse to place it or to read the prayers, which surprised me. I made them promise they would not leave or enter their apartment without putting their fingers to the mezuzah in the traditional way. To my credit I did not speak nonsense about supernatural protection. Loving gift, nothing more.

Later that week Orwig called. "I've done a survey of the literature over the weekend. With the exception of Cabbalistic practices by vestigial Hasidic sects there's really very little. Where the idea of the pushy Jew got in, I'll never know. Theologically, you're the least manipulative people on the face of the earth. But I've had a break in another direction and I'd like to talk it over with you. Oh, by the way, how did things go with the mezuzah?"

"Surprisingly well."

"Good," he said, "but it's only a beginning. Can you come up today?"

"This afternoon, about four?"

"Fine."

I had been too preoccupied the first time I had visited Dr. Orwig's office to notice much about it. It was a strange office for a professor of religion, even comparative. There were, of course, many bookshelves and the inevitable indoor plants along with a large plastic marijuana, a student's idea, no doubt. But there were posters on the walls, too— Fijian gods—and on the shelf tops Maori idols; a Salish totem in miniature; a *Venus of Willendorf*, naked and pregnant; Shiva with supple arms; Amaterasu, cloud-borne in silk near the window; an African war god, armed to the teeth. "Marvelous, isn't he?" Orwig said, as he noticed me looking. "You know, the Department of Religion has been moved in under anthropology in this school and in many others. We all ranted and raved at first, but it turned out to be more comfortable; it seems to fit here, especially for comparative religion—fewer value judgments."

"Allee Samee, as the man said?"

"Oh, no—many threads the same, many needs the same. All different. Students may feel that pull at the end of freshman year, to say that all religions are the same. Then we recommend a second year. No, certainly not all the same. Look at you, for example—a world full of incantations and spells, augury and mantic arts, of the most fearful chemistry, none of it available for you to unpack from the satchel of your own heritage."

"Have you tasted our traditional food? Maybe nobody needed black magic. Two Jewish feasts and out they go."

He laughed. "Yes, but that's killing the ones you love."

"As much as you find our reliance on a slow God admirable, you find our lack of ceremonial magic a weakness, don't you?"

"They're *your* aunts." We sat down.

"Tell me," Orwig said, "do you know the story of the golem of Prague?"

"A sort of Jewish Frankenstein's monster in the sixteenth-century Pale ... "

"Yes, very like Frankenstein's monster but with significant differences. First, he was always under his master's control—Rabbi Judah Lowe never lost power over him. The story was one in which the 'monster,' far from breaking out of control, helped and sustained the oppressed Jews against the greater 'monsters' outside the ghetto. Rabbi Lowe made this golem the way God made man—out of clay, and as he could not breathe into his nostrils the breath of life, he did the next best thing: he wrote the Ineffable Name on a scrap of parchment and placed that in the golem's mouth, and the golem became sentient."

"Where do I stand in line for a good golem?"

"Don't you see—there is a strong tradition in Judaism of the power of the Law's written word. The whole Cabbala is a meditation on the theme of numbers, words, and power. Other traditional myths are filled with this awe at the written word. There is also, worldwide, a belief in supernatural eating to gain power—the brains of slain enemies or a totem animal; the sacraments of peyote; the eucharist, which until recently was far more than a remembrance; ceremonial meals . . . "

"What are you suggesting?"

"That they eat their words."

I don't think I said anything but only sat for a long time and looked at the pattern the sun was making through one of the potted plants. Then I said, "It's impossible."

"Why?"

"They're not village people in the Pale; they're modern Americans. Four years ago, before they got too frightened, they were going to concerts and lectures, playing canasta or bridge in the afternoons. When my Uncle Milton died, Aunt Rose took over the business and ran it for years—"

"What are they now, both of them?"

"Frightened," I admitted. "Old and frightened."

"As frightened as any village women of the wolves or the Cossacks when they walk through the woods?"

"Perhaps."

"And what can we do to cure that?" I sat still. In the years when the Greeks were casting augury bones and the Romans read entrails, Jews were writing a body of Law. In the centuries of Druidic winds and Finnish knot-storms, the raising of incubi, and the haunting of graveyards for the stuff of spells, Jewish wives were happy enough to stare into egg yolks to see if they were kosher or not.

"Against Dracula, Christians can hold the cross," I said. "I always wondered what a Jew could do against such a force, a force no doors could lock away."

"The devil shrinks from Christ's symbol," Orwig said, smiling. "You Jews are so stubbornly monotheistic, so steadfastly set against idolatry—even a symbol—that the Star of David is simply your sign. It cures no fevers, confounds no demons."

"How can I get them to *do* it?"

Psalm 22, full of terror of things that are images for what cannot be named—the dog, the bull, the lion. Save me from the lion's mouth, my beloved, from the power of the dog. I wrote three verses on white paper. I wrote the words in Hebrew without vowels—why I did not know; perhaps it made the words more mystical, more secret, and more powerful. I burned the paper to a black ash and prepared a small honey cake, the kind they liked. I crumbled the ashes into the batter and baked it at 350 degrees for one and a half hours, a slightly slower oven than I usually use and for slightly longer—to give the burned words their full and focused power. If they were to believe, I had to believe to the limits of my ability. I could not fool them.

I made a special visit. I wore an old dress, torn, like a mourner's, no jewelry, my hair uncombed; why, I don't know, unless it was because great joy and great sorrow drive out fear and I couldn't counterfeit joy without mocking it. They were shocked, distracted by my outfit. For a moment they seemed more afraid of me than of the lion, the bull, and the dog. Oh, you old witches in dank caves, you dangerous midnight hags, you were no fools to wear your curlers to work, to let Macbeth see you with a safety pin holding your slip strap. "I have done some-

74

thing important and powerful," I said. "There is a special ingredient in this cake. I want each of you to eat two slices of it every day, one in the morning and one at night. They are not to be eaten with other food and are to be preceded and followed by fluid."

"What is it?" Aunt Gusta said suspiciously.

"Don't ask me that yet. Just do as I say. I have gone to an authority on this, and I have followed his instructions to the letter. Ancient Jewish customs and Laws are being followed here. I certainly don't expect great results right away, but there will be a gradual change, a very slight change. If you notice anything, please mention it when I come next week."

Then I left, giving them no chance for further questions lest I compromise the power of my fetish.

"You have done well, my daughter," said my subverter when I called him to tell him that the cake had been given. "Perhaps you should send some member of the family to check on them later this week."

"I'll send my sister Ruth. They don't approve of her very much, and it will put them off their poise if she comes for no special reason."

"Perhaps another relative then—"

"No, I have a feeling that being put off their stride is just what they need right now."

"You know," Orwig said delightedly, "I think you have a genuine flair for this, a real gift. I never thought of that, that part of the magic must be just keeping the client off-balance. Extraordinary. It would, of course, render the client that much more suggestible, less able to put up complete defenses."

"I know something else," I said. "I know that the claw foot of an eagle caught at midnight and dipped in murderer's blood is not a trapping but an essential tool. America does not stimulate creativity in magic."

"Nonsense." He laughed. "Remember Salem?"

"They were colonists," I said. "We were immigrants."

"Remember too," he said, "that we are not spooking cattle or drying up the breasts of nursing mothers or causing fits in the adolescent. This isn't macumba, conjuring devils, blinding our rivals; it is white magic, healing magic, magic to strengthen and give hope."

"*If* it strengthens," I answered. "*If* it gives hope."

Ruth was surprised but not put out as I had expected. "Yes, I can drop by on my way from shiatsu class. Did they actually say they wanted to see me?"

"It wasn't as strong as that," I said, "and in a way it was much stronger. They can't understand the nude encounter groups and your having lived with Randy, but they are feeling the whole family pulling away from them, pulling apart into a dozen pieces that don't make sense to them. You've had all that experience with change, with learning new things. They really need to see that you are not someone who's growing a third eye."

"I'm not going to lie," Ruth said, "or be backed into a corner."

"You won't have to discuss anything. Let them feed you cookies and tea and tell you whatever they want. I'm glad they've been asking about you so much. I've lost my objectivity with them. They seem so shriveled, so reduced, so imprisoned by fear that I can't stand to see it." Ruth, who loves objectivity, smiled graciously at me.

That week a family who lived in our neighborhood was murdered. They were on vacation in Wyoming, and they were found dead in their camper on a side road near the national park. The local papers had pictures and a story. There was coverage on TV. While we did not know them, I realized that our children must have gone to school with those children—a girl named Marcie who was twelve and a boy, Jonathan, nine. I started to break the news gently, and before I was finished, my son Richie interrupted: "Oh, that—yes, we know."

"We saw it before it was on TV," Wendy said. "They had an interview with some of the kids at school."

"Were they friends of yours—did you know them well?" Richie shrugged and stared at me, knowing I wanted something more from him and not knowing what that was.

"She was in a couple of my classes, but it's a big school and I really idn't know her. They just had bad luck, I guess."

Wendy, who was fourteen and older than those children, shrugged nd stared at me and said nothing.

I stayed at the table after they had gone, and tried to think how we ad all changed. When I was growing up this suburb did not exist. We ved in the city, in a neighborhood that was in many ways like a small wn. We never worried about going out alone to movies at night or lasses with late hours. We seldom locked our doors unless we were aving home for a long time. Terrors existed, but they came from ther quarters—loss of a job, sudden death, injury and accident, illess above all, and the deaths of children and breadwinners and young nothers. There were wreaths on the doors then, black ribbons with osettes, and for the Italians on the next block, pictures too, and dried owers. Mrs. Lambrusco's door haunted me for years with its wreath at had hung there for a month, made of ribbons and black, woven orsehair flowers. We always crossed the street to avoid the houses here death had been. We shivered at it; meeting to play after school, e told stories about those houses to scare one another. It was hanged, all changed. No longer credulous, our children, no longer the nakers of blood-chilling myths. Only the old keep that talent now. For ne young there is no deed without a name.

I can't believe it," Ruth said. "It's beyond understanding. They have big mezuzah on the door, and when I noticed it and mentioned it ney said I should get one myself. They even touched it and kissed heir fingers when they went back inside. I nearly fell over. And they eemed . . ."

"What?"

"Preoccupied."

"Maybe they were only uncomfortable and didn't know what to say you."

"But the sudden change—a mezuzah—"

"How did they seem to you besides that?"

"Less . . . less clawing, less grasping and groping. When I used to go there they always pulled me in and hung on like grim death. And they didn't keep looking around as though something would creep up on us all from the kitchen. This time it didn't seem so bad. They were calmer, I think, a little calmer."

"Did they say anything that bothered you?"

"Well, you know they can't let me get away without hearing about how I'm ruining Natalie by my 'escapades' as they put it. I'm too thin, I smoke too much, et cetera, et cetera."

I called Dr. Orwig the next day. "Maybe power corrupts but it also strengthens. We have reduced terror to fear."

"So far so good. Do you think you could get them to bake the cake themselves?"

"Yes, what's the difference?"

"There should be a series of activities, a complex series that absorbs them completely. Prayers at every ingredient, a complete weighing and measuring, an examination of every egg. The flour must be sifted seven times, and it should take a half day to make. To the cake there should be added the special words, looked over carefully and then burned white, this time, and a double dose. You do that."

"What are we aiming for?"

"Building the power levels, amplifying their capacity to use pure power."

"Where does this power idea come from?"

"It's in all magic and all of the suggestive magic of our day—the natural-food people use it, the natural-healing people too—acupuncture, for all I know. The point is that the patient be enlisted as much as possible in the mechanics of the magic."

"Perhaps I can get them to wear the words also—not a mezuzah—something special, close to their bodies."

"It's a good idea," Orwig said. "You know, you *have* a gift for witchcraft."

"I'm only impatient."

"All witches are. What else is it that makes them want to force creation, to summon the future, to render justice themselves, right wrongs, even scores, here and there, call vengeance—"

"Justice," I said. "Next Passover I will demand that the family put back the deleted Hebrew portion of the service, "Pour out Thy Wrath." It's the part where we call on God to bring our persecutors to justice. Reform Jews never use that section. We took it out because it makes our Christian friends uncomfortable and now we shiver at night because of criminals. I will have them bake the cake and sift seven siftings of flour. I will write the words and burn them white."

A dream. I am in the apartment, and the two old aunts are standing in the middle of their living room. They have their hair up in rollers, and they wear the flowered housecoats I gave them last year—drip dry and permanent-press. Looking with solemnity through their genteel bifocals they pore over the Bible, reciting in their light old voices the thousand maledictions that God reserves for enemies. Then as they read, the room changes, darkens. It is they who have darkened. Instead of the flower-sprigged housecoats, they wear long black robes; instead of the light-blue foam rollers, they wear the large varnish-stiffened wigs once worn by pious Jewish women who cut their hair after marriage. They speak the horrible maledictions, the high-water marks of God's past rages. They speak in Hebrew and read from slips I have written and then other words in other languages, languages that have never been domesticated with use in careful prayers to a God who Himself obeys the Laws He has made. Where they point, a force focused like a laser shoots light, and where the light touches, be it ever so gently, everything disintegrates—walls, doors, a scavenging cat in an alley, an old drunk curled up in a doorway, and all of the criminals skulking between their street and the river.

The dream should have been frightening but it wasn't; it was ridiculous. The sight of the aunts in hair rollers and housecoats magicking away made me giggle when I thought of it. It was the dream of an imaginative ten-year-old. I may have gone to Orwig and talked about mysticism and monotheism, but the subconscious was conjuring in pure comic book.

We baked. We took the best part of the afternoon at it, sifting and resifting with prayers and the white-burned ashes as Orwig had specified. The Psalms were carefully copied without error, vowels omitted so that their mystical power remained at its primal strength. While we worked I watched them. They were stronger, surer, less passive at their old household tasks. A month ago I thought I would never again see the lively, gossipy, generous aunts of my childhood. Now there were hints of them in the practiced way they beat the batter, the deft understanding that slipped the egg yolk free of the white. So, for a season, we would all be witches, they and I—no insult to the Lord, not really. They were old and powerless, I was middle-aged and helpless to change the rules, and we were eating cake with a higher carbon content than usual and no more. No children would be subverted over the Sabbath candles, no harm done.

Is it possible for anyone to write manuscript Hebrew and not feel some delight in the aesthetics of its calligraphy? The picture is now a letter, abstract and respectable, with a sound, but in the letter the picture is still remembered. The camel yet raises a dignified foot, the ox shakes his curved horn, the mouth opens to speak. The letters bend, wax fat and spin out lean, put delicate small feet out to trip the writer, wear crowns. The strange witch and the pious Torah scribe copy with the same punctilious exactness.

Sometimes in the jaunty stance of the *tav,* and the elaborate squared *aleph* I would stop and worry about things. Worrying is one of my few forms of prayer. Certainly my aunts were lonely and frightened, but my sister Ruth, for all her fierce and somewhat chilly independence, has fewer roots than they, and my niece Natalie almost no roots. Ruth moves often and is only temporarily here in mid-flight between her emotional fulfillment in California and her intellectual home in New York.

They were taking strength, visibly so, and I was content with my part in the mystery. A week after we had made the second cake they called an old friend and asked her to go with them to a matinee downtown. Being theatergoers of an older generation, such an outing demanded more than a home hair-wash and rollers. It meant a half day in the beauty parlor and a complete examination of the clothes closet. They had not had such an outing in two years. I was deeply relieved and so was the friend, who called me afterward. "They were such fun in the old days, those two," she said. "Of course, it's not the same now, but . . . " I knew what she meant, and for a while the two of us talked about how things had been. To Ruthie and me they had showed the same delight, rare in adults. I am not nearly so accepting of Natalie, my niece, whom I see as whining and waiflike, shriveled in the leaf. Ruth doesn't like my children either, partly because of our philosophical differences. She thinks they are repressed and uncreative, which are the worst sins in her catalog.

But Ruth too was happy about the change in Gusta and Rose, and their own children, as far away as California, were breathing easier.

It frightened me to hear how much Rose's and Gusta's children had wanted transformation all those months and how much hope they were placing on the fragile structure of my magic. Ruth hadn't told them about the mezuzahs, and I had told no one about the baked incantations. They would have been horrified, not because they are pious Jews but because they are pious and doctrinaire rationalists who would have seen their loving mothers in a madhouse before they compromised their agnosticism to the extent of a sign upon the door-post of the house, upon the hand, or for a frontlet between the eyes.

Orwig was fascinated by the whole thing—the family's grasping at straws and my disappointment and worry. At first I had felt a sense of release in our talks together. Not only was he sharing the secret, but his suggestions and help made me feel confident of success. Others had walked this way. It was mapped, and there were markers to keep the novice from losing himself in the entangling brush. Lately, however, I had had moments of feeling like the subject in a "dynamic" piece of anthropology. Was a monograph forming in Orwig's mind— Psychological Effects of Witchcraft on the Middle-Class Jewish-American Witch? With footnotes?

I did not see my aunts for two weeks, and when I rang their bell again I found myself listening for a change in their steps as they came to answer. When I looked into their faces it was to see if they had changed as Ruth said they had, as the friend said they had.

It was there. It was measurably there. I was about to go inside when Aunt Rose gently took my hand and placed it to the mezuzah and then to my lips. Only then did they draw me inside, greeting me and asking about the family. I looked at them carefully, studying their gestures, their postures, the expressions on their faces. It was true. They were no longer furtive or so fearful. I couldn't make them my aunts of twenty years ago, but the awful panic was no longer there. Then I noticed one thing more. There was no voice in the other room. The TV was off. "Is your set broken? You usually have something on," I said.

"We stopped watching it so much," Gusta said in her slow way. "We watched a program on violence last week, and I think it made me nervous. I couldn't sleep all night, and I think it made Rose nervous too. We watch some shows now, but only cultural things."

"And the news—?"

"A person *should* watch the news—" Rose said, "but . . . "

"But not if it makes him nervous all the time."

"But a person should be well informed—"

They must have argued about it, about being cut off from the information we are told is so necessary, all the horrors that bind us to the community of fellow feeling, to civilization. It was restful in the apartment with the TV off. We had tea.

"This isn't your usual tea, is it? It tastes different somehow."

"It's organic. All organic. Ruthie brought it to us."

"Do you like it?"

"Well, Ruthie says it's healthy. It makes your senses keener and cleans out your body, all your blood." I smiled.

"We're glad you came over today," Aunt Gusta said. "We've been wanting to discuss some things with you."

I waited. They began by talking about a grandfather, a man in the old country who was called Reb Yekel. I had heard of him before, a man of power and influence in the village from which my grandfather's people came. He was supposed to have had phenomenal strength and an imposing personality. Whatever he had been in those days, he now wore the mythic nimbus of an Old Testament hero. Why were they raising his ghost?

"He knew, he always *knew* when trouble was coming."

"Yes, he always had a way to get around whatever it was, by skill or strength, hiding or coming into the open, giving or withholding."

"A man of power," Aunt Gusta said. They stared at me pointedly.

"A man of power," Rose repeated.

"I don't understand," I said.

"Look at us—old women, falling apart. Any thief knows he could blow us over with a breath, any robber knows he could come in on us and we wouldn't have the power to resist."

"We no longer have our families to guard and protect us," Rose said. "We need other ways—other means of our own."

"Yes," I agreed. "I've given you the special ways I know—"

"We need something more. We are ready for more, something that will protect us from all this independence."

I had a moment of anxiety. Somehow when people have nothing, they live on nothing. When they have a little they begin to want more. Never had I dreamed that the women would want to raise this power to the wind and sail with it.

"You're getting this somewhere, this force," Gusta said in a low, tense voice. "We know it. We want you to go back, to see whoever it is, to pay them what they want and get us this so that we won't have to live always in terror, like moles!"

"You have power now—use it—build on it!"

"Is that what I said to you when you were ten years old and came to me because you wanted a dog so badly and your parents wouldn't get one for you? 'Beg them,' you said, and I begged them. And later, too, when there was that friend they didn't like and we let her visit over here—it was because you wanted these things, no other reason. Now we need, and we want!"

A month ago they were cowed old ghosts. Now they were defending their lives and their right to be defended. I didn't know what I could do. I nodded. They knew I wasn't the brains behind the plan. I hadn't known they were so conscious of things, so perceptive with all their fear. I nodded, feeling that at least I had returned to a more comfortable relationship with them. Once again things were as they should be—they as powerful elders, I as less responsible for them. Perhaps Orwig had come to the end of his gifts and I could retire as witch having given them something—enough.

I agreed to go to "them," and the aunts smiled, and suddenly it was all there, the memory of snowy Sundays spent baking cookies, the sight of the two of them sitting at the school play because my mother had been sick and could not come. The smell of their skins as I hugged them years ago. We sat over more tea, three women now, with gossip to knit up and cast off our needles before the afternoon went gray.

"I think Ruth is making a mistake with Natalie, back and forth like a Ping-Pong ball between here and there and God knows where."

"She has a modern idea of things, that's all," I said. "If life isn't rewarding where you are, the idea is to find another place. It's admirable, really, to try to improve a situation."

"Where can it improve when you bring the same silliness with you? Ruth is a silly woman—she should stay near her family where her silliness doesn't leave her daughter so much alone."

How could I tell them that the family was not really close enough to help anymore? They, the two sisters and my mother, had been the pins that had held it all together. The nephews and nieces had grown and gone separate ways. No one lived so close together that their homes were easily available to all the family children. The two old women had been taken up with their terror and had not been there to help. Besides, Natalie was not a lovable child and never had been. As a baby she had been whiny and temperamental, and as a little girl was sour and intransigent. She was one of those people whom one pities in the abstract. I think we all knew it, because we changed the subject without saying any more about Natalie.

I saw Orwig on Monday afternoon. Perhaps he was rushed, or perhaps he was getting tired of magicking in a darkening arena when most of the spectators had gone home. Perhaps there had been the early excitement of a monograph or two at the back of his mind and now maybe he wasn't so sure, but I was annoyed by his hurried manner and the obvious lessening of his attention. My aunts were getting sharp and perceptive now that they went armed into the daylight and strengthened into the night. I saw that they had also gotten a bit cynical as well. Had I? What happens to the armorer who knows that the metal he has made for his prince's hauberk is not metal at all but papier-mâché? Between interruptions I told Orwig about the problem. He seemed not only impatient but annoyed that it had not already been solved. "But your aunts aren't having nightmares anymore—they are going out now, they are strong enough to turn off the TV—the main source of their fear. What more is there to do?"

"They want something specific, a power more immediate."

"What are you asking for?"

"I don't know. Can't you see that I don't know anything about magic, about spells and amulets, about power blown from the spark of words! All the years we had the Talmud, we never hatched spells with it. And do you know what happened? All over the world people began to speak of us as 'the little Jew' . . . 'there was this little Jew—' "

Orwig looked at me hard for the first time that day. It was a look of puzzlement, I thought, and something else. I am not clever at reading looks. Besides, it was getting late and one of his students was standing outside waiting to be seen. I left.

The Emperor's New Clothes. The trouble in the tale doesn't come, as far as the swindlers are concerned, until the emperor shows himself to the populace and the inevitable child. Talmudic Law forbids the overdecorated letter, a letter for art's sake and not for the formation of legible words. Test the letter, say the Holy Books, by calling in a child, one who has just learned his *aleph*-bet. If the child can read it, it is a true letter and not a design, which would bring notoriety to the artist and not glory to God. The makers of papier-mâché armor must take heed and keep their princes from the populace and the inevitable child.

Orwig didn't know what to do about Rose and Gusta's demand. Neither did I. Perhaps we could put them off until they tired of the wait and developed a strength sufficient to their needs. My next visits were made quickly between other appointments, dropping in in a friendly way that they could not fault. The truth was that for no reason I could identify, I did not want them to go beyond the protection they had, the simple amulets and formulas that they needed to placate and calm themselves. I remembered that I had met Orwig at a drug seminar. The next time I spoke to him I would remind him of it and tell him that I did not wish my aunts to step from patent medicines to hard narcotics.

But then he called me and he was jubilant. "I've got it! It's perfect!" he cried. "I only wonder why you people never used this yourselves."

"What is it?"

"Come on over and let me show you."

I wanted to tell him that I had thought again and that what we needed was to move slowly now, to tie the magic to the foundation posts of law and reality.

"I'm really sorry about last time," he said. "It was finals week, and I had so many other things on my mind. When vacation started I was able to get to the problem." He sounded so sorry and so sincere that I told him I would come whenever he wished. I did not mention my misgivings.

"Look at this," he said and drew a box about twelve inches long and two inches wide from a desk drawer. I began to feel nervous. What did he have, a shard of the leaf spring of Elijah's chariot? The ferrule of Moses' rod? A branch of the burning bush—still burning? He opened the box. "See," he said, "see?"

It was a silver yad, quite a lovely one. "I got it from the museum. They have a small collection of ceremonial objects, and the curator and I were students together."

"But this is just a pointer. It's so the reader won't touch the scroll with his fingers and wear or stain the letters. It's not magic, but Jewish housewifery at work."

"It's of silver, a precious metal, and it's fashioned in the shape of a hand with a pointing finger."

"Yes . . ."

"It is potent magic."

"It's a pointer, a fancy version of the thing the sixth-grade teacher uses to show Madagascar on the map."

"It is—it *could* be ceremonial protection of great power. Did you ever hear of 'pointing the bone'?"

"It kills enemies—I mean it's supposed to kill enemies at a distance, isn't it? Say the spell and draw a bead on the enemy. Three miles away a man's fire goes out, leaves on the trees around him shake and are blown in no earthly wind from their branches. The casual alighting bird drops from its perch, dead. The man's eyes dry in their sockets, his mouth fills with dust. There is no escape."

"Well," and he smiled, "that's the general idea."

"My aunts have no enemies—"

"Your aunts have a million enemies."

"A million isn't one. Whom do you go after in streets full of alien faces and foreign tongues? Do you cry to men whom you fear will watch you robbed or beaten by one of their own and not raise a hand to stop the horror?"

"You go after the fear of the people, not the people themselves. Those two, as you describe them, are less fearful under the protection of their amulets, but that's only in the home where the amulets are. They need mobility, which includes not only the means to strengthen themselves but powers to weaken their enemies."

"And this yad, pointed at Fifth and Market, will clear the streets before them, cut a swath through the living, bank up humanity on either side like the Red Sea held back for Moses?"

"They can feel that they walk in an aura of power, a magic zone."

"I don't think they'll do it. Swallowing baked words is one thing, but waving a wand and saying things aloud—"

"They did that when they put up the mezuzahs, and they want more from us, don't they?"

"Where does it stop?"

"With this, I think. There's plenty of power there."

I had gone to them before as a mourner, but I had been in costume. This time I wore ordinary clothes and sensible walking shoes because the sorrow was real and I needed the comfort and stability of working clothes. When I came to the door I rang the family ring. This time there was no groping and fumbling the length of the door on either side, no whispered consultations and fearful questions, the answers to which were scarcely heard through the pervading terror; there was only one simple chain and one simple call to me as it had been in the past, love coming forward through the door before it opened. If magic had wrought this, was it only squeamishness on my part to deny them more? Was I only thinking of how it would look, waving wands?

And they were dressed, not in their housecoats but in street clothes as though they could go out if they wished, through the battleground streets to the store, the play, the concert, and the whole world of choice. It was early for lunch so we sat down and they asked about Sam and the kids. The talk was general but not idle. They knitted while they talked; they belonged to a generation that believed the only hand empty of work should be the hand of a corpse. I had brought mending. When lunch was over and the dishes were cleared away, Aunt Gusta came back from the sink and sat opposite me at the table. "So," she said, "you went to them? What did they say?"

"*He* said you should be free to go wherever you want in safety." They smiled. "You already have power against your nightmares and the fear—"

"There are things we need to do—"

"There are places we need to go—"

"I know, but—"

"Give us the power we need."

"The weak have no dignity."

"The worst thing about old age—"

"You are young yet. You don't know how it is—"

I reached into my sewing bag and brought out the box. They drew in their breaths. Before I opened the box I told them about the formula. It was the same psalm as before, but this time read, and read facing in four directions and repeating the formula letter-perfect. Then I opened the box.

I think I expected the inevitable child, that they would stare at the lovely artifact and tell me what it was. "But it's just a yad!" "It's like the one the congregation gave Rabbi Jacob when he retired." They only stared and said nothing. I took it out of the box. The intricate and graceful silver finger shone in their winter-dim kitchen. "This one is very valuable," I said. "It's an antique and shouldn't leave the house." Silence. They were staring at it. "I am going to leave it with you now, and in a few days I will have written out the formula. You know, don't you, what it does?" Aunt Rose turned to me and nodded. I tried to read her expression but I couldn't. There was something tremulous about her look. I thought perhaps I saw tears forming.

Our family are closet extremists, natural radicals brought to heel by law and hard facts. When my sister Ruth went into yoga it was a total commitment. When disenchantment followed, that too was complete. When cousin Bernard became a Communist he was soon chairman of his group. At his change of heart, he changed root and branch, hating communism as totally as he had loved it. Now he preaches Armageddon at street corners, and he is the most devoted of all the Children of Light. I had taken on my aunts' rehabilitation. I expected to give great energy to the work.

I was making dinner early that evening. Wendy and Richie were watching TV in the living room. I was still depressed and abstracted, thinking of Rose and Gusta. I wasn't listening to the kids—they only talked desultorily during the programs. Occasionally there would be a phone call for Wendy. After one such call I heard their voices raised in anger, and that too was not unusual. They sometimes flew at one another for no obvious reason. I had long ago given up trying to mediate, but Richie's tone was urgent, and I heard him cry out, "She is not!" I began to listen. Wendy was hissing at him, a thing she does that I particularly dislike. "She is too, she is! It's all there for anyone to see, the way she acts and everything. Mom is having an affair!"

My first reaction was to want to burst out laughing. Instant communication, total openness, family life and sex ed. at school, and now everyone knows everything in a pop-psych, literal, pea-brained way. If Richie was defending me it was because he didn't believe anyone over thirty capable of making love. Wendy had been aiming bitter and savage remarks at me lately, and I had credited it to the usual stresses of her adolescence. I too had read the fashionable books. I knew though that I couldn't laugh or pass it off. I went into the living room and stood in front of the set. As I did, the laughter left me. Something in their faces or their limp postures woke an anger in me that was more than the necessary amount to make me forceful. "You demand your privacy and you demand our trust whether you earn it or not. Kindly give me the same privileges. I am not, in fact, having an affair. I am trying to help two old women whom neither of you seem to recognize as being quite human. If I come home preoccupied, elated, or depressed, it is because of what is going on with them. You don't think that the behavior of two old women could elate or depress anyone, do you? What has made you so self-centered, so unthinking?"

Rhetorical questions. All the child-rearing books denounce them. So do I, or try to. When times were better I would have to ask Aunt Gusta and Aunt Rose if I had ever faced them with that placid, flaccid condescension.

As I thought about it later I saw beneath Wendy's mistake. I had been preoccupied, my mind and time too taken up with the changes, good and bad, in Aunt Gusta and Aunt Rose. If I had not been sexually unfaithful to my family I had been spiritually so, a condition for which my precocious daughter had no word and no concept. I would have work to do at home when my aunts could walk the streets, go to matinees, and argue the way home about the motives of the characters.

The next day I was busy as a scribe. My letters were still far from perfect, but I was learning, picking up speed and competence. Who knows, if Sam's business should fail there might be a whole career for me as a maker of spells and amulets, special charms for suburban living. Are your children zombies—numb and dumb before the TV? A page of Proverbs dusted into the dust of the pepper shaker, and they will rise up and call you blessed. Later, for the PTA, I could dress in black and go by night to the local fast-food place with Ecclesiastes (12) written in special ink on special paper and burned white. Into the taco sauce and the pickle relish, into the chocolate shakes and the soft ice cream: "Remember thy Creator in the days of thy youth." Group rates, of course.

But although it wasn't perfect I was proud of the job I had done, and before it was destroyed I felt the need to show it to someone. Didn't God make man so He could show off the other five days of creation? Didn't He make angels so He could show off man? The only one I could show my finished work to was Orwig, so I called. He was free and wanted to see the work. Besides, he had, he said, something to tell me. I packed up my pages carefully and went.

He was surprised at the care I had taken. "But what a shame to burn this—" he cried, and then, turning in his chair, he steepled his fingers and put them to his lips. "I wonder how much fine art gets destroyed in just this way. Do you think that what we see as native art can, in many cases, be lesser work, rejected, perhaps for the greater, which ends in the sacred fire or the sacred lake?"

"Or the sacred pancake," I said. "Definitely."

"Do you think we could take a picture?"

"Nix," I said. "Ruins the spell."

"Yes, of course."

"You said you had something to tell me?"

"Yes, so I do. Last year I put in for a field-study grant to do some work with a group of Indians whose social units have proved to be very cohesive in spite of their assimilation into American life. Their religion is one of these cohesive forces. If we can learn how—"

"You're leaving . . . "

"I'm afraid so. I'll be gone for six months. You see, I never imagined the grant would come through. With all the competing applications for a very limited amount of money—"

"When are you leaving?"

"Next week."

"And of course you're going to be busy planning and packing . . . "

"Yes."

"I'll be all alone."

"But you're doing beautifully. You're a natural. You have an intuitive sense of—"

"The whole thing's gotten too big for me. It scares me, and without you—"

"When I'm settled I'll send you my address. We can write—"

We sounded like lovers breaking up, his voice defensive and placating, mine imploring and louder than I wished. A student passing by looked in quickly and too quickly went away, smiling perhaps about good old Orwig. It took the spirit out of me. I gathered up the pages. "My last days as a witch," I said.

"When I come back perhaps you can make a piece of calligraphy for my wall."

"I'd love to," I said, and left. It wasn't until I was in the car that I saw his wall again in my mind. Goddess Amaterasu cloud riding; the gods of the Dogon; Shiva, majestic in destruction, his foot on a human skull; and next to them all, what?—the words of our contract with the Almighty? It would be my fault, not Orwig's. For Christmas I'll send him a picture of myself in witch's robes, I thought, but not the words. The words will be burned to keep them from profanation. Nowhere will Tiamat or Kali open idols' eyes and read the letters, the graceful letters that comfort our tiny, stiff-necked people.

The next day I delivered the pages to Rose and Gusta. They were in new spring dresses. "I feel like having a party," Gusta said, "now that spring is coming. Maybe we should do some entertaining and invite all the children and grandchildren." As they talked about it I noticed that the curtains were open in the living room and there was light coming from the bedroom, also. When they had given me my tea and talked the requisite amount of time they stopped. The whole apartment was silent in its light, waiting for me.

There was so much I wanted to tell them and couldn't. I put the folder with the pages in the table. "I've gone over it all twice, word for word and no mistakes. I put the vowels in one copy because you'll have to read the other letter perfect. I suppose it would have been easier to transliterate—"

"It wouldn't have worked then." Gusta smiled. They took up the pages and began to study in a low mutter, correcting now and then. I had demanded they read with Sephardic pronunciation, the one now used in Israel. I did not want an eastern-European sound to the Hebrew, one that recalled ghettos and persecutions. They were deep in study when I left.

Ruth called me at the end of the week. "Are you going to be home tomorrow? I'd like to leave some cartons off." Ruth had a corner in our basement where an ever-changing array of boxes and trunks were kept—the California things when she was in New York, the New York things when she was in California, her outgrown hobbies, and Natalie's outgrown clothes. When the stack got too big she would let me call the Salvation Army. Our local branch featured tennis gear, batik equipment, and pottery-making supplies.

"Oh, Ruth, not again, not so soon!"

"I just can't stay here—my life isn't *moving* anywhere! We're both at a standstill. Natalie's school isn't stimulating, and this place is dead spiritually."

"Where to now?"

"Oh, we won't be leaving for a few weeks, but I think we need a complete change, some place like India, a place of spiritual resonance."

"If you want spiritual resonance, what about the Sinai, or the Western Wall or the Golan or Safad or Kinneret or the settlements by the Jordan—" I found I was getting too angry to stop myself. "Are those places not spiritual enough? Ruth, if you need commitment, you and Natalie, why not go where you are really wanted, really needed by your own people?" We had spoken about this before—she knew my feelings. I hated my compulsion to begin it all again. Her voice chilled. "This family has never understood my needs, never. You would like nothing better than to bury me on some kibbutz in the desert."

"As opposed to Tibet. Ruth, why is the Gobi better spiritually than the Sinai *always*?"

"You wouldn't understand."

"I suppose not," I said, and made myself let go. "I'm sorry I raised the issue. Of course you can leave the boxes here. What should I do with what's here already?"

"Do I have stuff there now? I guess I do. I suppose I should look through it all. Some of it might be usable." She sounded disappointed. Ruth hates "looking back" as she puts it, finding suitable graves for the old styles and enthusiasms. I didn't want her to leave angry.

"Come over anyway—I have the day free. Please?"

She came up the walk looking young and sprightly, and I went to the door trying to keep disapproval off my face. Ruth loves new beginnings, the times before there are ambivalences, complications, results. I often wondered where she got it from, that weekend-guest view of life. The endings were usually sad, but at beginnings she was always fun to be with. "Good morning!" she cried and hugged me. "I've been thinking about what you said, and you know, you're right. The Orient isn't the place for a growing girl. Natalie needs balance and tradition and a sense of continuity. You know the only place where all that still happens—Mexico. I thought we'd go to Oaxaca first. When I was at Esalen—"

I caught myself quickly, and the next thing I said was, "Let's have coffee first. Then we can get to the basement."

"Great!" Ruth said. "I've got two trunks in the car." In spite of everything it was a pleasant morning. I was happy because I like her when she's feeling good. There'd be things to get and plans to make, so she wouldn't be leaving for a week at least. Perhaps I could get them over for a good-bye meal. Ruth sped away at one, leaving me three trunks full of clothes and hobbies. When she called again at four she was another person.

Natalie had collapsed at school and had been taken to the local hospital. She was conscious but very weak. They did not know what it was but suspected some kind of blood problem. Could Ruth come and stay with us for a while until they knew? "Of course!" I cried and hung up the phone guilty for being obscurely happy.

It is in the real adventures, in true crises, that Ruthie shines. Her worry about Natalie made her gentler and more patient. She had no sense of martyrdom or self-pity. She was not melodramatic. As a houseguest she was a pure pleasure—helpful and often guiltlessly cheerful. She even began to know the kids a little and developed a friendly natural ease with them that amazed me. Sometimes in the evening we would clean up the kitchen together and reminisce. We had shared the years of her childhood and my adolescence, and because of the age difference we had experienced them in very different ways. I answered a dozen questions Ruthie never knew were puzzling her, and she amused me with her perceptions of our parents and my friends from those days. Forgotten names and people came back. The kitchen rang with laughter. Sam, knowing a reunion when he saw one, left us pretty much alone. He had not liked her, but now there was a grudging respect between them. Our joyousness amazed Wendy and Richie. Their amazement gave me pause. Had I always been so dry and literal? At first they tiptoed past, wide-eyed and quiet, skirting the tribal laughter and the lighted hearth-place. Now and then they crept closer to the edge of our camp. I could see their unblinking stares just beyond the circle of light. Soon they might not fade away into the darkness but come closer, sit on soft haunches, and listen. And later still they might join us in a howl or two at the moon before I spoke incantations, spread my cape and rose hie-up-cap-and-over on the night-rack clouds and sped away. As I observed Ruthie laughing and relaxed I knew that she too had been solemn and responsible in her own way with Natalie and that she relished the release from her role as guide, example, and saint. How we all long to explode and free ourselves of bonds; how fragile they are after all, the customs that tie us to each other and to the world.

A week went by. Natalie was no better and no worse. There were new tests, new guesses. Ruthie went to the hospital every day and came back no closer to an answer. The doctors were magicking too, their tests escalating in complexity and pain, their reasoning more circuitous. They were sailing beyond themselves and their tiny isolated rooms of proven truth. I knew the feeling. Aunt Gusta and Aunt Rose called a few times. Was there space enough for Ruthie in our house? If not, they would be glad to take Wendy for a visit. "Sisters should stay together when trouble comes," Aunt Gusta said. "The family," Aunt Rose echoed, "that's what's important." I asked if I could drop by on my way downtown. They were hesitant. They were going out today, and tomorrow there was the science show at the museum and their library day. Could I come over on Thursday? Ruth, who had spoken to them also, was puzzled. They had asked after Natalie in a general way but had gone into detail about herself. How was she spending her evenings? How did she get on with my family? "I told them that outside of worrying about Natalie I was fine and happy enough. They sounded—*satisfied*. It was the tone of voice you hear from a mother when her six-year-old does well in company." I didn't acknowledge the remark, and when Ruthie looked over at me I looked away.

I went over on Thursday and for a reason I didn't examine, I brought something—a bottle of good wine. The aunts welcomed me in. They couldn't have lunch with me, they were sorry. They were going downtown to help a friend's granddaughter with her wedding shopping. How was everything? Fine, I said, considering Natalie was still in the hospital. More tests and still no one seemed to know what was wrong. Ruthie was a joy to have—we had never been so close, but when the reason for it all was illness and suffering— Gusta came close and put her hand on my arm. "Don't worry," she said, "everything is going to work out. People will do what they must, and things will come right."

"Look," said Aunt Rose, "how Ruthie has changed in the week since Natalie's trouble, how Natalie herself has changed. We saw her yesterday. She was glad to see us—none of her old snippiness. Of course it would spoil everything if Ruthie were told just yet why things need to stay this way."

"Of course she won't tell," Gusta said. "How can she and not destroy herself—even her own children!"

"Right now it's Ruthie and Natalie who must be considered. They'll come to see the rightness of this when they settle here at last in a place close to yours. We've given it a lot of work and a lot of thought. We want you to get her to some work—maybe office work in that big Jewish center you have out there. There's one of those divorce groups out there, isn't there? A nice man with a child or two—that's what Ruthie needs."

"But—"

"And Natalie will be all right when the right things happen, when Ruthie sees her duty to her family and does it."

"Old people need secure worlds, close communities, families around them," Gusta said. "If people can't do what's right they must be made to."

"We know, for instance, how busy you are with all you have to do, but it's been months since the children came to see us. You'll attend to that soon, won't you?"

"We wouldn't want to have to become hard or tyrannical, of course; you're our favorite niece."

"Is that all that keeps you from tyranny, that love you say you have for us?"

"Who can depend on love?" Aunt Rose said. "Fear is so much more stable, and stability is what we need, people our ages."

"We blackmail with love until the love is no more, and then with fear."

"The yad—"

"The power didn't corrupt us, the weakness did. See to them, the things we told you."

They turned into their soft new coats, and after a touch of the talisman at the door, waved lovingly after me and went their ways through streets full of rationalists and vandals.

PALIMPSEST

Dr. La Doux hears that it's already morning. Wataska is small enough so that the roosters kept by two pensioners east of town still break the day. He gets up quietly, leaving his wife to sleep the extra hour, and goes down to his study to spend what he has come to think of as the gracious time.

His chair faces the backyard and the two old trees whose lower limbs are smooth with his children's climbing. The grass, once mowed weekly by patients, is now high and ragged. His wife has tried to get some of the young people in the neighborhood to come and cut it, but none of them wants to enter the hospital grounds, or not for what the doctor is willing to pay. It's a holdover from the past, this fear of the place, and especially illogical to him since the "asylum" is responsible for Wataska's existence and has been the single dependable source of its employment for thirty years.

The hospital was built with care and concern, according to the finest liberal thinking of the time. Crowded slums, filth, poverty, disease, and despair made of the industrial part of the state a breeding ground for insanity. Mothers who bore child after child went staring strange, sitting bolt upright before open gas jets. Fathers went screaming mad through the tenements with knives. The aged drifted into starved senility, unnoticed and unfed. In 1893 a group of Quaker ladies led by the redoubtable Ernestine Van Zandt convinced the legislature to build in the lovely, rural northern part of Wataska County a haven for these broken souls. When he came in 1962, Dr. La Doux had been given this history and a talk on the architecture of the Main Building by his predecessor, Dr. Linville. It was, or had been, an elegant building, on which much care had been lavished. It was Victorian in feeling but with simple lines. One saw the original effect in the picture hanging in the superintendent's office, taken in 1902 when Main was all there was. Trees had been planted around it, and the patients had their garden plots in back where they grew vegetables to supplement the institutional rations.

No one could have predicted the trebling of population in the slums that fed Wataska. Restless blacks from the South, the immigrant poor of Europe, the failed farmer, the strange child whose condition did not yet have a name. By 1930, when Coulter had his picture taken at the front gate, six buildings clustered around Main. They were the hurry-up constructions of terrible need. The trees were gone, the garden plots paved over for the security section's exercise yard. In 1945, when Linville came, there were eighty-nine hundred patients in the hospital. Then the mill closed. Wataska State Hospital was the town's industry.

Dr. La Doux sometimes thinks about the hospital in his gracious time, but it is always in such general ways—its history, his predecessors, certain patients who stand out in his memory. He does not allow current problems or administrative cares to intrude on the time. He cannot see the hospital from his backyard, only the big trees planted by himself and the others—Linville mostly. There are fashions in such things, too—open views versus closed, vistas versus privacy.

The coffee is ready. Before he pours it he goes from the kitchen to his front door and down the walk to his mailbox. Across the street one side of Main and parts of three larger, later buildings are struck with early light. He takes his newspaper from the box and returns to the house. When he is ready he will sit in the study and spend the remaining time reading the news. Part of him will read the news. Part of him will savor his reading, the hot coffee, the stillness, the simplicity of this hour. Then, at the appointed moment, his wife will stir and he will take her some coffee. The day will open. While showering he will review his appointments. While shaving, he will contemplate his problems. It is all bearable because he has been armed with this healing stillness.

The cup steams in his hand. The paper is waiting. He sits back and unfolds it. The international news is grim but predictably so, and therefore a comfort. The editorials. National news. State. His eye lights on a smaller piece on the last news page: STATE RATIFIES PATIENTS' RIGHTS BILL.

In recent years he has heard a good deal about such plans. He is surprised that a bill would come so soon. His own experience with the state legislature is that its actions are taken with glacial slowness. Yet here . . .

He skims the article: "blanket removal of legal adjudication as mentally incompetent . . . right to treatment . . . right of refusal of treatment . . . choice of 'treatment modalities' . . . civil rights . . . driver's license . . . voting rights under law . . . change of commitment procedures . . . inspection of medical records . . . rights of review . . . "

It will not change very much for him. Even before he came, the overwhelming number of patients in the hospital were voluntary. The regional mental-health centers now take care of most of the sudden-acute cases, leaving to Wataska the brain-damaged, the senile, the chronic, the continually violent, and those so dependent that they cannot find their way in a free society. He is pleased. Perhaps now there will be more respect in the community for the patients, fewer examples of casual abuse and cruelty in and out of the institution. In the hall, the clock strikes the hour. Dr. La Doux finishes his coffee and rises to the day.

By nine he is in his office. His secretary, Miss Rulliger (whose mother had died in Main, a patient) commands his first three hours. The legislature has not voted sufficient funds for an administrative assistant, so most of the medical records, releases, insurance forms, and inquiries regarding present and former patients must come across his desk. She seems slightly distracted this morning, but her usual reserve makes it impossible for him to question her beyond a neutral-voiced "Am I dictating too fast? You seem a bit perturbed."

"Well, didn't you see the article in this morning's paper?"

"Which article?"

"About the Patients' Rights Bill."

"Oh, that. I don't think that will affect us much." He tells her what he has thought out in tranquil stillness over his coffee. He is glad that he is able to give his ideas in so balanced and organized a way.

"But the bill says the patients may refuse medication," Miss Rulliger persists. "People will stop taking the tranquilizers they need. Everyone will get . . . overwrought . . . the way it was years ago . . . before the drugs. And they'll be going away, leaving. They'll all be able to *leave* . . . "

"One way or another, most of them can do that now. The sad thing is that there's no place for them to go."

"And the violent ones?"

"They'll have a choice—here or jail." He knows she is seeing her mother again, all those years ago, fighting and screaming, out of control.

He turns back to the letter he has been holding. "I don't think the new bill will bother us, Ms. R.," he says. She likes it when he calls her Ms. R. She smiles and is mollified.

"Oh, yes," she says, "Miss Annie and Miss Jane want to see you this afternoon. Are you free?"

"I guess so," he says, and sighs, "but only for fifteen minutes. Then buzz and tell me I have an appointment with Dr. Allison."

Miss Annie and Miss Jane are two of the patients who have established themselves as special in the hospital. They have been here for upwards of forty years—through booms and busts, work therapies and chemotherapies, shock treatments and psychodrama, additions, subtractions, modifications, and religions—and they have stayed the same while psychiatry and society changed around them. Miss Annie was hospitalized when she was twenty-five. It was rumored that there were politics behind the commitment because she had been a prostitute with the best room in the best hotel in Wataska, which had, in the thirties, been up and coming as the county seat. She is ugly and obese now, but because of the heartily transparent quality of her guile and her false-naïve, cajoling manner, she is at the head of every line, eats what and when she likes, and commands the TV shows and the room of her choice. Years ago, Miss Jane, the beaten outcast of some obscure family horror, was brought in, in a rigid catatonic trance. (Strange, one does not see catatonics at the hospital anymore—what has happened to them all?—they once decorated the corners like caryatids.) Through some unexplained affinity she was "adopted" by Miss Annie, bullied and cajoled from stupor to become a faithful lieutenant with whom Miss Annie fights and schemes the years away. They have free run of the institution, and they see Dr. La Doux whenever they please. They have not insisted on this privilege for a month or so, although he sees them on his daily walk through the shrinking wards of his care.

He is now able to walk his wards in half a day. Rollins and Hawley buildings are closed, awaiting some other use, and the temporary "holding" wards in the converted barracks are long gone. Sections that had once bulged with six times their capacity now house almost the number of patients they were built for. He wonders for a moment what the women want this time, who has fallen under their censure. He will know soon enough. Miss Annie is nothing if not direct.

It is also his habit to lunch in the dining room at Main if he can. If there is not some official function at noon, he will saunter over and go through the line among the patients, choosing a table at random. The patients will be uncomfortable in his presence, he knows, but they will also have the message that he is available to them, and he will be able to sense changes in the tone of the place. Sometimes it is important. There are still dangerous people in this population, still instances of violence and abuse, still, with all the drugs and tranquilizers, a need for immediate accessibility and compassion.

He looks at the schedule. Some of the day-shift staff has been wanting to speak with him; there is time on Thursday. He marks it on his calendar along with a note that those concerned be called. A sheaf of requests. Changes in the Medicaid law for him to study. At noon he gets up and walks slowly across the grounds. Few of the patients are out even on so lovely a day. He knows how debilitating mental illness is, but he never fails to wonder at the gifts untaken, the possibilities unexplored, the challenges refused by these patients time after time— even so simple a thing as a spring day.

There is an undercurrent in the dining room, a new tone, but he can not define it. He feels the excitement—a nervous, wary quickening of voices and gestures—not in everyone, of course: the chronically depressed still stare out at him from blank faces, the senile are light-years away. But the tone of the place is higher, shriller. From a distant corner Miss Annie sees him and stands up waving and shouting a greeting. She sits down in a flurry of attention. Some of the patients look at him and then look away as though they are embarrassed; he is puzzled.

At two o'clock he is trying to find out why maintenance is unable to fix the antiquated plumbing in Main. Miss Rulliger buzzes him to tell him that Miss Annie and Miss Jane have arrived. It would be more convenient to have them wait until he is finished, but he knows that if he does, they will blame Miss Rulliger; thwarted, they can become searingly vindictive, and she is vulnerable. He sighs, rises, and opens his door to them.

Until the mid-sixties there was a hospital uniform for patients, a kind of jumpsuit for men, in brown, gray, or green, and a hoover apron for women, in flowered calico. When Dr. La Doux came he ordered that the uniforms be made optional and was surprised when the great majority of patients continued to wear them. For many, the neat suits and wraparounds were the best clothes they had ever owned. They laundered well and were replaced by the institution when they wore out. Miss Annie had never worn hospital dress. Years ago she had cut up old bed sheets and created the Statue of Liberty costume that was her trademark, complete with torch and tiara. Miss Jane was less successful as Uncle Sam, or what Dr. La Doux guessed was Uncle Sam. Without the beard. From time to time, other adornments had been added. On Miss Annie's dirty arm are a dozen or so greening-brass bangles. Her fingers are stiff with rings. The tennis shoes she wears have been cut away at the tops to reveal polished toenails and an additional half-dozen rings. She winks broadly at him. "How you keepin', Doc?" Her lips are heavily coated with a purplish lipstick. She puts them out in the moue of a kiss, then turns, barking over her shoulder. "Jane!" She is filling the doorway—he has a feeling of being inundated by her, swamped, suffocated. "Jane, come in here! Don't you see how tired poor old Doc looks? You been workin' too hard, Doc. You been lettin' these here crazy people walk all over you, been wor-ryin' about 'em, God love you—" She wrings his hand. He thinks he can see a tear forming in her eye. Perhaps it is caused by the heavy mascara and eyeliner she wears. She waddles into the office and Miss Jane follows. The gray men's jumpsuit has been modified by the addition of painted red stripes and an old blue blazer cut off high in front to simulate a waistcoat. There is also a top hat of heavy card-board painted in stripes of red and white with a border of blue. After someone's comment that the outfit looked mannish, they had added a few necklaces and also makeup and lipstick. A new doctor had de-scribed Miss Jane's looks as "death at a rummage sale."

"Hello Doctor," she says shyly and holds out a limp hand. He shakes it once and it slides away. She seems to disappear then, leaving only Miss Annie and himself in the airless room.

"You made a big mistake, Doc." Miss Annie booms. "The civil rights put the niggers in the same wards as us. I didn't say nothin', I acted like a lady. The women's rights give us that new doctor, Grace What'sername, walkin' around in pants here, and I didn't give her a kick in the ass like she deserved. Now they gone too far, and I see you need our help right away. Jane and me, we discussed it, and there ain't but one way to save your buns, and that's for us to get on top of things first before anyone else gets too much time to think. You agree with that, don't you, Doc, bein' you're about the smartest one around here?"

"I don't understand."

"Shit, Doc, there ain't nothin' *to* understand, just that we're on your side and gonna give you all the pertection you need, ain't we, Jane? Tell him that." Miss Jane opens her mouth, but Miss Annie goes on, "Why anyone that'ud try to mess on you, I'd fix him, and you can bet your ass on that!" and the torch of freedom trembles in Liberty's hand. "You're a good man, Doc, good man, and don't you worry one damn bit, 'cause me and Jane here are goin' to sew things up good!" A grin, a wink, and they are gone, leaving the unquenchable flower-oil smell of their perfume going stale in the air.

He shakes his head and calls for Miss Rulliger. It seems to him that not only are there few catatonics but not so many eccentrics in the hospital population as there once had been. Tranquilizers have altered the picture of the "lunatic," by blunting the edges of panic and rage, but over the years there have been other changes that drugs and new methods of treatment cannot explain. Hysteria now is rare, conversion symptoms fading. Depression is now the largest category in the hospital, greater than all other syndromes put together, and the flowering eccentric madman, eater of bugs, preacher of world's end, the raging Napoleon, the self-martyring Jesus an aging and dying minority. It is strange. He wonders if there has been research done.

In another gracious time two weeks later, Dr. La Doux opens his newspaper again and learns what Miss Annie and Miss Jane meant by their offer to "get on top of things." The article is on page 4, a simple announcement made without comment. Miss Annie and Miss Jane, quoting the new Patients' Rights Bill have, the very afternoon past, announced themselves as candidates for the offices of mayor of Wataska and sheriff of Wataska County, respectively.

Dr. La Doux's first response is to laugh. Whoever had cooked up the story had, no doubt, seen the women in their costumes and remembered that Pat Paulsen and W. C. Fields had made hilarious fun out of campaigning for the presidency. But Fields and Paulsen were conscious of what they were doing—were sane. This joke was ridiculing his patients in a way he had fought to stop since he had come to the hospital. Some of the serenity went out of the morning.

Later from his office he called the newspaper. It was a long-distance call, and he was some time getting to the right person. "I can understand your upset, Doctor, but this is not a joke. The filing was done in a legal, formal way. To the best of my knowledge it was done by the women themselves."

"These women are mentally ill—they're both long-time patients here. They're incapable of a day's functioning outside a hospital—"

"Been there for a long time, have they?"

"Forty years."

"Then the residence requirements are okay."

"They're ignorant, half-literate, mentally ill people!"

"Mental illness is no longer a bar, Doctor; any franchised person is free to run. The state of their literacy is irrelevant also, since 1965—that was the Jones case—*Jones* versus *Sleasor* et al. If they're as sick as you say they are, they won't campaign much—they probably won't get many votes."

Later he calls the attorney general's office and receives the same information. There is nothing he can do. The head of the Department of Institutions, whom he calls later, is not aware of the problem. "The Patients' Rights Bill was a long time coming, George, but if those women are as crazy as you say they are, why don't you try to talk them out of it? Get them interested in something else—you know how suggestible those people are." Dr. La Doux remembers that the head of institutions has no experience with mental illness—his field had been retardation. When he hangs up the phone he sits at his desk thinking. What Miss Annie and Miss Jane have done is legal, lawful, possible. The electors of Wataska County number some six thousand souls. They are people of long patience and of a quiet, fatalistic stillness. They endure. The population of Wataska State Hospital is four thousand. The election will pit apathy against madness.

Miss Annie and Miss Jane have long enjoyed free run not only of the hospital and its grounds, but of the town, where they are usually seen on Saturday in full regalia, cadging sodas at the Chip 'n' Dip.

The town caters to them with amused affection. They have not waited in any lines for years nor been shooed away from any ceremony great or small. Their more-bizarre statements are treasured and retold, and their doings supply a unique source of town humor. To his relief, through the enervating days of summer, Dr. La Doux learns that the candidates are not actively stumping in the town. Mayor Thorne's annual Fourth of July picnic is, of course, attended by both Liberty and Uncle Sam, but there are no confrontations and the ladies do not demand equal time. In September, Sheriff Runciman begins to put up his posters—it is said he ordered fifteen thousand of them when he first declared in 1957 and is only halfway through his supply. They are flattering to the man he was. It is October now, but the face of Miss Annie enlivens none of the county's barn walls or billboards.

Miss Jane does not take the stage either, or grant interviews through the barred gates from which the locks have, at any rate, been taken.

But inside the hospital they are as ubiquitous as television, as Thorazine, as waiting, as despair. And never in his wildest dreams has Dr. La Doux imagined what their campaign would be.

From a two-minute spot by Miss Annie at the first sitting of dinner, October 2, 1978, and repeated in rambling and altered form by Miss Jane at the second:

Crazy people have sold themselfs short actin' harmless and tryin' to make people love 'em 'cause they ain't dangerous. Well, that's fine and it has give us rights and that. But what Sanes give they can take away. Don't some of these-here politicians in the poor countries act crazy so's people will be scared? They ain't the genuine thing. The youth admire us because we are the real thing. The youth say society is crazy—I seen that on TV somewheres, but people ain't afraid of us no more, and that's a mistake we made that's gotta be fixed!

Posters appear, one showing a sheet with two eye-holes and the word, *Boo!* One poster has a picture of Miss Annie and Miss Jane leering in their regalia, and underneath, *Beautiful Madness*. Another is a simple logo, no message but a drawing of a straitjacket, the long sleeves spread out and dangling in cruciform.

It is then that Dr. La Doux realizes why the ladies have not taken their campaign out of the hospital. There is no need. The commissioners have long since gerrymandered Wataska into a very favorable voting ratio as regards the rest of the county. Votes cast in Wataska proper count two for one. It has kept county-seat people at the county seat for years. Now, if the state hospital votes as a bloc, the rest of the county can vote as it will. Liberty, cracked in the bell, will be mayor of the town of Wataska; Uncle Sam, its law enforcement.

A manifesto, printed on the hospital press (occupational therapy):

To be in everyone's mailbox or milkbox or whatever and up in Eckert's store where they sell the money orders and over Coe and Clary where the niggers live. 1. I am crazy and that's for sure. I'm gonna ride this town and this county like Deacon Ripley rides his girl friend. I'm gonna whip you all down. 2. Disobey me or break the law and I'm gonna kill you, and you know how? No, you don't know how because I'm crazy. 3. When my right hand in the preliction and form of Miss Jane comes by in her squadcar and picks someone up smokin dope or speedin or drunk or actin simple or a bad dresser, maybe she will kill them and maybe she will shoot em in the cheek or right through the hand or maybe she will smile and offer em a dip of snuff and you never know, do you, what a lieunatic will do and me, I'm the same way up in the mayor's office for plots or subdivisions, zoning, water and fire and that. 4. Money can not buy me off because crazy people don't have no sense, and don't try reasonin with us or fairness or nothing like that. 5. Crazy people have super-human strength and they know what you are thinkin so WATCH OUT!!!

It is the first week of November. There is an autumnal slowness, woodsmoke smelling and warmed now and then by the rueful sun falling at an ever-more-acute angle. The mellow silence takes hold of the inhabitants of downtown Wataska. The elections, even the presidential ones, do not cause great excitement here or unduly speed the blood in its circuit. The truth that filters down from the national to the state capital reaches these streets already so diluted and compromised as to be indistinguishable from the lie already in residence. The sheriff and his hand-picked opponent have faced each other in stylized mock combat for years; the mayor has created his nemesis to rise before him on September 24 at 2:30 P.M. precisely, and to disappear on voting day with words so well known as to constitute classic ritual. Wataska's local politics is a theater of maximum drama and minimum surprise.

But inside the Wataska State Hospital there is no woodsmoke, no nostalgia. Sewing teams are busy over new splendor for the candidates. The signs proliferate, the manifesto circulates. The staff is pleased. The patients are taking an interest in the community at last. An arrangement with the precinct, under State Law 25.287, is causing the installation of a polling place in a storage shed behind the generator building on hospital grounds. It is more convenient to the staff, and they are happy with the change. What no one seems to think important is that since the second of June when the Patients' Rights Bill went into effect, the hospital's inmates have been drifting down to the courthouse by twos and threes to be registered. They say what Miss Annie has directed them to say, and if they are too sick to remember, they are coached by others who go with them. Bowing to convention, they do not give their addresses as Wataska State Hospital. They give one of the twenty-three numbers on four streets assigned to the hospital by the post office for mailing purposes.

Gracellen Grimes Mundy is Wataska County's voting registrar. In 1948, Carson Grimes, the county assessor, faced the fact that his daughter's marriage to Augustus Mundy was a love match, and that Augustus was hopelessly inept at anything else. He and the boys at the courthouse fixed up the job as registrar for Gracellen. In the years since, the office has been run so as to cause everyone to be happy with Carson's idea. Gracellen is hardworking and punctilious to a fault. She handles all of the assessor's "clean" bookkeeping and does whatever other work is asked of her. During the dark times of the Civil Rights Movement, when most voting registrars suffered unbelievable pressure from both sides, Gracellen weathered the storm in tranquility. The movement affected Wataska very little since the part of the local government that was corrupt had for years been corrupt without reference to race, religion, or previous condition of servitude, and because the town itself and all the areas surrounding it were steadily losing population, those vigorous and energetic enough to protest the civic apathy and corruption chose relocation over reform. The result of all this is that Gracellen has developed no eye for coincidence, and during the past three months when an unprecedented three thousand people presented themselves at her desk for registration as electors, she expressed her amazement only to the courthouse's cleaning woman, and casually, to Augustus. The new electors were now liable to jury service and to seek political office themselves. Gracellen is proud of her office's efficiency. Consequences flow naturally. The old voting machines are taken up from the school basement and sent to the new precinct. New jury rolls are made out in Gracellen's careful script. New tax-assessment blanks are ordered. There is suddenly a great deal of work to attend to.

It is the first Tuesday after the first Monday in November. Election Day. Dr. La Doux walks briskly through the windy streets to the elementary school that his children once attended. Only when he sees the notice on the door stating a change of precinct does he remember signing something some months back that would enable his staff to vote more easily at the hospital. He goes where the notice directs, to the north entrance of the hospital, and there follows a rather intricate and winding course to the generator building behind which is the shed. There is a substantial line at the shed. With a start of surprise, Dr. La Doux recognizes that the overwhelming number of people on the line are patients, some of the sickest of his patients, and they are lined up stiffly, working at being on the line, facing front and moving when the line moves. It is not a game, then, or Miss Annie's joke, and he is well beyond the idea that decisions made by the two of them will have a glimmer of sanity in them: they are comfortable only in madness, too fragile to see the world as it exists apart from themselves. He turns, wishing to do something, to say something, to make some move that will stop all this, but there is nowhere to go. The governor has told him that the state's hands are tied; the attorney general, who has not taken him seriously, has laughed that the "little game is legal" and that 'Thorne and Runciman and the upstate boys need a little perking up, something to make 'em campaign a little closer to the bone." The attorney general has sent him clippings of recent campaigns for governor by two gurus and a revolutionary, each of whom got a hundred votes or so from followers of revealed truth and nonanimal protein. As Dr. La Doux stands blank and undecided, he sees old Jesperson coming across the lawn. Jesperson, an orderly, has been at Wataska for as long as most people can remember. As he sees Jesperson, the doctor has a sudden burst of inspiration that sends him walking swiftly toward the old man, calling out to him. "Good God, Jesperson, has this been going on all morning?"

"Strangest thing I ever seen!" Jesperson answers. "That old bag has gone through the wards and got up ever'body that ain't nailed down, give 'em sample ballots, showed 'em how to work the booths, exactly what to do and where to push the levers."

"These people are not competent to vote," La Doux cries, almost grabbing the old man's lapels, "and you know why: they are all heavily drugged—there's enough tranquilizer in those systems to dope an army. We can stop it on *that* basis, even with the Patients' Rights ... "

"Sorry, Doc, but half the medicine cabinets in this country got Librium in 'em, and a quarter of the people I know on the outside are takin' tranquilizers regular. It won't do, Doc. We're gonna get somethin' more than a harmless nut for mayor *this* time."

Dr. La Doux sits down on the dry lawn and contemplates the line. He is seeing more than a conquest of Wataska County. He thinks he is seeing a change in the nature of the condition he has been studying and treating for years. The change is not because of the Patients' Rights Bill. The bill has been on the books for five months, and while

its provisions make some things harder, other things are easier. Th
victims have changed. Instead of unjust commitments there are u
just releases, people signing themselves out against medical advi
and killing others or themselves, or trying to. Yet, on balance, l
thinks the effects have been good. Those who come are less frightene
more amenable to treatment—of which there is still too little, becau
rights or not, the legislature has not given them the money to empl
trained staff.

The change is in the patients themselves. He looks again at the li
before him, moving steadily. For years, Miss Annie has queened
over Miss Jane, the patients, and the staff, and, yes, the town, with
the careful limits they allowed her, as a spoiled child might. What ha
saved everyone before was the nature of mental illness itself. In th
worst days of the cruelest years of the "asylums" there had never bee
riots or rebellion. This was not because the mentally ill did not fe
their suffering, but that they were unable to organize, to come t
gether for any reason, to reach across the barriers that kept the
caught in their separate nightmares. Defiance is a kind of affirmatic
of which very few are capable, group defiance a response demandin
trust and a knowledge of others light-years beyond their power. Wh
he was seeing here, then, was no less than a change in the nature of th
illness itself.

Mental illness is as old as man. It is universal and appears
different forms in all cultures and at all times. But there are fashior
modes of expression, that change as though by secret agreement b
neath the anomie and isolation of the single sufferer. It is as thoug
each prisoner in the Bastille, separated from all other prisoners t
walls too thick to transmit the tap of a message, never meeting, facir
out to different directions, would each at the same time, speak
refrain from speaking certain words. Catatonics, a majority of the
men, were a staple in the state hospitals of the forties. Now they a
gone. Where did these men go? Recent residents in psychiatry trav
the nation's hospitals without ever seeing "catatonic excitation," ar
some now declare that it must never have existed at all. Anorex
nervosa, once extremely rare, has now multiplied itself into group

and subgroups, and doctors are writing texts on it. It is a woman's expression. From where do these women come? From mania, now out of fashion? From the hysterias, banners under which no one now marches?

So the styles change. The metaphors change. The symptoms are fashions to be discarded or sewn in new lengths, let down, taken up, let in, let out, and trimmed to the time. The world outside defines the causes, and these also change. Possession by demons, possession by guilt, a defect in the will, a weakness of the brain, a split in the personality, a rift in the character, an inability to confirm reality, and now . . . a political act?

Political. Who sends the message that sets the style? Where on the outside is the consensus made that sets the Bastille singing its songs, adding new verses and dropping old ones? And is the old anomie the ground tone of madness also to be changed? Dr. La Doux says aloud, "I don't think so."

Some of the patients look at him, and he suddenly has the feeling he knows he has elicited in them often enough, of being caught with his guard down.

There is a group coming toward him across the hospital grounds. It is another band of voters from the wards, and at its head, resplendent in new sheets, Miss Annie. She has been making this trip back and forth all day. As she comes on he realizes that it has been years since he tried to peer into her mind, to get behind her exotic, simple, and near-perfect defenses and look at her straight on. She has used herself as a figure of speech for so long, as a symbol and nothing else, that he wonders why she should wish to change now. She is old and easy in her loud, vulgar, Miss Liberty persona. It has gotten her very far, secured for her all manner of privileges and perquisites. She is herself an institution, and they, he knows too well, are slow to change.

"Well, howdy, Doc!" She bellows ahead. "Watchin' the votin'?" As she comes abreast of him she shoves the leaders of the small group ahead of her and booms to them, "I can't come within a hundred feet of there, 'cause one of them judges we got said somethin' about electioneering. Go on and vote like I showed ya!" She plumps herself down beside the doctor. "Doc, you look as lonesome as a miser's turd. Why don't you get up and go vote?"

"Miss Annie," he says, "what made you decide to do all this?"

"Look at it this way, Doc. I'm saving you people from yourselfs. You people have been dehuminizin' us for years. I heard that right on the TV. We been *institutionalized*—that's a bad word now, Doc, very bad. Institution. We got to end all that. All institutions. Everyone needs to be in the community. *Community* is a *good* word. I done all this because I decided *I* gotta be the one to tell the difference."

"The difference?"

"Between what's a community and what's a institution—what the bars keep in and what they keep out. Go on in, Doc. It won't matter now, but folks like you always feel better votin'."

He gets up and goes to the line. "Don't fret, Doc," she cries, "your job's safe. I'll be movin' city hall out here, but you can stay on. We'll reopen Rollins. That was where I first come, Rollins. You'll need to take care of somebody won't you? Fill out drug prescriptions and that and sign up patients—'cause *we'll* be sending you patients, now—we'll be decidin' who's crazy and who ain't. After all, Doc, we can't see all that state and federal money goin' by us, can we?"

As the line slowly shuffles into the shed, Miss Liberty, framed by the edge of the doorway, blows him an obscene kiss.

LIKE A BANNER

Richard Rampling (this is degrading) sits reading Plato in his wood-paneled bachelor penthouse. He reads carefully, intently, in the original, referring only occasionally to the leather-bound Greek dictionary beside him. (Why do I do this? Why do I have to do this?) As he looks up now and then to meditate on what he has read, he can see the lights of the city below him slowly going out one by one. (It's been part of me so long, and without it—) On the table beside him is a glass of brandy. Now and then he sips it, and when he is finished, Porter is at his side. "Will there be anything else, sir?"

"No, thank you, Porter, nothing more tonight."

They smile at one another, and Porter says, "Well, sir, I hope not." Then there is a signal, a discreet toneless beep over the Secret Network. At the moment of alarm Richard Rampling stands up; Porter disappears and is back immediately with the white cape and cowl. Rampling slips into the outfit while Porter says quietly, "I'll ready the machine, sir." From a sliding panel in the wall a button is pressed. At the end of a secret shaft a light goes on. A door closes and another opens, and the purr of the great, low engine fills the small space. Dr.

Life is ready. From Porter he takes his equipment case, mounts it in i
special sling, and slides down the pole into the darkness. A roar an
the car is gone. Through rain-slick streets Dr. Life rides on his mi
sion. He pulls up at a curb where an injured child lies, does ca
diopulmonary resuscitation expertly, and when the child is breathin
on its own and he hears the ambulance coming, vanishes leaving n
trace. No one dies as Dr. Life leaps ready from his car. Better yet, n
one vomits. The burned girl (they never get facial burns) smiles up a
him as he applies the special dressing that will heal all injuries an
ease all pain. "Who was that?" the fine old man whispers as the othe
help him up. "I felt so comfortable—my pain and fear left me when h
was here . . ."

"Oh, it must have been a visit from Dr. . . ."

There is a grinding buzz at his ear. At first he thinks it is the engin
of the marvelous car, but then he comes awake. Norris is shaking hir
"What is it, a call?" Runkle mumbles.

"I'd say so," Norris answers caustically.

Runkle gets up quickly and pulls on his boots. He has been dozin
fully dressed and is ready except for the uniform jacket. The flat voic
of the dispatcher has been telling them where they are to go. It's a
accident with injuries. Two cars.

His shoelace breaks. "Shit!" Norris says. He fumbles at knottin
the broken lace, then gives it up, and they go to start the ambulance.
is an old vehicle as ambulances go and has had to endure the tinkerin
of four different drivers. For what seems like minutes it will not star

It's better when they are on their way. Running red-light-and-sire
down the early-morning street there is at least the sense of speed an
competence that Runkle yearns for. Norris isn't the brightest of part
ners, but he knows his stuff and he drives well. There is time fo
Runkle to sit quietly with the sleep-shards of Richard Rampling an
Dr. Life, the tyrants of his youth.

The fantasy hasn't changed much since Runkle was twelve or thir
teen. Rampling is still a wealthy bachelor with a secret life. Hi
brandies have names now, his clothes are less flamboyant, and th

girls who look on in adoration have gotten riper and more frankly sensuous over the years, but Rampling himself seems frozen in creation. He has no friends, no confidants except Porter, no enemies except death. He has no politics, no doubts; he knows no indecision, no ambivalence, no despair. As Dr. Life he is invulnerable, invincible, inhuman. He has changed in his medical knowledge, of course. The magical hypodermics are still there, the mystical burn salves, but the life-support techniques are properly named, the veins, arteries, and muscles properly placed. What bothers Dick Runkle most is that Richard Rampling and Dr. Life have made him what he is: that a twelve-year-old boy with a comic-book mentality has been holding a twenty-two-year-old man his captive and hostage, having baited the trap with a boy's dream of omnipotence and sprung it with a boy's dream of heroics.

"Shit!" says Norris again at his side. "This looks like a bastard." He is right. A head-on. The cars are indistinguishable from one another. The police are trying to route what traffic there is around the mess. Norris moves in as close as he can. "Step on it, you guys," the cop says, "there's gas all over the street."

Both drivers are dead, impaled on their steering wheels. Four teenage boys are in one car, the front passenger has internal injuries, and the two in back are very drunk. One is not hurt at all, the other has a broken arm. They wonder why Runkle has examined them quickly and left them. "Where the fuck are you going!"

He is going to the passenger of the other car. Norris has shouted to him to come. It's bad. She is bleeding from the mouth, which may be the broken bones in her face, but she is beginning to choke on her blood. They suction and give her an airway. The light is not good enough to tell where the blood is coming from by its color. Her responses are slowed. They work quickly.

The boys in the other car keep up a continual noise. They think they have been left until last because they are young. Their language is vile. Runkle and Norris get the woman onto a backboard on her side, and the police help get her into the ambulance. Runkle wishes there were another person on the team. They have put in for the third person on nights, but the hospital has turned them down. He doesn't understand why the night always goes short.

Runkle goes back to the other car. The boy in the backseat behind the driver is so drunk or doped he is not aware of the accident. His mind wanders in a sordid dream or memory from which he keeps muttering, "Stick it in her, shove it at her. Make her scream. Make her scream!" He says this over and over, rising to something like excitement and then falling back to muffled muttering. The boy in the front has begun to go a little spacey with shock. His vitals slip a little. Runkle starts oxygen and an IV. The other boy in back continues to curse them for their slowness. Runkle is surprised at his energy. "Stick-it-in-her" rises and falls in the background. As Norris and Runkle are working, the dead driver stares glassily at them. They get the two serious victims stabilized in the ambulance, then go to work on the fracture case. It is a while before they can radio in. With another person on the team they could have saved so much time.

They get to the hospital as fast as they can, hoping the emergency-room people will have things ready. Runkle has often been impatient when a busy night made them wait. "All we can do is what *we* do," Norris always says. Our job is . . ."

"I know, but a person goes through hell waiting for—"

"We can't remake the system. We can only remake our part of it."

Norris is the sixth partner Runkle has had. Evans was grossly incompetent and didn't last long. There were three others—medical students who had come on the service for book money and had lasted only as long as it took to get them through another semester—and Minify. Runkle suspected that Minify had asked to be assigned to another partner because of Runkle's fussiness. "Relax, it's only a job," Minify would say, and when Runkle kept reliving their difficult runs, wondering aloud how things could have been done better, Minify would slam out of the service muttering and leave him alone with Dr. Life's disappointed sneer.

Runkle was nineteen before he saw Dr. Life as an idea—something that could be thought about and sifted for meaning like any other idea. The realization took him by surprise. Dr. Life and Richard Rampling and Porter had been with him for so long that they had seemed like facts of existence, no more to be questioned than the color of his own eyes and hair, the shape of his own fingers. When he began to think about the idea of Dr. Life, he saw how important Porter was in the fantasy. When he was a boy he had imagined Porter as the one who took care of the daily, tiresome jobs of existence—valet work for Rampling, maintenance of the car, and all of Dr. Life's marvelous equipment. It was during his tour in the army that Runkle saw Dr. Life as something apart from himself and also how vital Porter was in the embarrassing play. It was Porter who savored the mystery, Porter who engineered the effects, Porter whose sympathetic knowledge of all that Rampling was made Rampling not single, lonely, and bereft, but a hero. Even in the breast of the secret hero burns a desire that someone know, share the plan, applaud the act, know to praise, know to pity.

Seeing Porter in this new way, it occurred to Runkle with horror that his fantasy must be the creation of a homosexual mind. Who but a queer would have that quiet, faithful, approving male voice always at his ear: "Mr. Rampling, sir, the night has been very hard. I took the liberty of putting out another glass of brandy!" "Mr. Rampling, you've been hurt—was that you at that train wreck, saving all those people? I should have known, sir."

In fear and revulsion Runkle went to the army psychiatrist. He did not tell the substance of his fantasy; it was too childish to confide to a grown man, a doctor. He did speak of "someone taking care of me." After a few questions about his own life and his fantasies during sex the doctor smiled and said that Runkle was a normal heterosexual male and that the faithful sidekick fantasy was a common one and perhaps one of the more helpful ones since it resulted in the male ideal of loyalty to one's friends. Nevertheless, after his last chat with the doctor, Runkle decided to give up Richard Rampling, Porter, and Dr.

Life. If the fantasies weren't homosexual, they were puerile, which is worse. What if he were sent to Vietnam and wounded there, and in his delirium went into the stupid scenario, that kid's Saturday-afternoon dream? He would be a laughingstock, a joke. He could hear a nurse telling an orderly: "You gotta dig that bird in the fourth bed there; it's really something. 'Put the special serum in my utility belt, Porter, there's plague all over the island.' 'But sir, there's no way to be inoculated against it, and a horrible death for anyone who—' 'I've got to go—no one else will take the risk.' 'God be with you, sir.' " They double up laughing.

But Dr. Life would not die. He could be put aside temporarily, if Runkle flooded his mind with more acceptable fantasies—but denied for any period of time, Dr. Life took elaborate revenge by invading Runkle's most ordinary dreams and fantasies with his bizarre presence.

The girl is lovely, the lights are low. Soft music is playing on the record player. She has already told him of her desire for him, and he is turning to kiss her when the lights go on and he finds himself in Rampling's apartment. At that moment Dr. Life in full-flowing costume comes in from some catastrophe or other. The girl leaves Runkle's side without a backward glance, and goes to Dr. Life as naturally as a cat seeks the warm corner.

It was the Dr. Life dream that influenced him to train for the medics. Emergency medical training was as close as one could get to Dr. Life's secret work. They could be, in a sense, colleagues.

And Runkle (How he hated that name!) was good at his job. "Alert, conscientious, skilled, and compassionate," his ratings said. He was close to the top of his class in the theoretical part of his training and tied for the top in skills. With his rating he was certain he would be sent to a front-line assignment, a field hospital or med-evac. The other top man, Spaulding, was assigned to a trauma surgical team. Runkle drew an army hospital in Dakota, the psychiatric ward. He kept requesting transfer overseas, but his Nam was North Dakota.

Through the remainder of his time in service, Dr. Life and Porter and the missions became a long-spun, heavily addictive narcotic to him. He couldn't go to sleep without a visit to Rampling's softly glowing wood-sheen-and-leather study, listening for the soft tink of crystal on silver as Porter decanted the brandy. And always the call, the white costume, the gleaming instruments, the marvelously equipped car. It would be wonderful to have a car that carried all kinds of lifesaving equipment like Dr. Life's car . . .

Norris pulls up to the ramp and signals. Ryder and Blakely are there, and they unload the patients quickly. The woman looks a little better. When the emergency-room people have taken over, Runkle and Norris clean up and ready the ambulance again and back it into its place. Then they go to their little office to write up the call.

This is a time Runkle likes, winding down. He and Norris sometimes talk over their coffee and the reports. When he had first come on night duty he had used this time to replay the run. Since Minify, he is making an effort not to do that anymore. He feels incomplete without it and guilty for ignoring a chance to perfect their skills.

Looking around at the office he sighs and shakes his head. It is windowless except for the small panel that gives on to the garage. The lighting is bad, the furniture rickety and mismatched. The daytime never cleans up. It has somehow devolved on the night people to gather up the sticky cups and spilled sugar and sweep out. Norris says they had better leave a note for the day team about a shimmy in the steering wheel. "I'll stay on and have a look at it," Runkle says. "Let me drive the next call. If it's what I think it is, I can fix it here."

"Okay, after we finish these, I think I'll hit the books." Norris is going to school to become a mortician. All semester he has tried to get Runkle interested in the work. "People like us come out ahead because we've seen and worked with the dead and there's no big emotional jolt for us. The pay is good, and dying is really a growth industry " and he laughs. "No, I mean it—no recessions, no layoffs. If you start next semester I might be able to get you into the place where I'll be working, and after a while . . ."

Runkle is surprised and a little pleased that Norris wants him as a partner. He doesn't want to hurt Norris's feelings so he puts him off.

What can he say—that Dr. Life wouldn't allow it? It is true, neverthe-less. He is letting that stupid fantasy ruin his chances again, keeping him away from something steady, safe, and lucrative. The pay on this job was only fair, and the hours were awful; there was no advance-ment; it was work for the young. He sighs. "Think it will be a heavy night?"

"Why should it be?" Norris answers, "It's not a holiday."

The alarm goes off as Norris says "holiday," and they look at one another with raised eyebrows. Runkle takes a deep breath, wishing for the first time since he has come on the service, not to go, not to be where he is and what he is, to be shut of it, another man, slave to some other idea, some other set of laws and limits. They take their jackets from the hooks outside the door, and as the garage doors go up they hear the dispatcher telling them where to go. "Morning, Walter," Norris says quickly into the radio.

"Two-thirteen," Walter answers mechanically. Their time out.

The call is up near Van Allen. Head injury. Knowing Van Allen it is probably a saloon fight, broken bottles, lots of blood and swearing, and maybe an attack by one of the combatants. Runkle had been born near Van Allen. His people had left when the Irish were leaving and the Jews were beginning to go and the Blacks had begun to come in. Now it is almost solidly Chicano. They have many calls there. "What was that number?" he asks Norris.

"Three eighty-three Bisher."

Runkle turns off Van Allen and cuts the siren, leaving on the rotat-ing red-and-white lights.

It is an old house a block up from the projects and gently decaying. In this neighborhood a driver never leaves his vehicle unless it is absolutely necessary, then he locks it. Norris runs in to see what the trouble is and emerges a few seconds later with a heavy old lady dressed in a man's long topcoat.

"I thought you turkeys would never get here." She puffs and plumps herself into the front seat. "God, my head's killin' me. Can't you birds move it?"

Runkle sighs. A pensioner. They use the emergency room as their clinic and the ambulances as their taxis. There is no money on the old-age budget for transportation except by bus. The teams have been told to run empty rather than encourage them, but Norris and Runkle ignore the rule. They might just as well take her. "Lady, next time, please—"

"I know, Buster," she says, "I know."

It has happened two or three hundred times in the last three years, yet now he finds himself unreasonably angry; it is all he can do to put the lights out with forced calm and start the engine up again. He knows it isn't anger at the old woman or impatience at the system but something deeper and more corrosive than that. He feels like wrecking the ambulance—driving it into a wall. He couldn't go into a wall. Who would they call, another ambulance?

Back in the dispatch office they fudge the reports a little. "Patient in severe pain." Actually, she had chattered all the way to the hospital. It is 3:00 A.M. The physical weariness he had felt before is gone. Norris too is not in the mood for sleep and apparently not ready for study. He pours them both some coffee and sits down, motioning to the clipboard where he had just posted the call.

"Dick, I can't figure you out."

"I'm a hard case to figure," Runkle says.

"I mean being gung-ho like you are, I'd have thought these nothin' calls would bother you, but you seem to take them in stride. When I first came on nights and we had that gunfight up on Bisher—remember that? We ran out of gas on the way back because the day guys had forgot to fill the tank." He laughs. "I thought you'd have a shitfit."

"The victims were such bums—they were fighting me in the back trying to get to each other again—and then to be held up by our own incompetence—"

"But it wasn't *our* incompetence, it was the day guys. The rule goes—"

"I know how the rule goes, but there's a way things should be done—"

"Yeah, yeah, grateful patients and a superb medical staff, brilliant and alert. You've been watching those medical shows again." Norris was from Texas and he liked to use it sometimes. "Ever' tahm I lit you at that TeeVee, Rodney, you go al! simple oan me."

"I am simple. I guess I want to believe the TV stories about the grateful patients and the superb medical staff. It's not the pensioners with headaches that bother me. At least she wanted to live. She didn't curse me for trying to help."

"Last night is still on your mind, isn't it," Norris says. "No calls for two nights and then five of them one after another. And that one at the end."

"She *spat* at me," Runkle says. "She spat at me and cursed me for trying to save her life."

"She was crazy." Norris shakes his head. "You must have had that happen to you before—"

"Yes, it's happened, but I didn't seem to see it, to feel it before. Maybe I was too busy with whatever I was doing, but last night the— the ugliness of it got to me all at once. The language she used, the hate in her eyes, and then spitting at me—and I was trying to help her, not hurt her—" Why hadn't he seen the ugliness before? What had started the change in him, the anger, the feeling of loss? He had once been so happy and fulfilled in this work, its worthiness, its direct, uncomplicated good. Now he was afraid, because if so direct and uncomplicated a good went dim, what things were good or worthwhile at all? He sits in the battered office chair, his mind back in the dark hall—a middle-aged woman, her face grimacing with pain and hatred, fighting him, her breath and body giving off the smells of her sickness and fear, and as he reaches down to help her, to calm her—

"Dick—?"

"You're right," Runkle says. "Too much TV."

It's a call, Tenth and Vandalia. Accident with injuries. One victim. He is tired, dead tired. It has gotten very cold. Vandalia is mobbed with traffic, which is strange so long before dawn. Even with lights and siren it is hard to get through. A car has broken down in the middle of the street, blocking everything. He tries to back out, but he is already hemmed in by cars. At last things clear a little and he fights through the rest of the way. A meat truck has run into a wall and turned over. The back has sprung, and sides and quarters of beef are lying all over the street. Already people are running up to cut at some of it, and two or three together are dragging whole sides and quarters away. There is a festival air about it all, people laughing and the smell of meat rank in the air. Crushed under the truck is a sports car, a low, white one, its hood flattened almost to the floorboards. He gets an extrication bar and calls for help, but no one can get through. The crowd on the street has become a mob. He has to fight his way to the wreck. He tries to look inside with his flashlight but can't see for all the jammed metal and broken glass. He hears a sound inside, a voice saying over and over, "Please . . . please . . ." He uses the bar, making no headway until a fireman comes and helps him. They spring the door, and Runkle bends in, almost flat.

At first, he can't make out anything and he yells for some light. The fireman brings it. Impaled, twisted, and bleeding from his mouth, his white outfit torn and dirty, is Dr. Life. Runkle moves back in terror, calling at the top of his voice for help. Going in close again he tries to pull the steering wheel out of the way. Something else gives, and Dr. Life moans.

"I'll get you out! Just hang on till I get some help!" Runkle cries. He calls to the policeman again, but all the police are trying to disperse the crowds. He calls for Norris, but Norris isn't there. He tries getting the bystanders to help, but they laugh and turn away.

Then he begins to move the glass and broken metal out of the way himself, gritting his teeth when Dr. Life cries at the movement that tears his wounds deeper. At last he can bear Dr. Life's pain no longer. "Where are they now!" he shouts at the dying man. "Where are all the people you saved?" Dr. Life can barely speak. He is looking at Runkle, his head not turned, but twisted toward him on a broken neck. "Don't you know?" Dr. Life says very clearly, and with the shadow of a smile. "Don't you know that the first one I ever saved was you?"

He wakes shivering and confused. He has been sitting up in the desk chair with his feet on the desk and has almost fallen. Norris is in back studying. The office is cold, and it is almost morning. The dream has left him lonelier than he has been since he was a boy. He sighs and tries to turn his mind to ordinary thoughts about the day. He would be on duty until nine this morning, but he has told Norris he would fix the shimmy in the wheel. He might go home then and take a nice long bath and maybe get a good meal for once. He thinks about his apartment, a tiny studio in a small building within walking distance of the hospital. Because he spends little on clothes or food and has no car to keep up he is able to furnish the place with nice things. He is saving for something better, maybe with a pleasant view, a window at which he might sit with a small snifter of brandy now and then. He goes into the garage to get a blanket from the ambulance. It is abnormally cold for April, unless it's just his own sorry, bereft feeling. He sees Dr. Life's broken body again, the terrible wreck of the car, and he has a sudden desire to go into the emergency room and talk to the nurses so that there won't be such pictures in his mind. He gets the broom and sweeps out the office and goes to the john that is off the emergency service.

He is in the john when he hears the box go off again down the hall. Hurrying, he gets his zipper stuck. Richard Rampling never gets caught in the john. Richard Rampling never goes to the john. Richard Rampling and Dr. Life are dying now after all this time, all the shame of their existences and the shameful need of them, a kid's toy taken into a man's world. Rampling, his rival; Dr. Life, his tyrant. He hurries out to the ambulance.

Norris is behind the wheel. "Caught you again, did I? Why not finish the crap, for God sakes, I can wait."

"I'm okay," Runkle says. "Got my zipper stuck is all." He works on it as they ride.

"Okay, hotshot," Norris says, "you know it's going to be another pensioner with dyspepsia or a guy with an IUD caught in his throat. Why the uproar?"

"Dedication!" Runkle hisses. "Dedication!" It sounds more bitter than he means it. Norris gives him a quick look and says no more.

They get the stand-down when they are almost there. The party had apparently decided that the trouble wasn't that bad. They kill the lights and siren and slow to an easy speed down the tree-lined residential streets, noticing the morning crispness of the air, the stirring of the neighborhood getting ready for work. Runkle opens his side window and catches, or thinks he catches, the smell of bacon frying somewhere. He remembers that he did not eat last night. He stretches, and his stomach, silent in the tension of the call, begins to gurgle. "You're disgusting," Norris says, "and I don't intend to sit beside *that* all the way back to the hospital. I'm stopping at the Big Dipper, where I expect you to spring for something." Stopping off was frowned on, but all the crews pull into drive-in places now and then.

The Big Dipper's carry-out isn't crowded, and the food tastes particularly good to Runkle. Beside him Norris is talking about this and that, but he is staying away from the subject of mortuary school. Runkle is grateful.

He stays to fix the ambulance after the regular day crew comes on. He likes Soames and the other day men. He relaxes as he tightens the bolts then drains the oil and adjusts the valves on the oxygen equipment. He is good at this; he likes it, and it demands little of him.

As he works, calls come in for the other ambulance and there is a daytime feeling of alertness and activity—people coming and going—that Runkle misses at night. Strangely, even though he has caught two catnaps the night before, by eleven Runkle is fighting sleep. He leaves Soames to polish the vehicle and walks home yawning, to collapse on the bed half dressed.

They are underground in Dr. Life's secret laboratory and garage. On the stone bench where Dr. Life had done his own chemical experiments and medical studies, Rampling lies. He is obviously dead. Someone else is moving in the shadows. When he comes into the light Runkle sees that it is Porter, carrying a tray of instruments. Porter works quickly, efficiently, his face set. As Runkle watches, open-eyed,

Porter strips off his butler's uniform and stands bare-chested. He takes a large syringe and needle from the tray and, after applying alcohol to his left chest, plunges the needle into his own heart.

Runkle, horrified, sees Porter stagger backward. Then, with a heroic effort, Porter forces himself forward again and, gritting his teeth, holds the plunger steady. The blood flows up the barrel of the syringe in the rhythm of the pulsing of his heart. When the syringe is full, Porter extracts it and injects the blood directly into the victim's heart. Porter has not noticed Runkle's presence, or if he has, had made no sign. Runkle sees that there is movement, life in Rampling's body now. Its color has changed—blood is beating at the carotid pulse, he can see the little throb; the eyelids are trembling, the rhythms of breathing and swallowing begin. Rampling opens his eyes. Porter, on the other side of the bench, leans close. "Mr. Rampling, sir," he says quietly, "it was almost too late this time."

"Was I dead?"

"Yes, sir."

"How did you bring me back?"

"It was too late for ordinary methods. I had to use cardiation."

It is one of the miraculous treatments Runkle had dreamed up when he was twelve, along with the all-healing dressings and the instant pain-killer. Cardiation is the exchange of blood from someone of power and purity to a dead person. Dr. Life has used cardiation on the deserving dead of train wrecks and airplane crashes. It is the only procedure he uses that involves pain to himself, and he is obliged to choose the people on whom he can endure to use it. With Runkle's maturing medical knowledge, cardiation has slipped away into the past, but every now and then in a burst of wishful thinking it is reborn in a fantasy or a dream, the last, best weapon of the dream king.

"Porter," Rampling says quietly. "You risked your life to save mine."

"I considered it my duty, sir," Porter says with dignity, and then his voice changes and he says, "Where would we go, sir . . . what would we do?"

When Runkle wakes he is sweating. The heat had come on full while he slept, and the room is stifling. His window is dark and he can't tell what time it is or how long he has slept. He turns and looks at the clock. It is seven; there is just time to wash up, shave and go to the hospital, get something to eat, and go back on duty. Duty. "It was my duty, sir." He feels like crying.

"You know," he says to Rampling as he shaves, "you could have been anyone—a sultan of a harem, a Roman emperor, someone of subtle judgments and great wit. You could have been Voltaire or Einstein and learned philosophy or at least a little math."

"Why keep us if you hate us?" Rampling answers, as Runkle shaves. "If you want to be free of us, stop waiting up for me. Stop sitting in my leather chair and reading my Plato, and my Anacreon, and drinking what's left in the bottom of my glass!"

"Why can't I?" Runkle whispers to Rampling. He stands looking at himself with the lather on his face and he silently curses Porter and Richard Rampling and Dr. Life. He walks to work trying not to think about need of any kind.

Occasionally, when Runkle is feeling sorry for himself, he counts his love affairs, irritated that he can still count, that he remembers each and remembers the quality of the time he spent, the texture of everything with clarity and in detail. Other men seemed to have more affairs than he and to have them matter less. He had been close to marriage several times, and his relationships were intense, full of joy, terrible pain, and long periods of convalescence. He was convalescing now. It is only recently that he can eat his meals at the hospital cafeteria again without being flooded with emotions of loss and sorrow. He has been making himself use the cafeteria, coming early to sit socializing for a while before going on duty. This evening he finds some people he likes and stays fifteen minutes over, just to catch Norris's look of surprise.

It is a slow evening. They read and do bookwork, chat with the emergency-room people in their coffee room, and go over the vehicle until 2:00 A.M. Runkle is just sitting down again to his dinner in the cafeteria when the call comes. He runs back to the service. A three-car pileup. The trouble is on the underpass of the Van Allen freeway. "Three cars—" Norris sighs as they swing out. "It's going to be hairy. Dispatch is calling other services to assist."

"Good," Runkle says. They do not talk anymore. It is better to wait, not to imagine the difficulties they will encounter.

"What the hell!" Norris cries and slams on his brakes. Ahead of them in the street a construction sign and barrier are sticking out into their lane and a car has pulled in front of them and is proceeding with terrible caution down the single open lane. Their lights and siren must have panicked him because he is creeping along erratically, veering in the narrow lane as though to let them pass, then pulling out again. "I'm killing the lights and siren," Runkle says.

"What!"

"How else can we get that jackass to hurry up! He's practically a basket case now," Runkle growls, "but if he calms down enough maybe he'll be able to think a little." Norris curses, and Runkle turns the button from "yelp" to "off." Nothing happens. He tries again, and still nothing. Ahead of them the car is weaving its way along slowly, and by the time the construction ends and a lane opens up on the right, Norris is pounding the steering wheel in frustration. The car begins to signal that it is going to pull over but makes no move to do so. With a curse Norris swings around past just as the driver finally begins to change to the right-hand lane. For a moment Runkle thinks there is going to be a collision, but they clear by inches and pull ahead, leaving the other car swerving back and forth and probably out of control in their wake.

They turn onto the freeway ramp. Runkle is leaning forward trying to kill the siren. "We've got to get this knocked out by the time we get there, or nobody will be able to hear a damn thing!" The underpass is straight ahead, a tangle of cars, police vehicles, lights, and people. They come up as close as they can and pull in. Norris reaches over and pounds the siren switch. Nothing. Already the police are glaring at them. Runkle jumps out and runs to the man he takes to be in charge. "Damn siren—"

"What?" the man cries. "Hey, can't you kill that thing?"

"Broken!" Runkle howls, making broken motions with his hands. In the ambulance, Norris must have gone for the wires and pulled them. The sound stops in mid-note. Runkle runs to the cars.

The crew of another ambulance is tending to the first car, a big boat of a Buick overturned. The firefighters are beginning to pull the doors off so they can get to the victims. The middle car is a Volks; the driver is wedged in behind the wheel, and a passenger has been thrown free and is lying in a heap some yards away. Another ambulance has pulled up and is getting to the third car. Runkle takes it all in as quickly as he can and goes for the Volks, seeing Norris coming up behind him. The stuck siren has given him a headache. A panicky driver has cost them precious time, and now this. As he runs he notices that the extrication is almost finished with the first car. Norris goes to the driver of the Volks. Runkle moves around behind the car to get to the thrown victim. He doesn't know how the perception that there was someone there registered on him. In the dark, made darker by the hard glare of the lights nearby, the body looks like a pile of rags or refuse. When he comes close and kneels down he sees that it is a woman. He feels her breathing, and when she moans softly he smiles in the darkness with relief. He calls one of the police for light and Norris for some equipment, and using his little penlight, examines her quickly. There is no obvious bleeding, her eyes are reactive, and her breathing, although slow ... she has stopped! She is no longer breathing. He cries again for help, and adjusting her head to airway position he gives the four quick deep breaths that could start her again. There is no obstruction the breaths go in. He feels for a carotid pulse. There is nothing. He knows that death in trauma like this is seldom reversible but she was alive for him only seconds ago—blood going in its courses, breath in its channels, eyes adjusting to his light. He starts CPR, pacing himself, fighting the natural wish to breathe hard and fast; every now and then he yells for help. At last Norris appears with a kit and begins to unwrap things. "Better check pulse again," Runkle says on an exhale. Norris leans close and goes for the carotid.

"Negative," he says.

"Eyes?"

"Negative."

They start an IV, continuing CPR, Norris compressing the chest, leaning in and back. Runkle keeps on with the breathing, using pure oxygen, breathing it to her through a valve in the mask. They key their rhythm carefully in and out, crying for help now and then until the firemen come and spell them. They intubate, use the ambubag, forcing oxygen.

The time they have taken was necessary, but now they are almost alone. The other patients have gone in other ambulances. The wreckers are there. But they are not getting a heartbeat. There is no pulse. "We've got to take her in," Runkle says. Norris quits and goes to get help while Runkle and a fireman grind on. When the woman is on the stretcher, Norris asks Runkle if he wants to drive. Runkle shakes his head. They will take a fireman with them to help. As the woman is lifted into the ambulance, Runkle works. They run with lights and horn. Runkle and the fireman grind on, five pushes, quickly released, then a breath, counting on and on in an exhausting rote.

She is not responding on her own. At least five minutes have passed since her heart has stopped, but with the method they are using she can still be saved. He is tiring. He has been working alone for much of the time, and doing compressions in the ambulance is difficult. He is sweating heavily now though the night is cool. He hears his own whispered voice strange in his ears, not counting easily anymore, but ragged: "Pump, damn you, pump!" to her stopped heart.

In the monotony of the work, his mind moves away from what he is doing, the count and the rhythm working by themselves independent of his knowledge or his will. He is thinking of the comatose passenger in last night's accident, the boy who had kept saying over and over, "Make her scream." Then he thinks of the woman who had spat at him, of the foul-mouthed drunks he has picked out of wrecked cars, and the dying addicts who have cursed him and his meddling in their deaths. How ugly and grotesque his world is. And the inner lives of some of those people—how dark and violent they are. What must it be like to live in a continuous bath of hate and lust, to lie down every night in such ugliness? Dr. Life and Porter are silly, cardboard characters, caricatures, really, but they save lives and value the lives they save. No one is degraded, no one shamed by Dick Runkle's mind in the moments before sleep. And even now, as he begins to despair of this one, he sees his hands—Dr. Life's hands, pushing, grinding against death, and the last thought he has before they arrive is a simple picture, a picture outlined in the white light of his own breathlessness. It is a glimpse of Dr. Life's gleaming car speeding away on another case, in a world where there are no slow-ups or stuck sirens, a world where no one suffers needlessly and God is not mocked. He sees Dick Runkle, boy and man, standing on the sidewalk as the wonderful vehicle passes. He sees them raise their hands to wave at the speeding car in a gesture of affection and respect. Then they are at the ambulance ramp and others are taking over. Runkle is exhausted. He sits on the ambulance-squad bench and thinks of nothing.

He feels queasy. The sweat has gone cold on him. The woman is gone and so is Norris. He gets up and goes to look for them. He finds Norris coming out of the coffee room with two Styrofoam cups of coffee. "I was just getting you this," he says. "You looked so beat. I told you to let me take over. Even Superman can't do CPR for as long as you tried to do it."

"How is she?"

"She's not breathing on her own yet."

"Oh."

"Why don't you sit down!"

"Yeah, I'm a little dizzy, that's all."

He is resting on the cot near the door. He is tired and still a little sick. He turns toward the wall so he can face the lights of the city from Richard Rampling's study. On the table are two glasses of Rampling's fine brandy. In the chair Rampling is reading quietly one of the articles on medieval history he regularly contributes to learned journals. Porter, looking in to see if either of them needs anything, smiles at them and receives their good-nights.

"Oh dear," Rampling says, looking over at Runkle, "I see they've made a typo in my piece."

"Aythorpe will love that. He's been trying to get one up on you for years."

"Here, take a look. By the way, that woman—will she live?"

"I don't know. We can't do cardiation, you know. It doesn't work for us."

"Oh, the magic is fun," Rampling says. "I've always enjoyed it, but it's not the point, is it?"

"I always thought it was," Runkle says a little sadly.

"Of course it isn't. Didn't all that equipment look like magic when you first saw it? It's your knowledge that changed that, your knowledge and the experience of having used it and failed all the same. You made me without failings in order to keep the magic. But if you're really sick of the dream, I won't press it anymore. I hate to think of myself as your jailer." Runkle smiles. "Where else is there a leatherbound library—a brandy as old?"

Rampling looks around the room. "You know, it *is* a wonderful life you've given me; even the excitement is tasteful. Porter is the perfect butler, and it's a joy never to have to go out in bad weather, never to have the misery of repulsive or wretched victims. You've never even given me a suicide. I stay dry when it snows, and afterward there's always a fire and a good game of chess."

Rampling is setting up the board when Runkle falls asleep.

ON TIPTOE THEY MUST LEAVE, THE PIOUS OF ISRAEL

They must have finished dinner by now, although, looking through the little window, it was hard to tell. Sarah pushed the bell. Chimes. It was the husband who opened the door, and she said, "Good evening, Mr. Waldman, I'm your neighbor from down the road." He asked her in. He was a nice-looking man, very young, but Sarah quickly adjusted her expression of surprise. She knew it was her own age that made him seem so young.

"We're just having coffee," he said. "Come and have a cup." He called to his wife who had gone to the kitchen, "Get another cup, Clar, we have company."

"I met your wife yesterday, on my walk," Sarah said shyly. "Please don't bother about coffee, I just came by, collecting." She smiled up at him to show it wasn't usual with her. "People are always coming to me for the UN and the Cancer and the Girl Scouts and all diseases, and now it's my turn, I guess." He motioned her to a chair and sat down again waiting. She didn't have the box or the file of cards the collectors usually carried. Mrs. Waldman came in with a cup and a dish of cookies, and she smiled too until she saw Sarah, and then the look went cautious. "Oh, hello," she said. The tone was so equivocal that the man noticed and glanced quickly at his wife.

"I'm here for charity," Sarah said to her and then turned back to the husband. "Yesterday I passed by on my walk, and your wife was working outside. It's nice, now that everything is built and finished and you're all moved in. When I heard your name, Waldman, I thanked God. A family, a Jewish family here at last." She saw him stiffen slightly and she laughed, her hand to her mouth, "Oh, I forgot to introduce myself. I'm Sarah Levy. I live in the old house by the highway. Maybe your wife told you—I mentioned to her that we once had a store here, my husband and I. We were The Jews then, all alone, for years . . ." She brightened. "Well, that's not why I came. I came about a charity. Every year I give to a certain cause. They send me an envelope and I give. And it's so little. Now, with you here, maybe there will be more. It's the Home Hospital for the Pious of Israel."

At the world *hospital* they relaxed a bit. Mr. Waldman smiled. "We've given money to Israel before. In fact, I've already sent this year through my office, but I think we could spare a dollar or two for an Israeli hospital." He began to get up.

"But it isn't in Israel," Sarah said. "It's in Long Island, New York. It's for old people, who need to be taken care of among their own. Don't you think you could give, well, fifty dollars so that a rabbi maybe, could live out his days according to the Law, without worrying if his food was prepared right, if . . ."

Mrs. Waldman had sat down with a kind of defensive finality. "We don't believe in any of that," she said. "Israel, well, that's different, but we're not kosher, we don't go to a synagogue, and we don't believe in Jews separating themselves."

"But the Jews who do—" Sarah cried. "What about the Jews who do?"

"I don't know," Clarisse Waldman said, "and I don't care. I certainly don't want to pay for their narrowness. We don't believe in supporting a ghetto Jew's idea of God."

"Don't believe in it?" Sarah cried. "I bet you give to Biafra, to India; do you believe in those gods? The earth on a turtle? All over the world you give, and the more religious *those* people are, the better. An American Indian says, 'By my religion, God is snakes'; you nod your head and open your wallet."

"We believe in being responsible toward others."

"Is *every* god better than the God of the Jews, of America? To a synagogue in Russia you might send money, why not Long Island?"

"We don't believe in maintaining all of that!"

They argued about the nature of the cause, about the reputation of Jews as generous and charitable, about the fact that they, the Waldmans, were the only Jewish family between Sefton and Tonopha, not the first, the only, and that she, Sarah, was not part of a family anymore, but only a shred torn from a garment that was once whole. It went on for almost an hour, getting louder, and then when they remembered the children, sinking back. In the end they sat, red-faced and out of breath in silence, collecting themselves.

"So that's that?" Sarah said.

"Yes," answered Mr. Waldman, having taken over for his wife halfway along, "that's that."

"Well," Sarah said, "then the only thing left is blackmail."

Mr. Waldman began to laugh; Mrs. Waldman put her hand to her lips. "I beg your pardon."

"Blackmail," Sarah said. "Oh, no, wait, blackmail is for something in the past, or written; maybe it's extortion I mean." The Waldmans both laughed then, and their laughter and the sight of her, wide-eyed with her small, withered face like a child's made up for a play, made it impossible for them to dislike her.

"I'm quite serious," Sarah said. Mrs. Waldman bit her lip.

"Let's have some more coffee," Mr. Waldman told his wife. "I've got to hear this."

"I mean," Sarah said grimly, "that if you don't give something to the Pious, I will tell people that you are Jews."

Mr. Waldman looked disappointed. "That's ridiculous," he said. "People know. We certainly never kept our background a secret."

"But I will tell them so that they *know*."

Mrs. Waldman came back from the kitchen and sat down.

"You see," Sarah said, "my husband and I had a store here when all of this," and she waved out over Mulberry Road and Juniper Road and to uncounted miles beyond, "was farms. We were the only Jews. My husband came through here in 1919 with his pack—a peddler— and after he got a little money together, came back again and settled. We were one family, 250 miles from a synagogue. In those days people read the Bible, and some, even the farmers, would memorize whole books of it. We were of a strange, cursed race to them, but so were the French. We were foreigners, but the Bible, the words of Salvation, was our book. So, occasionally, the minister would come of an evening and ask my husband the meaning of certain words or customs, and some- times a farmer would come bringing a worn King James and point with his broken nail to where two texts seemed to disagree. In those days they didn't think to reconcile their thoughts about us as Christ killers with their respect for us as beginners of their Law."

"Well," said Mr. Waldman, "what has that to do with us?"

"I'll get to it in due time," Sarah said. "Over the years things changed. The city people started to summer here and then to retire, and then Dillar, which was only a village when we came, got big during the war, and people came here to live. Now it's starting to be a suburb. People have an acre or so and they build their houses, but they still commute to the city. We were the only Jews, my husband and I and our children. My Hyman, may he rest in peace, died, and the children went off to college and married and live in other suburbs, far away. I was the only Jew, until you came."

"What has this to do with us?" Mr. Waldman asked. "One family, then another."

"But the *Christians* have changed!" Sarah crowed with delight, "altogether! The people of the suburbs are modern; they want to understand everything; they must experience all there is. You won't find them coming with Bibles worn with reading; they want the true facts straight from the Jew himself, and they don't care what he thinks, only what he feels. They will invite you as a stranger, politely, and they will want to hear all your feelings explained, the Jewish view on every subject, all to be experienced by them and explored. On

138

Passover you will be the Jew on the fellowship committee; you will explain in the schools, you will explain in the churches, you will bare your souls in the Cultural Exchange Fellowship of the Women's Auxiliaries, and at the Literary Guild, and for the Hour of Reconciliation. Every Jewish holiday will be a spiritual last chance, in case the thing should get away."

"It sounds as though you're bitter," Mrs. Waldman said, "as though you don't want us to be understood."

"Can we be? Totally? And who asks the ones who might know, the sages, the pious? At any rate, you'll soon learn how much of our God-wrangle can be understood by people who expect religion to bring them peace. They take the Boy Scout troops to each church once so that they may know about all the major faiths. I will leave you to them."

"And unless we contribute to this mad cause of yours, you'll loose this on us."

"Exactly."

"Well, we won't do it, we'll just say no," Mr. Waldman said.

Clarisse Waldman looked at her husband incredulously. "Of course we won't be able to say no, Arthur. How can we, when this—"

"Extortionist," Sarah said helpfully.

"When this *woman* tells everyone that we're Jews, observant Jews! Would you laugh and say, 'No, we really don't believe in any of it'? It would make us look like hypocrites or liars, trying to fend them off, rejecting their offers of understanding." She turned to Sarah. "Do you really—would you really do a thing like that?"

"I wouldn't even have to say you were observant Jews. They know that Jews are all alike, that Jews believe deeply enough to have come from Mt. Sinai to Minsk to Miami without losing a single one of their own except to the gun and the gas oven."

"It's crazy, it's just plain arrogant and crazy!"

Sarah smiled at them, conciliatory wrinkles wreathing a sad mouth. "What am I asking of you? That your sons be Bar Mitzvah? That you *bensh licht* Friday nights so that I can see from my old woman's house my history moving past me? That you have a Seder on

Pesach and a menorah on Hanukkah and invite me? All I want is fifty dollars for some stubborn old Jews who are too stupid to die quaintly in Russia. Hey," and she grinned at them, "the black people hate us, and we give them money. The Israelis despise us and we give *them* money. These old Jews hate and despise us more than any of them could in his wildest moment. Who can hate like a brother? Now, if we Jews must pay everyone who hates us, why, we should make these old men princes, walking jewels!"

"Fifty dollars?" Mr. Waldman said.

"Fifty dollars. I wouldn't tell a soul!"

That first encounter had been in September, when they were new in the house, busy with decorating and shopping and becoming familiar with the neighborhood. They never ran into Sarah at the library or on the street or at the supermarket, but in November she was back at their door one evening with her eyes wide, and huddled in a man's sweater as though having grabbed the nearest thing in her haste.

"I was afraid you wouldn't want to let me in," she said, her face yellow in their porch light, "but I'm so worried I had to come even if you slammed the door in my face."

"Don't be melodramatic," Mr. Waldman said. "Come in."

She came in shivering through the foyer, but she seemed to expand in the warmth of the living room. "You really made this lovely, this room— Look at that fireplace, these couches, this rug—lovely." It struck him as being too much like an inventory, and it made him defensive. "What did you want to see us about?"

"Oh!" She cried as though she hadn't heard him. "How grateful and surprised they were, those old men. After the miserable bit I send them each year, it was wonderful, wonderful! And right before the holidays, too."

"Fine," he said, imagining a dozen ancient men, bearded and side-curled, tallised and skull-capped, gorging themselves at a holiday table, their rage no whit diminished. "Is that what you came to say?"

"No, it was about the taxes, the income taxes."

Clarisse Waldman had come up behind her husband. "What's this about taxes?"

"Yours," Sarah said. "It's been worrying me for weeks. You made the check out to me, the check for the Pious of Israel, and I cashed it and got the money, yours and mine, and sent it in a money order. I was proud; I congratulated myself because I knew that then you wouldn't be getting notices from them and appeals for Passover, and that they wouldn't bother you, and the mailman and the garbage man wouldn't see anything incriminating at your house. Also, I was afraid if you got those appeals from the Pious, you might get upset and write a bad letter and maybe hurt their feelings. Then, in the middle of the day, two, three weeks ago, I was standing in the kitchen, and I thought, my God, his taxes! What will he say when the charities have to be listed? He'll have to tell the name, and my name too, everything will come out, about our . . . relationship."

She moved her hands back and forth ineffectually. "Wait, listen . . ." Her hands stopped and she suddenly brightened. "What if you got yourself a Jewish accountant, a nice young Jewish man to go over your taxes so it wouldn't bother him about the Pious of Israel. That way, these private things wouldn't come out, nothing about your giving to an unfashionable cause."

Mr. Waldman found himself waiting for more. Surely she was going to recommend someone, one of those vanished sons—perhaps, a nephew, a brilliant boy who hadn't found himself.

"Mrs. Levy," he said coldly, "I have no intention of changing my accountant. My tax work is done through my office in the city, and I couldn't care less about what the man thinks of my charitable contributions! You may say whatever you like to whomever you like, but I will not hire your brother, your son, or your nephew. And that, Mrs. Levy, is final!" Without his meaning to, he had let his voice rise until the house echoed with it. A child who had come downstairs at the sound of conversation had run halfway up again and was surveying the scene at a distance. Sarah turned to Mr. Waldman, her eyes misted. "My husband, may he rest in peace, used to shout like that.

'No, Sarah, and that's final!' " And she imitated the hollow boom of it. "A person misses yelling even, when it's part of someone she loves. I haven't heard that phrase in so long it makes me remember him like he was standing here now. I'm glad you got the wrong idea, Arthur, because otherwise I wouldn't have heard you yelling so nicely, just like Hyman. I have no one for a job. My one son is in the foam-rubber business, mattresses, you know, and the other is a professor. Physiology. They couldn't help you. As for me, I go to Alfred Saylor, here. He and Hyman were friends for years."

Mr. Waldman felt his face getting hot. "Mrs. Levy."

"It's all right, Arthur," she said and smiled demurely. "I'm a criminal, and who knows what goes on in a criminal brain?" She backed toward the door. "You've got a nice tax man in the city, and he'll take care of it all, and now I'll stop worrying about the tax and the FBI." She fumbled with the doorknob behind her and then opened and slipped through the door leaving a faint whisper of speech behind her: "So good to hear a man yell once in a while; it made me feel the world will still go on." Arthur Waldman turned out the porch light when she had gone.

"FBI," he muttered.

Sarah didn't bother them again until January, for a kind of semiannual report: extortion-client services. "There's a new minister at the Crossing. Very modern. He had to send to Rock Springs and offer money, too, for two Jews for the Judeo part of the "Judeo-Christian Experience." Four parts. Channel Five TV is trying to get people to demonstrate a Seder on Good Friday. It comes out of Cheyenne, but they want Jews from all over the state. Young Adult Conference, Christian Church: not enough Jews to go around for the inter-faith discussion group. Mrs. Vallins told me that—she's been trying very hard because she's on the program board. It's easy for me to refuse because of my age, but they really *want* younger people. People who give the Jews a good image. Three sensitivity groups starting at the college, all minorities wanted. Blacks and Spanish from militant groups, Jews and Orientals hard to find. PTA: *that* program is supposed to be on minorities too, but we're the only minority out this far, unless you think about old man Alhavaridian who has the garbage truck. Armenian Orthodox, but no children."

February and March were cold and wet that year, but the Waldman boys came home later than usual, saying they were goofing around near the bus stop. Clarisse wanted them to have a "healthy socialization" with the neighborhood children, and instead of asking that they come right home, decided to let them stay. She had cocoa for them whenever they came in, and felt provident and maternal when she interrupted her work or cut short the day's shopping to go home and fix it for them. On one of those days, Brian, the youngest, asked, "Why don't we ever have tea?"

"We do," Clarisse said. "You know, when Aunt Rosey visits or when you have a cold."

"I mean in a glass," Brian said, "with jam in it." Shawn, the elder, kicked him under the table, and the boys began to wrangle. "I do too, I do too!" Brian screamed. "Listen—a *glayzel tay, mit povidle!*" Clarisse ran to the upstairs phone and called the family persecutor.

"I don't want to talk to you," Sarah said. "To talk to a woman I can talk to myself. Wait, and I'll talk to Arthur. A man, it's better." As she hung up, Clarisse was struck by the fact that there was a slight Yiddish intonation in Mrs. Levy's speech where there had been none before.

If they expected conciliation they were mistaken. When Arthur Waldman shook his head at his wife's faintheartedness and called Mrs. Levy's number, he was greeted summarily: "Good for you, I'll be right over."

She came in, jaw set. "You, you take your sins to the city and they get lost in the rush. I have my sins at home to stare at me from the tables and the mantelpiece like owls. Do you know what it's like to be a blackmailer, a maker of threats, a savage? You start worrying about your victim, how he's doing, what will happen to him. You have to worry about fresh edges for the extortion, you have to shift the knife, as we criminals say. You have to be concerned about the rest of your soul, that the criminal part doesn't pour and flow into the untouched part, into the part, God forbid, where God is. Do you know that yesterday I went shopping and had a candy and didn't pay for it? You'll think, well, she's old, she forgot, she put the wrapper in her pocket to bring to the check-out and she forgot it. You'd be wrong. I was leaving with my things to catch the bus and I remembered the candy, and I thought, go to hell, all of you, and I got right on the bus with the paper rustling in my pocket. Who knows what I will think of next? The Larsens's dog runs into my garden and digs my bulbs. Will I give him poison? The Winters's boys put mud in the mailboxes for a joke sometimes. What will I do then, hide guns on secret wires that shoot them from the bushes? Dynamite? The truth is, Arthur, I'm too old for this life, too old to learn new evil. Mrs. Francis, who is program director for youth at the church, tells me that as a subject of discussion race is out and drugs is in. Relevance, she says, the church must have relevance. Mazel tov. So after only one client, I am leaving the extortion business to younger people. The worst part is that I went through it for one check, one check! All of it for so little. Arthur, crime hardly pays!"

"Mrs. Levy," he said at last, "you've been having our children in for tea and cookies. Was that . . . another edge, as you put it?"

"Not another edge," Sarah said, "another knife. Another knife entirely."

"Mrs. Levy"—he sounded tired—"you didn't think of harming them, did you? You didn't hate them because we don't believe— because we aren't your kind of Jew . . . ?" He had spoken softly. There was stillness all around.

"Three years ago," Sarah said, "I could walk to town and back with my little shopping bag and not be tired. Two years ago I could work in the garden all morning and forget, in my body, that I had done it. Now, a walk to your house, right at the top of such a little hill, is a walk for which I have to prepare myself, like Hillary on Everest. Another thing about extortion, I have found, is that it takes time; it's a seed that has to be planted, to ripen, as it were. Six months, a year. I had a thought in the beginning that maybe before I got too weak and old and had to go where my sons wished, I could make out of your children Jewish people. Then I could leave and the thing would grow in your own house. It wouldn't be a sin then: all children blackmail their parents with their innocence. For years I never crossed against a traffic light because of my children. Your gifts to unfashionable Jews would be the same—"

"And?" Mr. Waldman said, knowing the opacity of his children whenever he made the effort of imparting "values" to them. "Did you succeed? Are they Jews, my children?" He was astonished to see Sarah's eyes fill with tears.

"May the Most High keep us from all extortion. In forcing others we push them somewhere, toward something, and there we meet ourselves coming back. I thought, I will give them treasures, the great Laws, the great answers. I thought that in watching a Jewish woman, they would be watching the Jews. How could I have known the vastness of my own ignorance? Who goes to that rim of his own will and peers over? I made cookies for them and said, 'Listen how your teeth crunch; see how brown and lacy that cookie is; take it, taste it, smell it. How wonderful a gift it is, the power to do these things, each person singly, for himself!' They laughed at me, and I said, 'Laugh, God gives it to you.' I made tea for them, and I told them God listens, so they should be careful what they pray for. I told them that the sprinkles on the cookies were stars and planets, and to study the real ones was to collaborate with God, and that the world of men was their job, and that our men love God enough that they can argue with Him continually about the work He has given them. I told them the Shema."

"Was that all?" he asked.

"Yes, that was all, of two thousand years, of deserts and cities and visions and prophesy and the Law, built agony by agony for generations. All the time something was whispering, 'Tell them more, tell them the rhythms, show them the richness, the variety of it all, come, it's time for the great truths. Bring forward the greatest truths!'" She was weeping. "And all I could do was to give them cookies. I couldn't give them the Jews so I gave them tea." She sniffed and then reached into her coat pocket and took out a linty Kleenex. He became conscious that she was still wearing her coat. "Can't you sit down, here, wait a minute?"

She put her hand to her hair. "I must look a fright! Imagine thinking because I had God all these years, I had the Jews, too. It wasn't so. Now, the Pious will go their way, with their fingers to their lips, and I will go my way and never breathe your secret, and the Pious and I will leave you altogether in peace."

And so it was. A week later a moving van came to the old house, and, having watched it gorge itself with ancient furniture and close its jaws on all of it, the Waldman boys ran home to Clarisse with the news: "The Jew-lady's gone!" While she was trying to think of what to say to them, it having occurred to her that perhaps the children had never been told any more than that they were of Jewish descent, the phone rang. The voice on the other end was hesitant and pleasant as befits a stranger who is making a request. "Mrs. Waldman, I'm Irene Kennedy, and I'm calling on behalf of the program committee of Potter School. This year we've been having seminars about our community, and we wanted to finish with one about neighbors. Dr. Martin will be with us—he's been so good about coming down from the college—he's our nice black neighbor, and when we heard that there were people of the Jewish faith living right here in . . ."

DE RERUM NATURA

Dear Professor Shapiro:

As I write this letter I have before me your newly published book, *Understanding Molecular Physics*. It is a work of profundity—I know because I have asked learned people and they agree with the good notices the book has attracted. (You must have been proud to read in the *Times*: "Elegant exposition, and syntheses neat as a fine sonata.") It is surely a triumph to do anything that someone calls "neat as a fine sonata." It must give you a good feeling to have what you have produced weigh solid in your hand, to be picked up and looked through when you are full of pain and in despair, knowing the pain will not go away tomorrow or the day after, and maybe never.

I bought your book not because I am a student of molecular physics and wanted to know more or because I know nothing about it but wanted to impress others. To be honest, I bought it because I liked the picture of you that was on the back cover.

There you are, sitting in that wonderful book-lined study. The volumes behind you are not there for show, either. One can see that they have been used, read, made part of your mind and your life.

Mathematics, chemistry, physics, cybernetics . . . Best of all, over to the side, a set of volumes that I recognize—a collection of great literary classics. And this says of you that you are not a man who is content to burrow into his work, to use it to defend himself from the world. Your work broadens and deepens your scope. You never let your study of science take you too far from the human values common to all of us, learned or simple. You acknowledge kinship with those who are secure and also with those on the edge of volcanoes.

And it's a good face, too, your face. Warm and kindly. You have just taken your pipe out of your mouth, and a spiral of smoke is disappearing upward, winding as naturally as your thoughts must as you contemplate those worlds and processes too minute to be seen. I think it must be snowing outside that quiet study, because I catch a warm light that probably comes from a fire; I can imagine it playing on the polished cabinet behind you, and the bookcase. How good it must be to be a friend of yours, to sit long winter evenings with you in quiet talk. It wouldn't be banal talk, the kind that wears a person out, that wearies and saddens—the petty frustrations of one's job, the activities of one's children—

You dedicated your book to your son. You say nothing more in the dedication. There are no clues there as to what the relationship is like. Perhaps he is a lovely little five-year-old, playing with the creative toy you have given him, hoping that it will develop in him the "inventive mastery" it says on the box. Maybe he is seven or nine or twelve, and working with the chemistry set you have given him, able to come to you when he cannot understand a chemical reaction. Or is he in college? Is there a chair in that study for him when he comes home on vacation, and two tobacco pouches side by side on the low table where the talk goes on quietly through the winter evenings, he eager and full of wonder, you calm and thoughtful?

By now you must be impatient with this letter, wanting me to get to the point, feeling insulted perhaps at a fan letter from someone with neither the training nor the intelligence to understand your work. The purpose of this letter is to ask a question—two questions, really—about molecular physics.

Physics deals with processes—things moving and changing, developing and flowing, with force against force balancing and opposing, and, in all, the terrible, inexorable law of the passing of time. The consciousness of that was what made the study of physics impossible for me in school—that stunning ray of light shooting through space so fast that by the time I could imagine it, it had shot past me and I was in the dark again. All the terrifying, vast poetry of energy and motion had to be caught in a web of numbers and while I was gathering the folds of the net, the reality of the light, the crystal note of the sound, slipped through and was gone.

I wanted to be sure of what I had to define for you. I looked up *molecular* in the dictionary:

Molecule: the smallest part of an element or compound that can exist separately without losing the physical or chemical properties of the original element.

It is exactly what I need to speak of, the molecular physics of my situation.

You dedicated your book to your son. Is your son lucky to have you for a father? Please forgive the presumption of this question—I am not trying to be sarcastic or insulting or to pry into your life to find reasons in you that may excuse my own failure. I have peered and peered into the molecular physics of my son's soul and my own. Such inquiries should be a part of physics. Relationships move; they change as fast as that light traveling between the sun and the earth, and how long I have tried to hold that beam of light in my hand, to weigh it and make it yield up a number that I can understand!

He was not an easy or a happy baby, our son, not a loving child. Who was responsible for that? The books say we were. The books say that loving and responsible parents beget loving and reasonable children in the natural way that light continues to fall on its accustomed path, that molecules "remember" the original shape of their forming and seek that shape again. Some weakness or flaw in us, unbeknownst to us, flowed outward to make itself manifest in our gestures and breaths and voices, and, with an irresistible, biochemical force, froze the natural, loving instincts of his nature.

Does anyone know the true nature of man? Of any single person? Of anything, even the atom? We have a good marriage, we gave him a good home. There was money enough, good food in quantity, warm clothing, good schooling, friends. We taught him ethics and morals didactically, and, we thought, by example. We did not beat him and then preach kindness. We did not compound our hypocrisy with god-like posturings or make it corrosive with false piety. I seem to remember times when he understood the confrontation between what we wished to be and what we had to be. I seem to remember . . .

God help me, I am giving you the wrong impression again. By now you must think that I am apologizing for having begotten a rapist or a murderer. I see you flipping the remaining pages of this long confession to see if the signature is familiar—one of those terrible names of which we have a growing collection—assassins, terrorists, the violent men who hold the world at gunpoint. Forgive me, I am not agonizing over some sky-sweeping, incandescent lunacy. I am attempting to plot the trajectory of a slow, randomly moving planet, to map a star that gives no evidence of light.

Almost none. Now and then he'll call from Kansas City or Milwaukee. Money for a job he almost has, for a room he needs to stay in while he looks for work, for a suit he needs in order to be presentable, for a ticket out before trouble catches up with him, for a ticket in so he can try someplace new. And it's the same whether we catch him or let him fall: he learns nothing. Women, I think, support him. Older women. Tired waitresses, sad divorcées. I see them taking imitation-leather wallets from torn handbags to give him the few extra dollars they have saved; they know as we do that there is no future in the gift or the "loan," that it will never be repaid, that it will never remake his life or change anything. When he was younger, we "cut him off" for a time, hoping that he would learn, but he has a pleasant way about him. He is easily agreeable, and when we stopped our support, the poor, a whole world we never knew existed, accepted him as one of its own and fed him. He cadged food from restaurant workers, sold things (dope, I think, part of the time), did favors (I don't like to think what favors), and was repaid in indifferent food and precarious lodgings here and there. And women. One called us once when she was coming through town. Because we had been months without news and because we wanted to learn about him in a way we could not as parents, we asked her to come for dinner.

She was a sad, heavy woman, twenty years his senior. Her name was Bonnie Jean. She came because she thought we knew where he was, and she was stolidly resigned when we told her we did not know. The house amazed her. She kept saying, "I dint know he grown up so good, y'know what I mean," and "I dint know he had a family like this." When she realized at last that she was hurting us, she sighed and lapsed into silence. We could get nothing from her. She was not a perceptive woman and could not understand our interest in our son's personality or motives, what he thought and said, what he was like. She only said, "He's real nice, y'know what I mean. I mean he ain't like some of the guys that—" and then caught herself and sighed again and stared at us. At the end of the long evening we offered her a bed for the night. She smiled wanly and said no, that she already had a place, which we knew to be a lie. Confounded, we could only let her go, standing transfixed at the wonder in her voice when she said, leaving, "You folks are real nice. I mean you're *nice people!*" And all night to lie awake and wonder how he saw us and what he told his friends about us, out of belief or to play on their sympathies. Not long after, he called us, collect of course, from a noisy bar in Duluth, Minnesota, and we mentioned her name. He couldn't place her at all, but seemed surprised and a little put out that she had looked us up. It was as though she had violated an unspoken but basic agreement. I think he called us from that bar because we would think he was with friends. He often did that, preferring to shout to us above the noise and lose half of what we said because he had the advantage of being always called away, of showing us that he was wanted somewhere, waited for by busy and active people, that he lacked for nothing in a life fully apart from ours.

Except, of course, that in these calls he always had to ask for money. We often send it now because the face of Bonnie Jean haunts us, that puffy, slack face, and the purse, which was as I had imagined it, torn vinyl—I couldn't stand the thought of his robbing the poor.

Or is it robbery? This is where I turn in the dark and this is where I must unravel the mysteries of the universe. Because everything in nature calls out with all its force to equalize itself. Water and air, molecules and atoms, all seek a balance, a mysterious reciprocity, and to attain it they will break glass, crack timber, burst asunder walls of metal. We give and they give, those sad women. Does he give? If I could know that there is a balance somewhere, that the world of people, like the world of light and sound, air and water, is, at last, just and fair, that he too plays his part, fits, is needed, I could be content, I think. I could say, "They also serve who only run away."

Perhaps I am blundering again. I'm sure you are now shuffling these pages and beginning to worry about my stability, thinking perhaps that you will have to answer me very carefully and with the greatest tact because I sound so desperate. I'm not desperate, really, only sad; not mad with anguish, only weary and baffled. The sun rises in the east each morning and bathes the world in warm light. One must look carefully to note that the westward-facing sides are shadowed and only the northwest corners are still dark under the eaves of the houses.

My landscape is dark at the northwest corner, and because I am looking at that corner, what I see is darkness. Usually I can look at the bright parts and scold myself for wanting everything to stand forward in full sunlight. It's impossible, impossible physically and spiritually, and yet I yearn for it, as air yearns toward a vacuum, as heat yearns upward. Is it so with you? Do you sit before the fire in that lovely study and find yourself unhappy with your son's choice of friends or out of tune with his politics? Do your colleagues annoy you far beyond the usual differences in philosophy or personality? Are you also shadowed at some northwest corner? Perhaps you agonize that the wonderful book you were so proud to have published is now one among many and perhaps not selling as well as you would like. Perhaps there is pain in some joint that reminds you meanly and routinely that you are getting older and that some day it will come to stay. I know how it is then, how you then must recall who you are, hating yourself for the petty counting of blessings, all the things we discount short like damaged goods when we have them—health, love, fame, the lives of parents to see and enjoy those things with us.

So the counting of blessings leads me to my last question. In flame there are molecules that rise at the very moment of incandescence to become fire and change in that magic; there must be other molecules that rise more slowly and some that do not rise purposefully at all, but drift away aimlessly on the warping air. Do those molecules not envy the luminous few, not go sighing in sorrow down the currents warm and cold, too slow to be caught up in the law and transmuted? They must. Oh, they must!

MERGING
TRAFFIC

There must be no touching. It is the single constant rule. The cars come from left and right. Cleverly, with the minutest, most subtle of judgments of time and space, speeding up and slowing down, the cars weave in and out to and from the ramps and lanes of the highway. It's done with breathtaking speed, each driver guessing precisely where he may glide to the right or the left, acknowledging with a language of lights and position his wishes to the other drivers, unseen and unknown, and never, never touching.

To touch is to be demolished, perhaps to die. At the very least it is to stop the flow for long moments, breaking the secret contract the driver makes with all the unknown strangers around him.

The hard-worked precision of a ballet has nothing to equal this daily choreography of thousands over miles of interstate; fifty thousand dancers without conductor or composer, a corps de ballet, the members of which have never met and will never recombine in exactly the same way, who almost never glimpse one another's hands or eyes or faces, and who may share nothing but their presence in the dance and a knowledge of its laws.

I do it every day and I marvel at it. Here I am, an overweight, middle-aged matron, gliding with sweet ease into and out of the dance, unpartnered and unashamed. To others the trip seems boring. In the morning, riding the middle lane on Sixth, I look past the sun and into the car of the couple beside me. Perhaps he is yawning or scratching sleep from an eye, she is trying for something on the radio, her face sleep-ridden. In the evening, it is all impatience with the stream, feet tapping angrily on the pedals—they are all eager to get home before the dark comes down, to get to dinner and put the day away.

Only young people seem to enjoy the wonder of what the commuter takes for granted. My son's old car is a metaphor for himself: all things are still potential, the destination has not yet been seen. He hates the idea of compromise and adjustment. He prides himself on his singularity and independence, yet he loves the split-second need to anticipate give and take; he rejoices in the adaptations he must make to the oncoming traffic and he does not feel the paradox inherent in these things, and neither do his car-mad friends, who, if they had unlimited gas money, would sooner eat at the McDonald's forty miles away than the one around the corner. High school for my son is bearable only because of that car. When I think about my high-school years I see the paradox of all that jumping into cars and driving off. Never were our relationships so frozen and so hierarchical. For all our physical motion we were as fixed socially as flies in amber. I look at him and try to recapture what it felt like before some of the destinations were known. I am surprised, for instance, that he does not want a copy of his yearbook or even the class picture. I try to remember how I felt about high school at his age, whether I wanted to save the names and the faces, caught at eighteen and frozen forever in their webs of success, failure, or invisibility—the Popular Girl, the Easy Lay, the Comic, the Nice Kid, the Athlete, the Grind, the Leper, the Rest of the Crowd.

Then I remember that I, too, had wanted to forget it all, to leave high school behind, because it was a time of isolation and pain for me, of knowing the truth about myself as unworthy of note, although when and by whom the judgment had been made I was not sure. That a judgment is made and that it is made completely and irrevocably and as though forever, I am sure—a judgment so unanimous that no one, not even the one judged, questions it.

The society in high school is a tribal one with its own absolute laws enforced as they must be in primitive groups, without written codes. It is rigidly stratified and depends on complex understandings. Perhaps it is the acceptance of these understandings that teach the first laws and begin the delicate training in the choreography of traffic. The understandings depend on the acceptance of each member in the group of his or her place. My place was as Other, and as long as I did not try to change my place I was allowed to exist without malice and now and then was given a crumb to live on. Alinda Weber, campaigning for Most Popular Girl, let me pass out voting leaflets in the hall, and for doing that she allowed herself to smile in my direction. Charlie Cates danced with me once to show his indifference to Lucy Garland. Such are the uses of Others.

There were many of us—the ugly, the fat, the dull, the brilliant, the psychologically encumbered, the very poor. The blacks had a parallel order—Sweetheart and Hero, Cute Girl and Put Out, Comic and Grind—their roles were louder and more colorful, but still the same as ours—and while black-white relations were friendly and easy on the surface, the lines were side by side. There was no touching.

I've thought since that, had we wished, the Others could have banded together—all the pimpled and the plain, the dull and the different, the wearers of unfashionable clothes and bottle-bottom glasses—and taken over their world, boycotted their dances, voted down their queens, deserted their football games and events, left them with only each other and their few, hand-picked elect. I see it now. Then, all I hoped for and all the rest of us hoped for was a moment of inclusion—our hands on their velvet-trains, our places at their dances—a hope never real, but never quite put by, that Bucky Lewis or Charlie Cates would one day look and then look again.

So we made no common cause. Sometimes there were brief, shy friendships, but because the friendships had the flavor of defeat, of anything being better than nothing, they were for the most part spirit-less and resigned. Except for my friendship with Shirley Antin, I flowed toward nothing, merged with no one.

Shirley was short and heavy. She had thick glasses and brown hair. She was as statusless, as invisible as I, but she didn't seem to mind. There was no bitterness in her, and she looked at the worlds above us as though they existed for her pleasure. "What are you unhappy about?" she used to say. "You don't *love* any of those guys, do you?"

"I haven't had the chance," I would answer.

"Well, I don't, and as a reward I get to watch the whole show—what they do to each other and themselves. Very little is hidden from me because they don't consider me important enough to hide anything from. In addition, I'm getting a good education which I will use to get a scholarship to a better college than my folks could pay for. Which I will use to get an interesting job and to have interesting friends. Like you." Interesting. It was what you had to be if you couldn't be pretty.

For weeks at a time I followed Shirley's advice, trying to watch the world with the same humorous ease she did, the same lack of involve-ment, but at the first unwitting slight, the odd cut, the careless exclu-sion of my name for the fourth time—all the many marks of their indifference—I became aware of myself as a tragic figure and the game was lost again. Pear-shaped and plain, I let the school fill me with facts, because the real purpose of my being there had failed.

After high school Shirley went east to college and I went to the state university. I didn't see her again, but I thought of her often over the years and wondered what good things had happened to her. I see her kind oftener now; they are the people who hold the the world together, the stable, rooted wives and mothers, the dogged, no-nonsense wheel-horses in organizations lucky enough to have them. Shirley is Anne Simpson in our hospital's emergency room, Mrs. Russell at the school, Mrs. Peet at Adam's office. In my own mind when I meet these people, I say to myself "There's a Shirley" and feel neighbored. There are four of them on my job, and when we are scheduled together the work goes well.

The work. I'm in the lobby of a large Detroit hotel, thinking about it. In an hour I'm to speak to a group at the national convention, which has preregistered to hear me. I want to make Shirley-sense—practical and compassionate, tolerant and humorous—to the people who do the same thing I do. My thoughts are organized on the much-studied cards I am carrying. The problem is to organize my feelings. There are many, some ambivalent, some that will be immediately shared by others in the room, and while it's easy to evoke them, almost too easy, the darker ones must also be explored. It's important.

There are other conventions here—meetings, workshops, forums, panels, groups, associations, armies, for all I know. Now and then the doors of the Empire Room or the Bronze Room or the Gateway Room open and people with name tags drift out. "Hello, I'm ———," "ABRFF," "National RAD," "CJSJ," "Regional Advisory Group." I'm wearing a name tag also, with initials others do not understand.

The door of a conference room down the corridor opens, and a group of women come walking toward me. Their badges are round yellow smile faces, and they do not walk past me and into the foyer but stop before the door opposite where I am sitting. They are waiting for another group still deliberating. In addition to their name badges they have other tags saying HOME BRITE, and by the way they talk and the fact that they obviously do not know one another, I suspect that they are wives waiting for their husbands to come out of *their* conference.

There is a woman among them—tall, red haired, a little heavy—who for a reason I do not know, makes me stare at her. It isn't the face but the gestures, a way of holding her body, that forces me to look at her and to keep looking, to comb my past for her and then to try and read the name tag. ALINDA (MRS. R.) MCCOOK. I get up and go over to her. "Excuse me," I say, "but didn't you go to Union High in Plainfield?"

I expect surprise—it's been twenty-eight years, a lifetime ago. She only smiles graciously, like the beautiful sophomore, junior, and senior queen she was. "Yes, I did." She leaves it to me to say, "I did too—I was in your class. I was Ruth Sky then."

"Oh?" she says vaguely, and I realize that of course, she does not remember me. In a way I am relieved. My world has opened wider than I had dreamed possible, and I am not the same person I was. I see that perhaps she has more in common with the other Home Brite wives and that I am keeping her from them.

"I just wanted to say hello—" I say. "Maybe you need to get back—" and I gesture out to the women waiting. She puts her hand up quickly. "Oh no, I haven't seen *anyone* for so long. I saw Anne Beeler about ten years ago and we thought about a reunion, but we both had so much to do and there was all that organizing and calling and the letters you have to write."

She looks at my name tag, "Ruth Rubino . . ." "It used to be Ruth Sky," I say again, "but I don't think we knew each other well back then."

It isn't true. As with the great and famous, more people knew her than were known by her. Many more. I knew her habits then, her dreams and dislikes by heart. Her favorite songs were the songs we played on the jukebox at Ciavatti's. Her choice in class rings and pins was our choice, her whim was our command. She didn't know me because it would have lessened her prestige to know me, to know any of us on the outside of things. An anthropologist once said that in primitive societies, the danger in coming in at the top is that you will never leave it, never be exposed in any way to the bottom. The anthropologist was a woman, Rosalie Somebody. She must have gone to Union High.

After a silence, Alinda asks, "Is your husband at a convention here?" She is looking at my name tag again.

"No, I'm on my own. My husband is back home at work."

"Oh." She seems stopped by that.

"I work also," I say, "and my work has the usual meetings, forums, all of that. Adam isn't particularly involved in what I do, apart from being married to me, so he doesn't come to my meetings, and I seldom go to his."

"What does your husband do?"

"He invents languages for computers—ways of getting them to answer special questions."

"Oh," Alinda says.

"He's very happy in his work," and I smile. "God knows he's tried to teach us what he can, but with so many new things coming it's hard for me to keep up."

"We are part of the Home Brite Family," Alinda says, "husbands and wives and kids, too. Our kids help. Our Todd is going to get his own route when he's eighteen."

"That's nice," I say. "It must make for a nice family feeling."

"It does. Our family is what they call the Home Brite Ideal. Our Ginger is in every club in school, practically, and Bobby Junior's real up-and-coming."

"Tell me something, Alinda. Do you miss those days in high school—the big dance, the Harvest Hayride—all that stuff?"

Her eyes go empty for a minute and the Home Brite smile vanishes.

"Oh, yes," she says. "God, yes. I used to get the blues so bad, I'd just sit home and cry all day. Then I'd pick on Bobby and the kids, and Bobby'd go back to the bad habits. That's why I'm so glad for Home Brite. It brought us back together. I do the books and organize the parties and the shows we do. Bobby, he does the shows and takes the orders, and the kids help, too, with deliveries. The Home Brite Family—and it really is. I mean, they have weekly local meetings, and they give two conventions a year, one state and one national, and if it's a Home Brite Ideal Family like ours is, the kids get to come along, too, and there are special activities and everything for them."

"That's nice," I say. I find that I mean it.

She talks on for a while about their house (two TVs, a new microwave oven, plans for a boat) and the community, which is a small new suburb outside Indianapolis ("No riffraff—everybody keeps their lawns real neat.") She is not curious about me or my life or what I am doing in this hotel alone, not part of any "family." I see her point. I was not interesting or important in school; she remembers me only as a stick figure, a shape without a face. Ten of them make a bunch, one hundred a crowd, and because you can't be prom queen without bunches and crowds, those figures and aggregates of figures are pleasant to smile at and to have around. No more.

But after a while she does ask a question. Perhaps she had been told in a Home Brite training session that it is important to show an interest in Others. "Are you at a convention, too?"

"Yes," I say, "I am."

"Are you a schoolteacher or something?"

"No, I work in emergency medicine—I'm on a fire-and-rescue team." She looks blank, so I go on. "Did you ever think about the problem of all those cars on the highway together? How they can never touch one another? Sometimes they do touch. Occasionally they touch a bridge or a power pole head-on at sixty miles an hour. Sometimes they catch fire or explode. My specialty is called extrication— the problems of getting injured people out of smashed cars and trucks. I guess my job has a lot to do with touching. That's what I'm here to talk about."

I have shocked her, and I find myself enjoying it. "It's a little bit like the TV show," I say, "only instead of a bunch of handsome young firemen, there are some handsome young firemen and a few middle-aged biddies. The sight of us often surprises people because they have been taught to expect the handsome young men."

"You mean you wear—you go around, like in *fire helmets*?"

"We have different kinds of turnout," I say, "for different kinds of calls—one thing for fires, another for accidents. But yes, there is a helmet. For accidents we wear hardhats."

"You're a *fireman*?"

"Firefighter," I say. I am enjoying myself every bit as much as she had when she was describing her house and the qualities of the Home Brite Ideal. "My group has developed some new methods of care in auto-wreck trauma—" She is silent and uncomfortable. I see her working to say something. Surely it says somewhere in the *Home Brite Manual* that everyone is a potential prospect and that members of the Home Brite Family are always unfailingly pleasant to prospects. So she brightens and says, "Well, that must be interesting work."

"In some ways it's like being a combat soldier in a war," I say. She looks at me hard. The look says, Damn you. The Home Brite husbands have not yet come out of their meeting, and my own people are just beginning to collect at the door, and because I had never, not ever in all those four years of high school, when it mattered so much, gotten a single reaction from her, I go on. "It's like combat because nine-tenths of the runs are routine and even boring. False alarms, drunks asleep in overturned cars gone down off a soft shoulder, things that look bad but where no one is badly hurt. One-tenth are life-and-death runs—your life or somebody else's—the fuel truck that explodes in rush-hour traffic, the fire that comes running toward you faster than you can run away, dying victims pinned in a wrecked van. What makes it like combat is that you never know when you start out which kind of run it's going to be. You get the same adrenaline charge for all of them. Also like combat, there are really no regular hours. In a bad situation everyone gets called. Another way it's like combat is the trust you come to have in your corps mates."

I am being cruel and I know it. She wants only a pleasant validation of her reality from me, not a statement of my reality, a world completely different from her own and one that juggles easily with things she does not like to think about—fire and death and highway accidents. The TV commercial shows the new Rutabaga 6 flying alone and beautiful on the California coast road, not backed up on the obsolete feeder lanes that serve the interstate and not ever as it is sideswiped, rear-ended, in collision. I have caused her to think of these things, caused her, for a moment, to stop thinking positively, a goal that Home Brite has spent much time and money trying to inculcate. I have done none of this for her good, only for my own, because of what happened to us, and what we did and did not do to each other thirty years ago. I am suddenly struck with sorrow at what I am doing. God knows I have seen enough bodies in collision to know that at a certain level we are much the same, that the sandaled spiritualist and the slum savage, if they are both young, will die hard, and that Alinda and I can now make common cause for reasons I know better than she. Her kidneys and liver are not doing the perfect job they once did. There are little puffinesses here and there which are edema, and not the pleasant roundnesses of healthy insulating fat. Six weeks ago, in a gully, I tripped on a rock and pulled something in my leg. It has not healed yet. Healing is slower than it was, longer, less complete, and there are twinges in my left shoulder, and my wind is not what it was. Our traffic is merging, not touching, but merging surely and inevitably from our different roads.

So I change the subject. I ask her if she has seen anyone besides Anne Beeler. She names two names: Mary-Anne Dalrymple, who is married and lives in Chicago, and Barbara Faye. These were other popular girls with whom I had little in common, but I remember them and am warmed by hearing their names again. "You saw Mary-Anne—what's happened to her since school. You said she's married . . . what else did she say?"

"Nothing. Her husband works in some kind of office somewhere. They have kids, I think."

"Yes, but what's she like now?"

She stares at me blankly. "I couldn't tell," she says. "I mean she was on the street and I didn't see the kids or their car. She had a diamond wedding band, though."

"And Barbara?"

"Barbara got divorced."

"Oh—"

"My sister saw her at the doctor's office once. She said she was divorced."

"Does she work? What's she like now?"

Alinda shrugged.

"Did you ever hear anything about Shirley Antin?"

"Who?"

"Shirley Antin. She was in our class. She was a quiet girl, a little heavyset—brown hair—"

Again I have embarrassed her. Home Brite must give courses in remembering people's names. ("You never can tell who will be a prospect some day; even the old high-school gang can get your order books bulging. Reunions can mean big sales as well as a laugh and a tear, Home Briters, and Sweet Sue may run a mansion now, so the old memories in that yearbook may mean big sales for you!")

She doesn't remember Shirley, just as she doesn't remember me. I have given her still another impossible reality, and the defenses go up again; but I am committed, too, because Shirley is a point on which I will not give. "Shirley was brighter than I," I say, "and wiser. She watched and enjoyed the show, she learned a great deal about people just by watching, and she did not eat her heart out to join in and be accepted the way I did. For all these years I've wondered where she took that wisdom, how far it carried her. Now and then when I pick up a *Time* magazine and read about advances in psychology or sociology, I wonder if some day I'll see her picture and read about some new thing she's come up with."

The doors of the room opposite us open, and the Home Brite men begin to come out. They are carefully, conservatively dressed. As they come through the doors they look about them. These men have been rejected at many doorways. They no longer take doorways for granted. Their expressions, too, are careful. Home Brite's challenges are perhaps sometimes like crises. I'm reminded of the looks I see on the faces of my teammates as we approach an overturned car in the middle of a highway. Even before we get to it we are looking for clues, trying to see the possible means of collision, the signals of injury. It all has meaning if only we have the eyes to see it.

The wives move forward formally. They nod and smile. They are uncomfortable in the formal surroundings of this large hotel. Alinda also moves away from me and toward a tall, conventionally handsome man. He is not balding, as I thought he would be. His hair is thick and gray. She leads him back to where I stand, and as I watch him move I know that years ago, in some other high school he was on the First Team, a letterman, and a male counterpart of what Alinda was to us, popular and respected, sought after and imitated. They are matched, a pair the eugenicists would have loved, and they are as average as can be.

My own group is getting larger before its door. I look at my watch and see that it is time to start. I know that Alinda will smile and nod to me as I go, but she will not introduce me to her husband. Even with a name tag to help her she has forgotten my name. Also, I have confused and obscurely insulted her, and so I wave and move toward my group. The Home Brite people have made me look at them with new eyes. The two groups are not so different after all. We too are fairly conventional; we too are here to cheer ourselves on and comfort ourselves with our numbers. We too have our jargon, our little jokes—funny or painful—our private losses. We too believe fanatically in luck—that most impalements will spare the nearby artery, that the severe skull fracture will be open and vent the brain, that the eye and the ear, the creature's darling senses, will find their natural protection sufficient. We too are cautious at doorways.

The traffic merges, never touching but giving and taking in an elegant and subtle dance, begun in the smallest and most complicated neural tracery, duplicated by millions of bodies into and out of the heart of the city.

FLIGHT
PATTERN

He waited on the treeless plain. It was shimmering hot and without feature except for the single north-south cut of the blacktop. At first when the rare car passed, the drivers squinting and impatient to be done with sun glare and flatness, he had put out his arm, thumb up, but now he simply stood and waited. On his last ride up from Roswell, he had fallen asleep, an exhausted, haunted sleep from which he had continually tried to fight free only to be pulled back against his will. His ride had been a route man for a small company. The ride had talked on and on, but Ben had forgotten everything up through Vaughn to Santa Fe and into Colorado, north up U.S. 25, listening without hearing.

He had come from Mexico changed and still changing. What worried him now was how much more changing there was to do. He had always enjoyed hitchhiking before this: vacationers, businessmen wanting someone for company, honeymooners, a carnival, a bunch of phys. ed. teachers on a tour, rock musicians going to a gig. He had listened to all of them, learning things, seeing into their lives, relishing the different textures of their silences or their talk. This time it had been a drudgery performed unwillingly, a geography to be gotten over and done with, the rides a means and nothing more. And now this. "Sorry, kid," the ride had said. "I tried to wake you up when we hit the Springs. Go on to Burlington and you can go U.S. Seventy into K.C."

The middle of nowhere. He had been here for hours watching the road cook. He had long since eaten the two apples he had in the knapsack he carried. There were a couple of paperbacks in there, too, but one of the ways he had changed since Mexico was that he was now too nervous to read. Until three days ago, it had been one of the keenest joys of his life, to sit on a rock or against a tree somewhere and open a book. The rides stopped for him anyway and offered him lifts and then asked him what he was reading. Sometimes there was good talk all the way to the next place. Mellow people, readers. More often than not they would stake him to a dinner or go out of their way to take him where he was going. Now his books made him nervous and he couldn't concentrate. He found himself looking under the print or over it and back into Mexico or into the faces of the people he had seen since and whom he now suspected of suspecting him.

Tied to his waist and thighs with strips torn from a roller towel were eight small plastic bags each with two ounces of cocaine. It had been smuggled into Mexico from Colombia, and they could get twelve hundred an ounce for it in Kansas City. He had not yet been able to call Lewis or Grog to tell them he had done it. He was amazed at how simple it had been and how full of bad changes.

Lewis had had the name of a man in Mexico and a place to go. The plan had been for Ben to make the buy. Lewis would either send Grog or come down himself, get the stuff from Ben, and take it back across the border. They would meet well away from the border on the American side and ride back up to K.C. on Grog's bike or in Lewis's cousin's car. Ben himself would not be crossing any line with the stuff, and as a hiker he could come and go easily.

He had gotten into Mexico with no trouble and had gone immediately to the place Lewis had said, a door in a row of doors on a nondescript street in a nondescript adobe slum. He had given a name, and a tired-looking woman had motioned him in. He and his friends had fifteen hundred to deal with, their pooled savings. Ben had un-loaded boxcars all summer for his part of that money. When the man, a small, lean, well-kept man named Bedoya, came out of the cur-tained-off place at the back of the room, Ben had had a moment of misgiving, but Bedoya had seemed to understand how hard such things were. He made Ben sit down and poured them both a drink. "The purchase is pure," he had said in a quiet way, "but taste if you wish from all the packages. I trust your money, too, that it is good and unmarked. It is good for men to trust. This way you will come back. We are established."

They had made the transfer over the tequila, Bedoya speaking now and then in a meditative way. He was neither secretive nor tough, as Ben had thought he would be. The time he spent with Bedoya was the last good thing Ben experienced, and he remembered it as something he might have dreamed of doing when he was younger. When Bedoya had gotten the packages of coke, Ben saw that he did it without furtiveness. He also noted Bedoya's approval when he did not snort, but only ritually tasted from one or two of the packages with a moistened finger. From his height, Ben saw himself as reasonable and worldly, above the illegality of what he was doing. In these matters, the law was ridiculous anyway. Everyone he knew smoked, drank bootleg, laughing that Kansas was dry. Who did the drug harm, really? And Bedoya was an honest and untroubled man.

His own troubles began when he left the house. The door closed on him, and instead of being enveloped in the anonymity of the adobe-sided street, he found it had become, in the half hour of his buy, a corridor of eyes and judges, police, informers, agents, spies. The tired people seemed to be playing at apathy, secretly looking, only their eyes moving in their unturning heads. There were subtle gestures made—see—a hand rising, a half smile; we know, we know. Ben had gone to get a haircut, as they had planned—something that would make him look more conventional. The cocaine was in his knapsack, and after the haircut and the purchase of a secondhand football sweater in a run-down store off the Calle Obregon, Ben went to the bus station, paid his way into a stall in the men's room, and waited. No one. Nothing. He waited longer, counting his breaths by hundreds until they were layered too deep to count. He counted the pockmarks on the wall until he ran out of walls and ceilings. He waited aggressively, moving from one foot to another, tapping and clicking. He waited passively, trying to remember lost verses of old songs, trying to clear his mind, trying . . . It was late and then too late, and finally he had only the truth to face—that in this lone crapper in the only square on the north side of town he was waiting alone, and that no one, neither Grog nor Lewis, was coming, and there was only himself and one pound of pure cocaine. When he could deny that no longer, nor the wave of panic that had come up over him like a green sea, washing him in trembling and nausea that was not helped by the odor of the latrine, he realized that it was almost sundown and that the crossing was his alone to do.

It seemed to help, that knowledge. He had the cocaine, on which a huge profit was to be made. He had his honor—his promise to Lewis and Grog. The sun would soon go down, and he would have to act quickly, *doing*, thank God, and not merely waiting. Over the sink he saw a filthy roller towel. With his penknife he cut it and then tore it off the roll. He tore it into wide strips, lengthwise, and carefully bandaged the packets of cocaine to his inner thighs and waist. He tried to work quickly, but he had some trouble anchoring the bands so they would not slip. When he was done he felt deformed, bulging at the thigh, his pants fitting oddly. And surely the bulges would be seen. The police would strip him, strip him naked while they laughed at his stupidity because he had been caught, and at his body, which was almost hairless and very white. There was no place to go but toward the border.

They had not planned for incidental expenses, for any of the sudden mishaps that turn misfortune into catastrophe if you have no money. And the necessary waiting had taken all the time they had allowed for crossing. As Ben approached the border he saw how empty and foolish the whole plan was. What had seemed elegant simplicity was now only a terrible lack of wit. The timing was wrong, the deed itself full of bad vibes and bad karma. He wanted nothing so much as to strip himself, to get out of his smuggler's bonds and go back across the border unashamed.

Coming in sight of it he saw that the lines were long. He steeled himself and walked on. There were many pedestrians and bikers, a whole motorcycle club, it looked like, and some little girls in uniforms with their leader. Endless. He didn't know if he could wait it out. At any other time he would have picked someone out and started up a conversation or turned to whoever was beside him to smile and comment on the line. His beliefs had to do with friendliness, gentleness and the reknitting of a world that lived on wars and at the flesh of slain animals. As a half-convinced vegetarian he had argued this tellingly with his parents.

Ahead of him there was some kind of stir. The line, which had been moving slowly, had stopped. There were voices, a cry, and a feeling of terrible tension communicating itself with a bioelectrical suddenness the way a cell deep in a long bone "knows" that, at the frontier, an organ has been ruptured. The woman ahead of him turned to him and shrugged. She was a heavy Spanish woman with a huge rump and an apathetic face. She seemed to be going in the wrong direction, not homeward bound for the evening. It added to his sense of the mistake of the whole day. He kept his face blank. The line began to move again.

By the time he reached the customs shed he felt as though he had begun to die. He was chilly and had trouble breathing. Nausea uncoiled itself in his stomach and slid slowly upward. Far away somewhere in the 'mellow golden light of the ordinary world, they were passing people through. When they came to him, they asked silly routine questions, not seeing his terror and sickness, and then, in an anticlimactic, matter-of-fact way they looked cursorily through his backpack, patted his sides down, banged the stamps once, twice here and there on his passport, and waved him on.

It was as though soundless cannons were firing in his head, sending shock waves down all the pathways of his nerves. On the verge of fainting, Ben picked up his backpack, stuffed the contents into it, and half stumbled out of the shed. They had all said it would be that easy. Lewis had done it a dozen times, he said. And Ben and Lewis and Grog were rich now. He was rich and free and freezing cold. He had the football sweater in his pack. He sat down on a curb and took it out and put it on, but it did no good. The cold had gone to the bone.

They had planned a circuitous trip to avoid police and hassle. Having hitched for years he was familiar with the way a hitchhiker had to look and act to get a ride, and the route he was taking, off the major highways, meant short distance rides by local people up through Texas and into New Mexico. In Roswell he thought it would be safe to strike out for Denver on an interstate and then go with U.S. 70 straight east to make up some of the time he had spent in Texas.

A night and half a day in Texas, living with his change. At first he thought it was the people, the rides, with cold faces and restless, darting eyes, up through Odessa to Brownfield, skirting Lubbock to Plainview and then back toward the New Mexico border. Then at Muleshoe he realized with alarm that the trouble was with him, that the ranchers and the students and the salesmen and vacationers were no different than they ever had been, and that because it was he who had changed and not they, all the rides to come would be angry or despairing and full of suspicion about him. In Roswell there was the long ride and the deep, impacted sleep past Colorado Springs and beyond Denver. That strange sleep was costing him the dip back south again to Burlington. How many miles he was from Burlington he didn't know, but he did know that he was cooking in the glare of the afternoon plains. And there was nothing in any direction.

Now, there was something, off in the distance. A car. He began to hope fervently, almost to pray, that this one would stop for him. He had hunkered down some minutes before in spite of the strain to his pants and the cocaine. He got up and looked again.

There seemed to be something wrong with the car. It was listing, unless the road wasn't even, a dusty Buick, '38 or '39, the kind that was sure to be carrying an old rancher and his tired wife toward town. That kind never picked up hitchhikers. Too dangerous. He leaned toward the road as the car came close seeking the driver's eye—it was a man, he saw, alone and not old. The car began to slow and stopped about fifty feet ahead of him. Then, to his surprise, it courteously backed up as he ran toward it. He got in quickly and thanked the driver.

"You going to Burlington?" the driver asked.

"Yes, sir, I am."

They started up with a little shudder, but the ride was surprisingly smooth. Ben did not perceive the list he thought he had seen. "It's a mighty bad stretch," the driver said. "When I travel this road I'm usually the only one on it." Ben looked at him. He was about thirty-five, and ordinary-looking.

"I guess I've been waiting for three hours or so. I almost gave up hope."

"It's really been a little over two hours," the driver said, "but I can imagine your nervousness, seeing as how you're carrying all that cocaine."

There seemed to be a stopping in Ben of every function except fear. He felt the blood falling from his brain; he didn't, or couldn't speak or reason. His hands hung, his feet went heavy. He could only sit immobilized. The driver, after watching the road for a minute, turned to him again affably and continued. "Of course, it's worth a good deal of money—more than you've ever made before at one time. Oh, by the way, Lawrence is in jail."

"Lawrence?" He was surprised that he was able to push out the single word. Maybe there was still hope. He didn't know anyone named Lawrence. The driver continued pleasantly, "You call him Grog. Didn't you know his real name? Apparently the long wait for your return was too much for him. He saw life passing him by—he scored some cocaine downtown in K.C. and went back uptown to sell it. He cuts such an unprepossessing figure that the only buyer he had in three hours of dedicated hustle was Lujean Adams, a narcotics officer. Off duty. Lujean arranged another buy, and in two hours Lawrence was being read his rights."

"Is this—are you a cop?"

"No."

"Who are you, then?"

"I'm not a policeman. Definitely not."

"Are you . . . someone from the Mob?"

"The Mob!" The driver laughed. It was a surprisingly musical laugh. Ben's terror deepened. He had not known that fear could go so deep.

"For God sakes," he said very quietly, "don't . . . don't . . ."

"Don't *you*," the driver said stiffly. "Of all the emotions there are and all the combinations of emotion, fear is the one I least understand. The lack is mine, no doubt, but your terror is affecting the air around you, and because I am sitting so close, I am being upset by it. Ordinarily, it wouldn't matter, but in serious cases my vision gets extremely short, and while driving I might—"

"What are you talking about!"

"I'm sorry, but before I go stone-blind as a result of your terror I'm going to have to pull over."

There was no shoulder, no fence in the vast flatness. Ben had already begun to grieve for himself at this moment of his death, coming so suddenly and so unfairly. He felt a terrible loss for the body he already saw lying in these spaces, covered and uncovered by blowing snow, torn by coyotes and dried to half-rotted leather by the sun and wind. "I don't want to die," he murmured. "I'll do anything I have to do, but I don't want to die."

The driver laughed again. "We'll deal with that when we come to it."

The car had stopped. Absently Ben looked out the window and saw with sudden and surprising clarity as though for the first time, the prairie at the roadside. What an intricate, complex ecology there was. Tiny crickets and beetles struggled through small clumps of grass, and their dozen shades of green, olive, and brown proclaimed themselves to his eye. Here and there the tiniest of flowers opened starry umbels to him; small mosses hid purple blooms of incomparable beauty. How had he ever seen this plain as empty! His hands were trembling. It had never seemed so important that he live—continue to live. "Listen to me," the driver said at his side. "I'm trying to talk to you." Ben tore his eyes from the patch of ground at which he had been staring.

"I've been trying to tell you," the driver said, "that you are a fool. Fools, though you probably don't know it, are of particular importance in the universe. They test the limits of everything. Put a fool in a car and he will get drunk and push to the very outermost boundaries, the forces of gravity, metal fatigue, and the physics of propulsion and inertia. Fools are at the limits of all biochemical laws and exchanges, but their primary purpose is the constant testing and extending of the patience and resourcefulness of their species and the mercy of God. Whenever the Lord has been convinced to widen his mercy or extend his patience it has been at the behest of a fool. You are such a fool."

"If it's the cocaine you want, you can have it. We paid for it; it's ours. We didn't cause any trouble. It was a simple deal. It caused no harm."

"What is laughable is that you really believe what you are saying. You have no idea, do you, where you have been and with whom. How can the forces of Providence bear, I wonder, to extend so huge a protection when the protected don't even realize it! Perhaps I should introduce some reality into this simple deal of yours. Let us pool our information about these past few days. Please begin at the beginning—How did it all start?"

"Lewis had the name of this man, and he and Grog and I . . ."

"Lewis had the name of a man. Lewis is a psychopath, Benjamin. His place in the scheme of things is entirely different from yours and Lawrence's, but his kind uses your kind, and in his particular case, you were to be used as a blackmail victim after the deal was made. You were also to be used as a smuggler and as a weapon against a man named Bentanquez, with whom Lewis has been having a rather ugly affair."

"I . . . I don't know anyone named Bentanquez."

"You saw him once, but you didn't know it. What was important was that *he* does not know you, and that was why Lewis gave you the name of this man Bedoya. But the Bentanquez business is another story. Let us proceed."

"I got to Mexico and across the border all right, and to the place I was supposed to go, to that room or apartment, and I found Bedoya."

"Bedoya would have found you if you hadn't. He had been told you were coming. Your approach to him, by the way, was one of the high-water marks of naïveté, and the memory of it, for the day or so before his death, was the source of all of Mr. Bedoya's lighter moments."

"Bedoya is dead?"

"Oh, yes, his throat was cut because of the mistake made in your case. The death was unpleasant because he had twelve hours or so to watch it coming, and of course he tried, with admirable energy, to get the decision reversed."

"He was . . . he had a gentleness, a dignity . . ."

"Wasn't it wonderful! I know everyone will miss that special gift of his. Bedoya had a streak of greatness in him. He prostituted his sisters and every woman he ever knew, usually beginning with a gang rape. He robbed and cheated, regularly sold out his acquaintances, and was merciless to his victims. There was, I think, nothing to which he would not stoop for money or power, yet he was greatly gifted. He sized you up at a glance, saw which stereotype of a Mexican dope trader you most needed to believe, and produced it instantly before you, an original never to be precisely duplicated. Now, alas, never to be duplicated at all."

"But that's crazy—why? Why should he need to fool me—I was there to make the buy."

"But perhaps you would have been alerted to the immorality of it— you might have thought and then thought again and gone back to Kansas City without making the buy at all. His percentage would have been lost, and also he was getting something from Lewis for the Bentanquez part of the thing. Bedoya wasn't rich, for all his efforts. All he had, really, were his contacts, and the faithful greased-wheel workings of his swindles to keep those contacts pleased with him. It was necessary to keep you unsuspicious and naïve, and it was his genius to be able to do that in a delicate, artistic way. At any rate, he is dead now—let us proceed with your travels."

"I went through the streets until I came to the park, and I went into the john there. I waited. Then when I knew no one was coming I tied the little plastic bags of coke to myself and went to the border."

"You are not very good at making bindings, are you?"

"I used to be, but it's been quite a while. When I was a boy scout . . ."

The driver grinned. "This is the hallmark of a fool, you know, that again and again it is his ineptitude and not his wit or skill that saves him. It is possible, sometimes, to question the mercy of God, but never His sense of humor."

"Do you believe in God? If you do, you couldn't consider murder or . . . or . . ."

"Belief. Most of the time it's too much to ask. Luckily, He doesn't seem to ask it."

"Why did you say that about the binding, that I was inept?"

"Do you know it took you an hour to get ten packets bound around you? Who could have foreseen such clumsiness? Bedoya had subtly but strongly suggested that you should go as quickly as possible to the border. The men there had been alerted and given your description. You were to have been caught, stripped, and the cocaine sent back to Bedoya for resale that evening to another fool, a young girl from Baggs, Wyoming. It was to have been the twelfth resale of that particular cocaine. Your waiting and bandage-bungling made you terribly late. You can see that as a single action, your purchase was a small one, really—what was it, fifteen hundred? But if you assume sales between one thousand and fifteen hundred dollars and multiply them by hundreds of resales, you will come to realize that touching the capital of such an enterprise is going to cause pain. Those who used Bedoya do not like pain and will inflict an almost infinite amount of it on others to see that they themselves are spared it."

"How come I wasn't caught then, wasn't even stopped or questioned?"

"But you were. They had given your description to a border informer and a man was sent to 'finger' you, as they say. You were so long in that bathroom that the man assumed you had slipped away and he thought to go to the border and head you off there. He was encountered by an old creditor and held up. Fortunately for you there was another young man crossing who looked enough like you to be mistaken for you by strangers given a simple physical description. The fingerer has also been killed. Do you remember a stir in the line ahead of you—perhaps you did not see, but it was a young man who also had some camping gear. You would not have been flattered. His first name was Jacob, and your last is Jacobs, which is the name you gave to Bedoya. By the time they ripped Jacob's clothes to shreds and tore the bottoms from his boots, dismantled his pack and subjected him to searches of every bodily orifice, you had gone through customs, fat, dumb, and happy, as they say, and, they thought, in the early stages of "Montezuma's Revenge." They wanted to be rid of you before you became ill in the middle of their busiest time. It is all understandable now, isn't it? Jacob, by the way, has been given a metaphor on which years of nightmares will turn. He was, in all senses except the metaphysical one, innocent, and so he felt his guilt strongly. In the jail where he now waits he has teetered between rage and psychosis, but I think he will swing back toward the primeval guilt, and given his background may leave the world for a religious order. The borders he will cross in the future will be spiritual ones only."

"How can he still be in jail? He's innocent, and they know it."

"Mexican law has few of the bourgeois legal safeguards you wave away so easily."

"I didn't mean . . . I never meant . . ."

"Of course you didn't. It's the fools' anthem."

Ben seemed for a moment to see deep into the canyon of his own stupidity. He saw himself tiny and antlike at the bottom, hurrying here and there, tracking and backtracking in his mindless work, the frantic eagerness to belong to the scheme, the misplaced confidence given so rashly, the physical haste of it all, and the mental sloth. He saw Lewis's plots and Bedoya's, and their scorn for his passivity and acceptance. A small-time punk smuggler. The easy ballast makings of a Mexican jail. For a moment the consciousness of all that stupidity came so fully upon him that he almost gagged with it, and then as suddenly, it turned in him. It was true, of course, that he had been stupid, a small fish, and because it was true, what was this man doing here? What was his purpose in knowing all of it? A thousand fools burdened the border every day—did any of them warrant such care in the unraveling of his biography, such a pursuit? "Who are you?" Ben asked again. "I want to know now, and I want to know how you know all this—my friends, my—what we were doing."

The car was still stopped at the side of the road. After Ben spoke there was only the buzz-tick summer sounds in the sparse prairie cover around them. The driver had turned to stare out the front window, flecked with the dead bodies of small insects. He turned again and faced Ben. "It's time to get out now."

Ben looked out again as though the geography might have changed in his moment's inattention. It was fearfully the same—flat, open, rim to rim to the ends of sight. Not a tree, not a rock, not a chance of escape. A gun could be raised and a trigger squeezed before he got fifty feet. If he got out the driver could sit comfortably in the car and shoot him down. Too easy, too goddam easy. "No," Ben said. "If you want blood, you are going to wear it, too."

"Get out, please," the driver insisted.

"Go screw yourself," Ben said. "I'm not getting out. Instead, you tell me who you are."

"You can understand so little," the driver said.

"I can understand this—I don't have to consent to my own death. I'm not moving."

To Ben's complete surprise, the driver grabbed him suddenly and violently and began to struggle with him. He found himself being pulled away from the door and halfway across the sprung seat of the old car. The driver, sitting at Ben's side, was able only to get his right arm in a positive hold; he struggled to bring the left over to block the blows by which Ben was trying to free himself. Ben punched the driver in the chest, but he had to reach across his own body and the blow was not strong. The driver got a hand in Ben's hair and gave it a fierce tug.

The places behind his eyes went red with pain, but as he continued to struggle, turning full length on the seat to come face-to-face with the driver, Ben suddenly realized that if the man had had a gun he surely would have used it by now. He hadn't seen a gun, he had only assumed—if there were no gun he would be better out of the car, to run or fight as he wished. The driver was strong, but Ben got the feeling he was inept as a fighter. He was older, too—perhaps Ben could outrun him.

He had jammed his foot up under the seat to give himself some leverage as he struggled. He pulled free and suddenly threw his weight backward, surprising the driver and throwing him off-balance. With his other foot he kicked the door handle downward, and with both arms, pushed away using the driver's body as a lever. But the driver's arm was across his body and the driver's fist was still in his hair. To the dismay of both of them, they overbalanced with the energy of Ben's push and both tumbled out of the car together.

When they fell over the running board the driver's hold was broken. With an agonizing wrench, Ben freed himself, leaving a hand of hair still in the driver's grip. He clambered to his feet. The struggle had winded him, but at least he was free. He realized also that he did not need to head off into the endless prairie. If he ran up the road, back in the direction the driver had come, perhaps he could wave down another car, could, in a mile or two, come to a house. Shadows were lengthening. Surely someone would be coming home over this road or into town for the evening. Whatever the choices of flight were, they were better than wrestling with a killer. And if the break was to be made it would have to be made quickly. The driver had begun to get up, so Ben pulled in all the breath he could force into his already tired lungs and broke into a shambling run up the road.

With all the noise of his breathing and the shuffle of his shoes against the gritty surface of the road Ben heard no sounds of pursuit. He picked up speed and was just beginning to think of hopeful possibilities when he found himself off his feet, airborne, flying, and then falling, slammed down on the asphalt, the air slapped out of him, leaving him gasping and blind with shock and pain.

The first thing he heard from the outside was a buzzing close to his ear. It was a while before he realized the sounds were words and another long while before the words had meaning. It was the driver. Leaning close and speaking not to Ben but anxiously to himself: "They said it wouldn't kill! It wasn't meant to kill. I have seen pictures of it done! Teams of men do it in play and no one is hurt!" The driver began to shake Ben who discovered that he had landed very hard on knees and elbows, and groaned. "Thank God!" the driver cried. "I thought you were dead!"

"Let me up!" Ben muttered, knowing he was unable to get up.

"Who would have guessed the technique would work so well!" the driver exclaimed.

"I feel sick—I can't breathe."

"Wait until I roll you over." With care the driver turned Ben over. It was done gently enough, but it came to Ben that the driver had never done it before, had never been in a fight as a child, or picked himself up or helped anyone else up after a fall.

"Leave me alone—let me do it myself."

"I can't let you up. Lie there, or we'll fight again."

"Who are you?" Ben demanded. "I mean, who the hell are you!"

"I'm a *malakh*," the driver said. "You have forgotten your Hebrew, but in English they call it an angel. I'm not using the English meaning, but the Hebrew one."

"Come on, if you're from outer space I can believe it—you don't have to lie to me. I know you're not from here, from . . . us. Are you someone sent to make contact?"

"Why is it so much more likely that I am from another planet than that I am what I say I am?"

"I don't believe in any of that."

"Irrelevant," the driver said. "What is relevant is my being, and my being here, and that I will not let you go unless you bless me."

"Let me up! Let me go!"

"Perhaps you want to fight some more. The tackling was very good, but you have recovered from it, and perhaps you need more struggle—"

"You've been taught some other holds you want to try, haven't you?"

"It's true, yes. Several. I'd like to do the tackling again, too, to see how it really works."

"No, no more. Just let me get up."

"You won't try to run away again, will you?"

"No, I don't think I could."

His pants were torn at the right knee. The knee and both elbows were badly abraded and sore, and at least one of the bags of cocaine had been broken. There was white powder on the ground. Ben sprinkled it over the raw places hoping to deaden the pain. After a while the driver helped him up, keeping a tight hold on him, and they moved slowly back to the car to get out of the sun glare, which the driver said was bothering his eyes.

It was getting late. Although he had no watch, Ben guessed it was sometime after five.

There were shadows welling the small pebbles and dust-whitened sagebrush of the plain. Ben had trouble walking and even more trouble sitting down beside the car. He was sure he had another abrasion on the outside of his left thigh, and he felt sore all over. How many of the bags of cocaine had been broken? "If you're an angel you should be able to get water from somewhere!"

"Men are far more gifted at technology than we. There is a method, though, in which one uses plastic to keep the water that condenses overnight—"

"It would mean dumping the coke, and that I won't do," Ben said, wondering if the driver was going to force him. The driver only shrugged. "Out here the plastic is more important than the drug."

"We won't be out here forever."

"There's also a good trick with urine, and I heard recently about using water from the radiator of a car. How does one get that water to come out?"

"Water from a radiator! Urine! Some angel!"

"*Malakh*, not angel. In the older Hebrew, the word has a different connotation altogether."

"I never told anyone I was Jewish—not Grog or Lewis."

"You seldom tell yourself, but that's not the issue here. I need something from you."

"Is it the blessing you spoke of before?"

"Yes, it's a sort of blessing."

"What is it? You seem to know everything about me already, about Grog and Bedoya and Lewis. Why don't you just read my mind?"

"I've tried several times, and I've been overwhelmed . . . the action of human senses is so intense—seeing, hearing, smelling, touching, balance, all at once. When I contemplate the feeling part of the human mind, I am confounded, out of my depth. I don't understand."

"What don't you understand?"

"*Appetite!*"

"You mean eating?"

"No, no, the hunger for food and sex was given you. It's vital, a key to your survival, but the other hungers. Take Bedoya. How he lusted and burned—and his burning had no sexuality in it. He used women but not for union. He hungered for various kinds of power over them. He hungered for power the way a dying man hungers for air—beyond all ability to use it, beyond all need or purpose. And you. You are young, and the young lust. I was prepared for that, and for your intricate and marvelously balanced physiology. How surprised I was at the hungers you have that seem so inchoate and so much more powerful than sex or even food.

"This vision you seek of yourself as a kind of warrior, a hero, a mythic personage larger than life—the thing that sent you on this lunatic trip in the first place. What is that passion that is not rooted in metabolism but in wish and symbol? What is this religious quest that lacks the goal of God, this quest in spite of God? I began to envy you that hunger. I began to envy something else."

"Sex?"

"No, surprise."

"Surprises aren't always good," Ben said, looking straight at the driver.

"No, but people are always surprised. For you every day unfolds without assurances. Will the cocaine be nine-tenths powdered milk? Will some corner be turned and some epiphany rise like a dew in the ordinary web of the day, transforming it?"

"If that's sarcasm, forget it."

"I'm not laughing. You cannot imagine what I lack. I'm a *malakh*, and we do not covet, but there rises in me a terrible wish to be so much invested in the day that I wouldn't simply bear it full upon my senses, but be pierced by those hungers as you are, and blessed by those surprises."

"How do you expect to do it—are you going to go into my mind . . . to . . . a kind of rape, taking my emotions and dressing yourself up in them?"

"God forbid. He does, you know, forbid our commanding your minds. The cost of keeping you from being our objects has been the savaging of human history. Such an exorbitant price."

"Don't envy us. We are usually very lonely."

"That too—that too was considered a fair price to pay for the first decision after the decision to make life-forms at all; that no two should be the same, not even a shell or a leaf, a fly or a wolf or a man. That decision haunts me now. Why is this singularity so vital?"

"Are you saying that whoever you are, martian or angel—"

"*Malakh*."

"*Malakh*, that you would prefer to be man?"

"Oh, yes, yes!"

"But why?"

"Haven't I just told you—the piercing . . ."

"Don't you know that we can't shut our ears to sound or our minds to a constant bombardment of thoughts and wishes, good and bad, fantasies, old songs, bad jokes? How can you want that? It isn't free will, it's free *whim*!"

Ben was suddenly aware that in their talk a considerable time had gone by. Their two shadows lengthened to the size of trees were laid down beside one another as though they were friends.

He had half expected the driver to cast no shadow. He pointed to the second shadow, and the driver laughed, "What do you want, wings?"

"Why not?"

"You see too much TV. You want the higher orders of creation as special-effects men."

"I want transcendence."

The driver laughed. "Pay attention."

He was wearing a white shirt, which, in the fight and tackle, had gotten rumpled and dirty. He unbuttoned it carefully and took it off. The undershirt was brand new. To Ben's surprise the driver turned around and began to flex the muscles of his back. "You see the large muscle that comes down the neck and attaches down the shoulder blade and the spine—it's the trapezius. Under it are muscles called the rhomboids. Here's the deltoid in my shoulder. They're big muscles, but they would never support a wing. You'd need muscles fifteen or sixteen times as big, and where would they attach? Do you want your angels looking like chickens? Like buzzards? I'm the model, take it or leave it."

"But . . ."

"Here, hold your hand like this and you can make a set of wings on the shadow."

Ben raised his hand to wave the driver away, and at that minute the sun went neatly down and both the shadows died instantly. They were left in the short, bright afterglow, all contour and no shadow. The warmth pulled away; Ben could feel it going. In the car was his backpack and in the pack the football sweater he had bought in Mexico. "Do you feel things, hot and cold?" he asked innocently. If the driver did feel heat and cold he might also feel hunger and Ben could suggest going into town in the car—someplace where they could get warm and eat dinner. There would surely be more chances of getting away. Anything would be better than the pitiful opportunities afforded by this treeless plain. Of course, if he waited here there might be a time when the driver would turn away and Ben could hit him with a rock and take the keys and get the car and ride to K.C. with the cocaine he had left, but even as he saw it happening in all his imagination's stark simplicity, he rejected it. It was too melodramatic. And what if he hit too hard and killed the driver? What if one blow was not enough and the driver took it and then turned in his rage and came back at him—what then? How hard should a blow to the head have to be to stun for fifteen minutes but not kill? It was impossible to know. It was impossible to speak of or to plan, but it was not impossible to imagine, and Ben drifted away into a long daydream of murder on the prairie with fence wire, fence posts, clothing, rocks, sticks, karate, and locoweed. He came out of his daydream reluctantly and without comprehension of the driver's words: "Of course, that's inevitable, don't you think?"

"What?"

"The problem I was describing."

"What problem?"

"The problem of heat and cold. Weren't you listening?"

"No, I guess not."

"What was it, one of those remarkable sexual fantasies Freud says humankind must revert to every fifteen minutes in order to discharge its fearful violence? If so, go on."

"Never mind," Ben muttered, "it's over."

"Well, as I said, there is a problem. If you are cold your sweater is in the car. I'll have to go first—I left the key in the ignition." He rose quickly and went to the driver's side.

The night had begun to come down and the warm metal of the car was losing its heat. Its bulk at their backs was only a darker form lost in the equivocating darkness of the huge sky just beginning to bloom with stars. The driver pointed upward. "One, two—Sabbath is over. If there is an Orthodox family in Burlington, the woman is beginning to cook now."

"It's lucky no one stole the car," Ben muttered, "with you leaving the key in it."

"If you remember, you were the one who ran."

"Do you think it will get much colder?"

"Yes, and I think we will soon need a fire. We can wait, though, till the moon comes. There is brush there and dung, if someone has run stock recently, and enough light canes for burning."

"And that's the miracle of one of God's angels?"

"For the last time, *malakh*, not angel. I'm not here to impress you or to turn you into a believer. Relax. I'm not even here to make you be good. *Malakhim* have other work to do. Suppose we get to the fire. I'm beginning to think that the miracle is man's conquest of his own sloth."

The finding of fuel was not difficult. Someone had indeed run stock on the plain, and the ground was covered with dried cow dung. The driver had told him to collect the discs in his knapsack and bring them with sufficient brush for starting.

At first it was a joke, kicking the dung lumps to see if they were dry enough, but the air was beginning to chill and the overwhelming sky made a fire necessary if only to keep Ben from feeling its vast emptiness. He had sought novelty and change for much of his life, but he now realized that his most extreme adventures had been bounded by the comforting presence of houses, people, streetlights, stoplights, law and order, instant transportation away from unpleasant prospects, food and drink on demand. Now, if he looked up, the universe dipped and wheeled overhead, an emptiness impersonal and cold as truth. He applied himself to searching out the drier dung clods by the light of the moon.

He was bending down for one when a picture caught in his mind and held him with his knees bent and his butt in the air. It was a simple picture, equivocal as symbols are, a metaphor full of humor and meaning. The driver had spoken of appetite and surprise, and Ben saw him in long hair and beard, dirty jeans, boots and helmet, a Harley between his legs, and no job come Monday morning. Draped over the handlebars was a slick leather jacket. Ben began to smile, and then to laugh. What would be on the back of that jacket? HELL'S ANGEL, as a lurid decal? MALAKH, in Hebrew letters? APPETITE & SURPRISE? Amen. He straightened up for a minute, and when he bent down again he was still laughing.

When he had filled his knapsack he walked slowly back to where the driver sat waiting. Ben was surprised to see that the driver had gathered dung also and some long dry stalks to use as starters. He felt better about the driver now that he had laughed at him. The laughter had not been secret either, since the sound of it had carried low and undistorted over the sandy ground for an amazing distance.

By the time they got the fire going Ben was cold enough to huddle close to it, grateful for its warmth. The fuel was perfect, burning hot and slow with long-lasting red embers and none of the stink Ben thought it would have. On the other side of the small glowing circle the driver squatted and waxed nostalgic. "This reminds me of the old days. Of course, the stars are different here, but the great spaces resonate with the same harmonics. I used to like to sit up late with the nomads wintering their sheep on the plains of Sharon and in the valley of the Jordan. It was before everyone began to expect miracles. Survival was the miracle then. How little they demanded for themselves and how much for mankind—"

"I'm not the one who goes on about appetite and surprise," Ben said. The driver laughed.

"Man changes and so do the *malakhim*. Surprises in the wilderness—quiet! Sh . . . !" Without a sound the driver rose and melted into the night.

Ben had been half reclining, leaning on one arm. He sat up, holding his breath. A series of short agonized animal cries came from the flowing dark, but how far away they were or from which direction he could not tell. He felt foolish and useless here, competent at nothing, knowing nothing. A lone Indian walking this plain before him would have been at home, his ears bringing him knowledge and not fear. Ben realized that his only referent to this landscape was the road, some hundred fifty yards away, hidden by the dark now and untraveled— useless to him. *Malakh* or not, extraterrestrial or divine, the driver was necessary to his existence. And what did the driver want? He smiled again. A Harley, a chick, and a hundred bucks: appetite and surprise.

Suddenly the driver was back. "I thought we might get a rabbit or two from a mousing owl and from a snare I made when you were getting our fuel. The snare is empty. The owl got the prey. We'll have another chance before morning and I'll set some more snares."

"But we have no knives, no . . . nothing to skin an animal with . . ."

"This plain is covered with razor-sharp stones," the driver said. "The only deficit is water, and we could have that if you would only . . ."

"Nothing doing."

"Suit yourself."

The driver sat down. "Tell me," he said, "about appetite and surprise."

"You're really serious about this, aren't you—you don't realize that it would mean giving up all that fine foreknowledge of yours. You would have nothing but feelings to go by. Is it worth it?"

"For the experience, the fresh act, lived out on my senses, my mind, my body—new, unsearched for, unlived until I live it—what a wonder that is, what a joy! To be as hungry as you are now and then to be filled, to hunger after the unguessable—what a quest!"

"You're sure?"

"Yes! Oh, yes! The Bedouin shepherds hoped and dreamed, but they were so poor, their scope was no wider than the desert they walked, their appetites no deeper than the deepest of their wells. One can hunger but not too far beyond one's present possibilities. I have heard people say the human imagination is infinite. They flatter themselves."

Ben leaned over and put a few more chips on the fire. "Then I am going to tell *you* a story. It's the story of what will happen when you get what you want. Ready? All right. Your senses, as you guess, are perfect, and I don't know where you get the money to buy one, but you are on a Harley and you are heading south and west into Mexico. You have a plan. Over a beer, two beers, five beers, you and your buddies have made this plan. There is a contact in a border town. He is an ex-convict, a pimp, and a murderer. You know these things, but you also know that the prize you seek, the proof, the adventure, the talisman won't be in the keeping of an archbishop. The point of taming lions is that they are lions. It is a test, and the test cannot be made with a toothless lion."

"Wait a minute—"

"No, you wait. I haven't given you the plan. Your beer buddy—and by this time the beer-blurred senses you envy will have convinced you that he is your friend, even though you know he is not, even though you know he is laughing at you, daring you to do this—this buddy says he has been in Mexico many times. He has friends on both sides of the border, and he says he will meet you at a spot he knows on the Mexican side. Your job is simply to go to 179 Calle Madrid and get the stuff from a man, someone like Bedoya. Your buddy says he is known too well. The streets are full of informers. You go to Calle Madrid and pick up the coke. Does it matter if you know that the dealer is teasing you, acting like something out of a Steinbeck short story? The dare has been dared, the lion's mouth is wide open, and what you *know* makes no difference. You go to the little square off Linares and in the guise of tinkering with your bike you disable it just enough so that it runs rough and stalls on you. Then you wait. At three o'clock you chain the bike up and go into the john. You wait. The plan is that your Lewis will come at three-thirty and make the transfer. You will go to the border at about five or five-thirty when all the tourists go back over the line and the maids and babysitters come home. Your nerve will be tested, but you will finally be passed without incident, and if searched, will have nothing to be found. Somewhere behind you, Lewis too will be waiting. You will not acknowledge one another. On the American side you will meet. You will have fixed the bike by then, and you and Lewis will ride home victorious. Cleverness, courage, discretion, appetite, and surprise. It's all there.

"But you aren't me. You aren't human. You never went to a carnival and ate everything you wanted and then were sick to death later. You never got roaring drunk on homemade popscull and spent the next day mute because the sound of your own voice tore through your head like a railroad train. This means that when the bike really *does* go out on you there is no terror in it. No possibilities explode behind your eyes one after another until you go blind with panic and have to sit down until your vision clears. It means that when that panic is conquered there is no other, slower one working in behind it. Lewis is late. Lewis is very late. Lewis is not coming. Now, anything is possible. Perhaps he has been caught and has told the authorities everything. You do not know him because none of us really *knows* another person, and because you, particularly, do not share an essential element with Lewis. You don't fear any of this. You don't fear anything. You don't abandon the bike, as I would have, in a panicky wish to travel light and knowing that with the cocaine on you and looking as you do, the authorities will search you and the bike minutely. You know you will have to hide the cocaine, and so you do, probably the same way I did, by tying it to your body with the same torn strips of roller towel. You are a *malakh*, but I wonder if you can anchor a bandage any better than I do."

"This scene you're constructing—"

"I'm not finished. You were brilliant at chasing down my Lewis's motives and Bedoya's, too. The moon is up and the dung burns beautifully. The ground is covered with flints you could use like a master. We'll come out of this warm and full and with rabbit-skin hats, no doubt, but I've been in the lion's mouth for two days, and it smells like hell in there, appetite, surprise, and all

"So, bound up, probably incompetently, you are ready for the border. Lewis has told you to go back around five o'clock. This you do with the broken bike. The idea would have been to leave the bike and cross the border on foot, to strike up a conversation with a tourist group or better yet a family—perhaps to get a ride back with them and be taken, in the rush, for one of them. But you do not do this because you lack a necessary element in your makeup, which Lewis has and Grog has and which I have. Instead, near sundown you push your bike into the line. A broken-down bike wheeled along by a suspicious character, wingless, but somehow not like other people. It hints at something far more serious than a little smuggling. A feeling, an instinct is alerted in the border guards. Perhaps this biker is a terrorist, the bike loaded with explosives, ready to be detonated as soon as it passes an agreed-on point. Is there to be a kidnapping or a raid across this border? You must remember that there's a flow of all kinds of illegal things and people back and forth. A little fear is always present at these borders, at any border. The happiest honeymooners feel it, the daily domestics trudging back from a day among the gringos feel it. You don't feel it, and you don't show it, and all that the guards can tell is that you are different from all the other people and therefore dangerous. So they don't wave you on; they stop the whole line, and sundown or not, they give you and the bike an elaborate search. And there it is, wrapped around your thighs like an extra set of muscles. Now they have a reason. It doesn't explain their anxiety about you, it just gives it a handle. They break down the bike piece by piece and they lay you open, and they don't do this gently. The less they find, the angrier they get, and because you lack that certain quality I mentioned before, they will shove you as they pass. You are not like them and they know it, and they may, depending on who they are and how much of this quality they have in their makeups, beat you. Can *malakhs* be killed?"

"*Malakhim.*"

"Can they?"

"Yes. I think you are starting now."

The driver had been working at the beginning, slowly bending some slender withes he had gathered, making snares, but he had stopped as Ben told the story, and now he sat staring moodily ahead of him. There was some more fuel left.

"You mentioned something I lack," the driver said. "Can you be more specific?"

"Wait," Ben said. "Listen—"

Something had changed around them, a quality of the night, nothing Ben could name at first. "Something's happening," he whispered across the fire to the morose driver.

"It's the rising of the earth," the driver said. "The dayrise." The driver pointed outward to the sky behind Ben, and when he turned and looked there seemed to be a line drawn, a thin line like a seam into which warm embers had been poured. At the same time he noticed a subtle lifting of the air, an almost imperceptible lightening, although the stars still poured in legions the whole half dome above him, rim to rim. The lifting, he realized, had to do with the change in sound. There was a different quality to the sounds around them—chatterings and clickings and a long repeated series of toneless notes like wood striking wood. "The night crew is leaving and the day crew is coming on," the driver said. By a degree or two it lightened, and the sounds like a ground mist rose all around them. When Ben looked at the stars they were gone, leaving not a mark. "You were going to tell me about appetite and surprise," the driver said moodily. "Instead you told me about some mystical trait I lack and you have, you and Lawrence and Lewis."

"Not mystical, but essential. Surely you saw from my story—"

"What is it, this trait?"

"Cowardice. You have no cowardice in you, none at all, and it means you probably wouldn't live a day in my world."

"If you're thinking of the qualms you have—"

"Only partly. Part of them I remember as fear—for the change in me. When I started lying I stopped trusting. That was spiritual, and not cowardly; but fear is one thing, terror is another. You have none. You would sail out so far beyond the limits that you could never swim back. Look at you out here, kidnapping me, fighting me, cornering me. What if I had been tougher than you? What if I had killed you? Don't you see that as you are you would drown in appetite, leap out into surprise, and get swallowed up the way I almost was by that sky full of stars? We deal with the smallest changes we can, we travel the shortest lines. Real heroes are rare, and they're not safe until they're reverently dead. A completely fearless man is not a man."

"How can you say that—you, who went over borders, smuggled, contemplated murder and death, coolly weighing methods, lied. Your heroism awes me."

"I only nudged the limits. If they had broken—if I'd really had Bedoya to deal with—good God, even this plain is too wide for me. Out there alone before I nearly died of it!"

"What's happened to you here? Why have you changed so suddenly?" It sounded like a reproach.

"I suppose I have changed. It doesn't feel any different. I'm certainly no happier."

"Where did you learn about all this, about cowardice?"

"Not from you."

"I see now! It's the other side of appetite and surprise!" the driver cried. "I knew it! It's the experience that's done it! Oh, I knew it would be this way!" He almost clapped his hands. "I keep forgetting there are so few other ways for humans to learn—they have to use experience almost exclusively."

"It makes no difference in your case," Ben said firmly. "Appetite comes easy and surprise easier still, but you will never, never make a coward no matter how hard you try. Your Harley will skid on gravel, you'll be lynched or jailed or beaten to death by your first girl's redneck fiancé."

Suddenly a band of light broke north of where they were. Before they could speak the whole plain was light, golden and warming. Dips and risings were divided, tiny bushes limned in radiance, small stones gleamed or were pushed back into shadow. The sun fled upward. The orchestration of sounds at the ground line settled into recognizable birdcalls and insect tickings.

The driver got up slowly. The withe he was bending to make a snare fell from his knees unnoticed. "Things have changed for both of us," he said. "Lewis is not to be trusted, and now you know it. Lawrence is in jail, and what cocaine you have left, and however much that is, now weighs on you alone and will weigh intolerably. You will have to sell it. To whom does a man sell such things? To people he can trust, his friends. Remember last year when you tried to sell your sleeping bag, the effort it took? If there is, as you say, a saving cowardice in you, you will keep away from Lewis and from the organizations dealing in evil. I envy you none of it. I must learn now not to envy you at all."

He turned away from Ben and began to walk out into the flatness toward the north. Ben thought he was going out there to relieve himself but as he walked on, Ben could see him unbuttoning his white shirt. Soon it flapped open around him and he shrugged it off, then the undershirt. He kept walking. In a few steps he had stepped out of his trousers and then he bent and undid his shoes. From his back something seemed to fall, unwrinkling and parting, like a garment. He shook it out until there were two huge wings, tightly folded then opening to spread wide in the sun. They looked wet at first, and they trembled like the wings of a moth pupa, but as they lifted up and spread, they seemed to strengthen. At full span they were eight or nine feet long so that they reached an arm's length over the driver's head and trailed behind him on the ground. Two huge beats and then he rose. Ben watched him catch light, a glow at each wing tip and along the upper edge of the wing. He did not circle, as Ben hoped he would, but worked, beating up and up, and was soon gone.

Ben waited until the sun was well clear of the horizon edge and the day in all its mundane heat and hunger was upon him. He shook out his knapsack and made for the car, but the driver had taken the keys, and, lacking the materials to hot-wire it, he was forced to continue down the single road that divided east and west, Everlasting from Everlasting.

THEOPHILUS NORTH
Thornton Wilder   53108 $3.95

Thornton Wilder, America's most honored writer, explores through young Theophilus North the lives of the saints and sinners, the rich and the servants, the gigolos and the fortune hunters in Newport, Rhode Island in the 1920's.

A CHARMED LIFE, Mary McCarthy   53884 $2.95

Mary McCarthy's celebrated novel of 20th Century love and decadence is set against the backdrop of a New England artists' colony. "A glittering tragedy."
The New York Times

AMERICAN BAROQUE
Lamar Herrin   77362 $3.50

An unforgettable story of the 1960's, and of the imperfect ideals and inescapable truths which sparked the imaginations and sensibilities of American youth. "Herrins's writing has vitality, humor, intelligence and vividness."   *The Washington Post*

THE WELL OF LONELINESS
Radclyffe Hall   54247 $3.95

This is the controversial and eloquent classic that movingly portrays a woman's love. It paved the way for the popularity of Virginia Woolf and of works such as Vita Sackville-West's THE DARK ISLAND, and Rita Mae Brown's THE RUBYFRUIT JUNGLE.

MASS APPEAL, Bill C. Davis   77396 $2.50

The stormy but underlying tender conflict between a middle-aged priest and a rebellious, idealistic young seminarian is explored in this "wise, moving and very funny comedy."   *The New York Times*

Available wherever paperbacks are sold, or directly from the publisher. Include 50¢ per copy for postage and handling; allow 6–8 weeks for delivery. Avon Books, Mail Order Dept., 224 West 57th St., N.Y., N.Y. 10019.

◢ New From Bard (cont'd)

DESERT NOTES:
Reflections In The Eye Of A Raven
Barry Holstun Lopez   53819 $2.25
In this collection of narrative contemplation, naturalist Lopez invites the reader to discover the beauty of the desert. "A magic evocation, Casteneda purged of chemistry and trappings."   *Publishers Weekly*

PRINCIPLES OF AMERICAN NUCLEAR CHEMISTRY: A NOVEL
Thomas McMahon   54122 $2.95
Set in Los Alamos, New Mexico in 1943, this is the story of the intellectual, emotional and sexual ferment that grips a group of American scientists at work on the atomic bomb. "A brilliant and important novel." Kurt Vonnegut, Jr.

A SHORT WALK, Alice Childress   54239 $3.50
From the rustic life of the rural South to the chaos of a Harlem riot to the revelry of a Depression Christmas, this is the moving story of one woman's passionate life, and a striking portrayal of 50 years of the black experience in America.

THE GROVES OF ACADEME
Mary McCarthy   52522 $2.95
In this wicked and witty bestseller Mary McCarthy deftly satirizes American intellectual life. "Brilliant ...funny...bitterly tongue-in-cheek."   *New Yorker*

Available wherever paperbacks are sold, or directly from the publisher. Include 50¢ per copy for postage and handling: allow 6–8 weeks for delivery. Avon Books, Mail Order Dept., 224 West 57th St., N.Y., N.Y. 10019.